ULTIMATE
GAY EROTICA

ULTIMATE
GAY EROTICA

EDITED BY JESSE GRANT

2009

alyson books
NEW YORK

Manufactured in the United States of America

Published by Alyson Books
245 West 17th Street, New York, NY 10011

Distribution in the United Kingdom by
Turnaround Publisher Services Ltd.
Unit 3, Olympia Trading Estate, Coburg Road, Wood Green
London N22 6TZ England

First Edition: January 2009
09 10 11 12 13 14 15 16 17 18 a 10 9 8 7 6 5 4 3 2 1

ISBN-10: 1-59350-090-4
ISBN-13: 978-1-59350-090-0

Library of Congress Cataloging-in-Publication data are on file.

Cover design by Victor Mingovits

CONTENTS

INTRODUCTION

OFTENTIMES I'M ASKED, what makes an erotica story "ultimate"? The truth is, I never have a straightforward response to such a question. Nor could I even begin to specify what elements I look for when picking out stories for Alyson Books's Ultimate Gay Erotica Series. Nothing is essential. Rather, it is the stories that break the mold and push the envelope that usually grab my attention. For me, good erotica (or any good story, for that matter) stays with me long after I have read it. The story—specifically the men involved—continue to grow in my head until I am vicariously experiencing each sensation and detail of their experience.

The stories in this anthology do just that. After all, we call it ultimate erotica for a reason. These stories will cling to you and just when you think you're done with them . . . that's when the fun begins . . . arousing you to the point of desperate release. The men in this anthology will take you on a whirlwind tour and leave you wanting more.

We saw a lot of change in 2008 that redefined the concepts *love, gay,* and *marriage*. The selected stories embody that evolution and lend different colors to our community's passion.

—*Jesse Grant*

JOCKEY SHORTS
ROB ROSEN

IT WAS THE MORNING BEFORE Saturday's season opening. Full capacity crowds expected. In other words, for the lucky few, big fucking payoffs. Hence my arrival the day earlier. The owners allowed the colts to be viewed by the heavy bettors. Good for business to spark some interest, they figured. Show off their wares. Get some major money riding on their investments.

Fine by me. Though it wasn't the horses that were doing the sparking. Least not for me, anyway. Well, now, not totally. Sure, I admired the animals for what they were. Top of the line, best of the best, and all. Still, it was the riders that really interested me. Got me down at the stables at that ungodly hour. Put some heavy lumpage in my shorts.

Yeah, truth be told, I dig short guys. Perfect miniatures. Pint-sized men. Guys that can bounce on daddy's lap. Needless to say, this peculiar penchant of mine, plus my predilection for the ponies, makes a perfect fit.

And the early hour? Beat the rush. Ringside seats. Well, *stall*side, at any rate.

The jockeys arrive early, too. Checking out the next day's racers. Making sure they're in tip-top shape and giving them a good brushing down so that they shine for the cameras. Strange sight to see, really. These elfin men alongside their relatively giant steeds. Strange and sexy, to be sure.

I strode along the earthen path, popping my head inside each cubicle as the colts got their rubdowns, their massive haunches quivering in apparent delight. And my cock quivered right along with them as each diminutive jockey came into view, determined looks on their angular faces, sinewy arms pumping back and forth against satiny hides. Too fucking hot, despite the morning chill.

With each stall I passed, my prick grew harder, steely against my cotton briefs. And then I reached the final one. I glanced down at the half-door. *Jersey Boy,* it read, printed across a wooden plank. I poked my peepers inside. The horse was a brilliant black, save for a pair of white circles around the rump. It looked up at me, shaking its head in greeting.

"Morning," I said to it, a smile now wide on my face.

"Morning," came the surprising reply, just as the jockey emerged from around the other side, wearing little more than a pair of denim shorts and knee-high boots. I gulped at the sight of him. At his muscle-tight, tiny frame, coated with a dense matting of curly black hair that trailed down before disappearing into his shorts, only to reappear along his equally hairy legs, thin and veined, bulging with compact, ripped sinew.

"Oh, hi. Sorry, didn't see you there."

He smirked, revealing a glorious set of pearly whites. "Yeah," he replied. "I get that a lot."

A red flush crept up my neck and spread across both cheeks. "Oh, um, I . . . I didn't mean . . ."

He cut me off. "Don't fret it, friend." He spoke with a strange accent, Slavic sounding, all wide vowels and truncated consonants. "Name's Gustav," he told me, reaching out and up with his hand, before quickly adding, "But my friends call me Gus."

I leaned in and down. "Stu," I replied. "Nice to meet you. And Jersey Boy."

We shook, my big hand engulfing his little one; though his grip was like a vise, probably from years of holding on to the reins so tightly. The shake lingered, flesh on warm pulsing flesh. He locked eyes with mine. His were a startling blue, laser-intense, drawing me in like a pool on a hot summer's day. The grin widened.

"You betting on the two of us tomorrow, Stu?"

I released his hand and grabbed for the program in my back pocket. Jersey Boy was running in the last race of the day. Ten to one odds. Not a hell of a lot of wins in his short racing career. "Not exactly money in the bank, Gus," I told him, as nicely as possible.

He moved in even closer, his small frame now leaning up against the door, allowing the sun to hit his face, causing his beautiful orbs to sparkle like the heavens. "Now, now, Stu. Just between you and me, Jersey Boy here is gonna win tomorrow. Make us *both* some money."

I moved in too, leaning on the door, just to the right of him. My elbow bumped against his, causing a spark to race up and down my spine. "And what do I get if you lose?"

He smiled up at me, lewdly, and with a wink replied, "Ah, you want a side bet then, my friend? Make it worth your while?" My heart began to race at the sound of the tone of his voice, now suddenly gravelly and husky.

"What did you have in mind, Gus?" I moved in closer, closer still, so that our arms were now abutting. "To make it worth my while, I mean."

He paused, his eyes taking me in as he thought carefully about his response. "Well, now, Stu, how about, if I lose, I fuck you silly until you don't care about losing your money."

I coughed, the red now returning to my face for a second time. "And if you win?"

He wasted no time in answering that one. "Stands to reason, Stu, you fuck me."

I reached out and ran my hand through all that dense hair, as soft as it was wiry, stopping at an eraser-tipped nipple, which I gently tugged and tweaked on. His eyes fluttered. He sighed. "Well, now," I said, echoing his grin with one of my own. "Do you think little old you can take on big old me?"

He backed away, the smile still very much there. Pointing to Jersey Boy, he answered, "Stu, if I can ride this big guy, I think I can handle you. Besides," he added, now reaching for the button on his shorts before sliding them down and around his boots, "I'm not exactly *small* everywhere."

A gross understatement if ever there was one.

Looking even more monstrous, especially compared to all his other appendages, his prick, already arching out and up before my very eyes, was seven meaty inches of thick flesh, with a wide, helmeted head slick with pre-come and two balls the size of lemons that shook as he started a slow, even stroke. Jersey Boy whinnied, clearly jealous of his rider's good fortune.

"A thousand on you to win," I relented. "You lose, I'm in for one hell of a fucking. You win—and man I hope you win—you're in for the ride of your life."

He slapped his cock, sending it springing from side to side. "Sounds like we win either way, my friend. A sure bet. This I like."

"Still, it would be nicer if you won. Icing on the cake. And then icing on that great chest of yours, and belly, and chin." My iron-hard cock was now pushing up against the stable door. "And if you win, do you think you can take what I've got in *my* shorts?"

He laughed and turned around, revealing the cutest little ass this side of the Mississippi, covered in the now-familiar matting that blanketed the rest of his taught body. I groaned at the sight of it. "See for yourself," he said, backing toward me, his cheeks splayed apart and his beautiful, pink asshole winking up at me.

I reached out and ran my palm across both cheeks and then down the crack before tracing my fingers around his hair-rimmed halo. Like the rest of him, it was small and tight and aching to be rode, just like the horse behind the man. "Great hole, Gus. But I think I got more than it can take."

He laughed. "Don't judge a book by its cover, my friend. Take it for a test drive, if you like."

I looked around. The stables were still fairly empty, as was the stall next to us. Quickly, I ducked inside. Gus turned around and melted into my waiting embrace. I bent down and brushed my lips against his, feeling the stubble that ran along his narrow face. He darted his tongue out and mashed his mouth into mine, instantly swapping some heavy spit. My hand instinctively grabbed his thick prick, now leaking copious amounts of sticky jizz. He groaned and sucked on my mouth. "Yum," I groaned back into his.

"The bottom hole tastes even better," he whispered as he stepped away and kicked off his shorts, so that he was now raging hard and naked, save for the boots. Then he turned and got on all fours, looking much like a smaller version of the horse that stood by our side, eating his hay as he ignored the shenanigans going on around him.

I crouched down, face to ass, my eyes meandering down the length of his hirsute, slim back and coming to rest on his pink, puckered hole. I leaned my face in and took a deep whiff. He smelled of musk and sweat, a heady mixture that pulled me ever forward, until my tongue took a sample lick and then a slide inside.

He moaned as my tongue entered him and pushed his heavy cock between his legs, allowing me to jack him off as I ate him out. "Now for that test drive," I told him, hocking a lugie at his asshole, slicking him up but good, and then gliding a spit-soaked finger up and in and back, feeling the smooth, muscled interior of his tight little hairy ass. A sight forever etched in my memory.

He moaned, low and deep, the sound filling the small space around us, as I added a second digit to the mix and craned my neck down for an eager suck and slurp on his long, hard tool.

"Three's the charm," he suggested.

I doubted his tiny tush could take it but did as he asked, prodding and pushing until he was getting triple-finger-fucked. His groaning grew louder as he bucked his compact ass into my hand and I sped up the stroke on his spit-slick cock. "Drives just perfect," I told him, now pistoning his ass with my fist.

"Oh, yeah, Stu. Ride it, ride it hard then."

Naturally, I did, until I felt the familiar hardening at the farthest reaches of his hole. With a furious final pump on his fat dick, he exploded, sending a stream of white hot come down to the ground below as his cock shot and shot and shot, his solid body quaking all the while.

Slowly, gently, I retracted my fingers from his tight little rump. He sighed, contentedly, and sank to the ground, rolling over to stare up at me. "Still don't think I can take it, friend?" he asked, the devilish smirk returning to his handsome face.

"I stand corrected," I told him and then joined him on the ground. "Make that, I *lay* corrected." And then I kissed him, soft and tender and perfect on his beautiful, full lips, running my hand down his amazingly tight, hair-covered body as I did so. "If you ride anywhere near as good as you kiss, I'm going to be a very rich man tomorrow."

He laughed, a rumble that ran over me like an avalanche. "I ride even better, my friend. Just you wait and see."

And wait I did. Thankfully, not for long.

As betting days went, I fared pretty well. Still, my mind raced at the thought of what was to come next. Or whom. Then the announcer proclaimed the final event. The crowd rose up, shouting, cheering, the sound nearly deafening me. Then absolute silence as the horses lined up behind their gates. A gunshot. They were off. Running. Hard. The jockeys perched atop their steeds, their legs braced tightly against thickly muscled flanks. Like a herd of wild animals pressed up side by side, impossibly close, the horses tore around the track.

All, that is, save Jersey Boy.

The ebony colt fell back, trailing one, then two body lengths behind the pack. My stomach sank. Not that sticking it to Gus would be a bad consolation prize, but still, losing was not what it was cracked up to be. Especially the wad of cash I had riding on this race. I sat my ass in the seat, my eyes glumly downcast. Then the announcer hollered that Jersey Boy was shooting around the outside. Again I looked up, stood up, shouted my obvious approval. Gus was pushing him on, fast, faster still, like a bolt of lightning. Little by little, he was gaining ground, passing each horse in turn, quickly moving into fourth, then third, then second place, running even, neck and neck with a brown colt, their bodies pressed up tight.

"Go, Jersey Boy. Go, Jersey Boy," I hollered, willing him forward. "Go, go, go fucking go."

The finish line drew nearer, and still they were dead even. Too damn close. Impossible to call.

The race ended. The crowd looked up expectantly at the megaphones. A photo finish was announced. Seconds ticked by like hours as my heart beat furiously in my chest and my stomach did a gastric samba.

Then the announcer wailed, "It's Jersey Boy by a nose!"

Half the crowd booed, the other cheered wildly. I, however, was already out of my seat, running to collect my winnings. *All* of them.

I met him outside the stall. In his shiny purple and gold suit, he led the triumphant Jersey Boy inside, smiling at me as he did so. "Told you we were going to win," he said as he passed by.

"Seems to me you had an extra good reason."

He returned, locked the stall, and replied, "Seems to me you're right. Had to make the race a quick one so I could get back here and get good and fucked. If you still want to, I mean." He looked up at me, coyly. Too damned fucking adorable.

"Hey, a bet's a bet. Where do I collect?"

The mischievous grin returned, as did the twinkle to his magnificent sapphire orbs. "Trailer's out back. Let's go before my cock explodes."

We rushed there and he led me inside. I instantly lifted him up and held on tight, smothering him with kisses, our eyes open, locked, watching intently, not wanting to miss a moment. "I can't wait to be inside you," I groaned into his mouth.

He laughed as I set him down. "Then you'd better hurry and undress me."

"Music to my ears," I told him, crouching down to untie his riding boots and pulling them off, then his long nylon socks, revealing his small feet, the toes smattered with the ever-present curly black hair, which I stroked with my fingertips. Then I stood back up and leaned down, kissing him softly, repeatedly, as I unbuttoned his satin jersey, dropping it to the floor before yanking his undershirt off. He giggled as I ran my fingers across his densely muscled abs, small and hard as oyster shells, though covered in the familiar soft down. I bent lower, taking a thick nipple in between my lips and teeth, biting down as I unbuttoned his trousers and slid down the zipper. He moaned, loudly, and shimmied out of his slacks, standing before me in nothing but a hard protective cup, and then that too was off him.

I stood back and appraised my work. "Damn," I said, with an appreciative sigh, "you are one beautiful, hard, hairy man."

"Speaking of hard," he said, pointing at the obvious tenting in my pants, "I think it's your turn now."

He watched, intently, as I shucked off my shoes, my slacks, my dress shirt and socks, and then my boxers, seeing me naked for the first time. He gave me an approving whistle. "Better than a garland of roses any day. Now fuck me. Quick."

Needless to say, he didn't have to tell me twice. And I came, literally, prepared.

I reached into my pant's pocket and removed a Trojan and a little tube of lube. I slid on the rubber, slicked up my prick, and hopped on his cot. "On your marks, get set," I said, smiling at him.

"Go," he practically purred, jumping on the cot and straddling my lap, perching his perfect ass just above my steely rod. I reached for the tube again, lubed up my fingers, and spread it around his chute.

I held him by his sides as he eased down, pressing his hole against the tip of my cock, pushing down, down, down, engulfing my prick in all that tight warmth and sending a million volts coursing from one end of my body to the other and then back again. When he was fully impaled on my dick, my balls lapping up against his hairy shores, he exhaled sharply, his eyes rolling to the back of his head before opening again, to stare into mine. "God, I'm glad I won that race."

"Ditto," I agreed, leaning in to kiss him, sucking on his mouth like a veritable Hoover as I reached down to stroke his swollen prick, already slick and sticky with pre-come, which leaked up and over his mushroomed head.

He mashed his ass down and his mouth in, grinding into my lap and my chest all at the same time, until I didn't know where my body ended and his began. Then he rode me like the pro he was, raising his rump up and then slamming it down, up and down, each time with a loud grunt, causing me to quicken my pace on his cock from a trot to a gallop in no time flat.

"Fuck, that feels good," he rasped, his mouth still pressed onto mine.

"Mhm," I agreed, my body now drenched in sweat as I pummeled his ass, ramming it with wild abandon.

"Make me come. Make me come. Make me come," he pleaded, the words hiccuping out of his mouth as I pumped his ass and cock.

I sped up, working his shaft rapid-fire fast. He ground his ass one final time onto my lap, forcing my cock to slam up against his granite-solid prostate. And then he shot, drenching my belly in hot, molten come, erupting over and over again, causing his ring to tighten around my prick, which then also shot, repeatedly, filling up that rubber and his ass with a massive load of my own.

Our moans and groans and sighs ricocheted around that trailer of his, which now shook as we rocked back and forth on his tiny cot. Then he collapsed into me, chest to fuzzy chest, sticky belly to sticky belly, his mouth nuzzling into my neck, a perfect fit if ever there was one, a giant puzzle piece and a much smaller one locking together.

We sat there like that, endless minutes ticking by as our breathing returned to normal. "Next time I might just lose," he finally whispered into my ear. "Just so I can fuck you."

"Easy for you to say," I whispered back, taking a diminutive lobe into my mouth. "It's not your money I'm betting with."

He shook with pleasure and pressed in even closer, if that was humanly possible. "You just made ten grand," he said. "I think you can spare it, my friend."

I laughed, reaching my arms around him in a tight embrace. "Not exactly."

"Not exactly? Didn't you bet on me to win?" I could already feel his cock miraculously begin to harden again, pushing gently into my stomach.

"Oh, that I did, Gus. That I did."

"But not the full thousand?" My own cock began to stiffen and fill up his hole, inch by rigid inch.

"Oh yes, the full thousand, five times over."

And then his laughter echoed my own as he slowly started to ride my cock again. "I made you *fifty* grand, Stu?"

"Mhm, enough for an entire season's worth of bets, Gus."

He leaned back out to look me deep in the eyes once again, those blue eyes of his eyes glinting in the light, as mesmerizing as the rest of him. "Sounds like a winning season then, Stu."

"Now *that's* a sure bet, Gus. A damn sure bet."

HUNK
MICHAEL ROBERTS

"FUCK ME, YOU BIG HUNKY STUD," he said.

"Oh, for heaven's sake," I said.

Timmy contrived to look inordinately hurt.

"You used to like to fuck me," he said, his lower lip quivering at about ninety miles an hour.

"I do like to fuck you. Most of the time. Some of the time. Occasionally."

He braked his lip and bit it and gave me his I'm-trying-very-hard-to-be-brave-but-it-isn't-easy look.

"What I *don't* like," I continued, giving him my I'm-exercising-every-bit-of-control-I-have-but-you're-really-testing-my-patience look, "what I *don't* like is the feeling that I'm reading you in one hand and jerking off with the other."

"Why, whatever do you mean?" he asked. He had adopted the tone of Joan Crawford in her why-are-you-beleaguering-me movies, wounded yet scornful. He drew himself up, trying to look imperious, an effect that was more than slightly marred by the fact that he was stark naked.

I was irritated and amused.

"I mean," I said, "that you seem to have read all the pornographic stories ever written and absorbed them en masse and in their entirety into your bloodstream. Then, when we're having sex—when I'm trying to have sex with you—you spew out every cliché you're ever read. That's what you are, a cliché spewer.

"Well, I don't want to fuck clichés. You're like a magazine. Turn to page 46 while I pound my pud and flip past the 900 telephone number ads and the photos of some guy sitting on a Harley, dangling his dingle over the gas tank, and pictures of another guy who's supposed to be straight but who's so gay he might as well be wearing neon lights —where the hell was I?"

"You were—" he said, and I held up my hand like a stop sign.

"I know where I was," I said. "I was turning the pages in this damned magazine to get to page 46 so that I can read another cliché about another guy's pile-driver cock plunging in and out of some dude's wet eager ass—"

"Oh, oh, oh!" Timmy said. "Pile driver—wet and eager—oh, wow, man! Yeah, yeah, my ass is so wet it's sweating! Your cock is like a machine—a big oily machine that's made to fit my ass!"

"Aaaah!" I commented. "If you don't stop with all the exclamation points, I'm going to knock your teeth down your throat."

"Oh, yeah!" he said, pitching his voice an octave lower. "S/M me, baby. Make me cringe, make me cry, make me suffer—just make me, master, make me!"

I think that I moaned. I sat on the edge of the bed with my back to Timmy, and I raised my face to the skies and shook my head as if I were asking for, and not receiving, help from something greater than I in dealing with my cliché-spouting burden. My nakedness contributed to the effect of the poor unprotected sufferer beset by vicissitudes beyond his control.

"Hey!" he growled. "Don't ignore me!"

I turned to him so quickly that I nearly gave myself whiplash. He looked, at that moment, so unlike himself that I feared that my forceful criticism had driven him to some sort of temporary (I hoped) derangement.

In alarm, I leaped to my feet.

"Pardon me?" I queried with icy inflection, conveying to him that he should abandon any hissy fit in which he intended to indulge—trying to convey to him, rather. The "pardon" emerged fine; the "me," however, emerged as a squeak.

"Look, *Davy,*" he said—using the short form of my name that he knows I hate. This was the Timmy to whom I was accustomed—reverting to puerile taunting to get what he wanted. "You cannot," he continued, "you cannot treat me so shittily." Ah—the typical Timmy vocabulary.

He sprang to his feet, nearly diving nose-first into the nightstand but recovering quite nicely.

"You see this?" he demanded, pointing to his crotch.

His prick pointed at us. Whatever Timmy's faults, his cock is delightful, a little wider and a little longer than standard size. Perhaps it was the angle from which I viewed it, but it seemed even wider and longer than usual. Certainly, I thought, I hadn't ever seen it jutting upward to quite that degree.

"You see *this?*" I snarled, gesturing to my groin.

My dick proudly exhibited its graceful curve as it stretched out to its full, firm length. It too is broader and longer than average, its attractions enhanced by a rightward swing. I had often presented this appendage to Timmy for my, and for his, delectation and delight.

Timmy swatted my schlong aside—not hard enough to hurt, just to sting. My boner bounced back.

"Big deal," he snapped. "Big fucking deal."

"Well, yes," I said, "actually, it is. As you very well know."

Timmy sneered. Until that moment, I hadn't ever seen him sneer. His expressions ran the gamut from puppy-love appreciation to queenly hauteur to dramatic detestation. (Timmy did not merely disapprove—he despised.) But sneering? That was bizarre. However, all his behavior had turned bizarre today.

"As I very well have led you to believe," he said, his upper lip curling in a manner that was both strange and frightening.

"Pardon me?" I said. This time, both words squeaked.

Timmy rolled his eyes—a response with which I was only too familiar. However, I was not in the least familiar with the timbre of the words that seethed from the lips that were now both drawn back over his teeth as if he were a piqued Pomeranian—some little yappy, yippy dog that might become more bothersome. Timmy's teeth appeared to be a trifle sharp.

What he so extraordinarily said was, "How many times—how many, many times—have I lain beneath you as you struggled toward some mediocre achievement, some meager climax—if you could call it a climax—how many times have I assured you that your efforts were transporting me to some exalted sensual plane? And how many times—how many, many times—has that encouragement been a fabrication, the most outrageous falsehood? How many times did I lie to you so that you would just finish your endeavors and roll off me and fall asleep and snore until you sounded like a 747 coming in for a landing? How many times—how many, many, many times—have I been so glad that you were asleep so that I could fantasize about being fucked by a real man?"

"Oh!" I gasped. I was, I admit, stung to the quick. It took a while to get to my quick, but Timmy was there. I wagged my wonker at him. "How many times—how many, many, many times—have you begged me to fuck you hard, fuck you long? How many times—how many, many, *many* times—have you been only too glad—*too glad*—to have my cock, my big hard cock, in your mouth and up your ass?"

"It's not the size of the wand," he said, looking down his nose at me, "it's the magic in the wand."

"Aaaah!" I remarked. "You cling to clichés like a—like a—you cling to clichés. Don't you ever stop clinging to clichés?"

Anger was reducing me to incoherence.

"*You* are a cliché," he declared, raising his voice a few decibels. "You are the cliché of the guy who thinks he's so fucking hot and so hot fucking, and he's really so cold, he's like the fucking South Pole."

"That makes no sense!" I shouted.

"Well, maybe *this* will make sense!" he barked, and, abruptly, he grabbed me by the shoulders, spun me around, and shoved me face down onto the bed.

"Pah!" I bleated into the mattress, and I was about to rise and ask him just what the blue bloody hell he thought he was doing when he threw himself down on top of me.

"You think you know what fucking is?" he whispered quite ferociously into my ear. "I'm going to *teach* you what *real* fucking is!"

"Now, you listen to me—" I started to say, or tried to say, since my mouth was squashed against the mattress.

He roughly grasped my buttocks in both of his hands and spread them, and I felt, I thought that I felt, surely I did not feel, the head of his cock pressing importunately against my nether regions.

I was expressing a variety of protests, unfortunately rendered unintelligible because I was expressing them into the Laura Ashley sheets on which Timmy insisted.

And then, the inexplicable assault upon me continued.

"You've been asking for this," he hissed into my ear, and bit it.

"Ouch!" I said. His dental attack had not been strong—his teeth had only nicked me. My muffled interjection was more of surprise than pain.

"Ouch, indeed," he said. "Let me show you what 'ouch' really is!"

At that point, he slammed his cock into me.

"Ow!" I said.

"How does that feel?" he asked.

I had not been a virgin for years—several years—so it wasn't as if I hadn't ever had a dick in me. It wasn't as if I had always been the passer and not the receiver. For some time, however, I had chosen to be a top.

And certainly there was no question of what roles Timmy and I were to play in our sexual drama—which was quickly becoming a melodrama or a comedy.

But if you don't use a road for a while, it becomes less easily driven —so to speak. And now Timmy's vehicle was charging into areas that had not been recently charted. "You haven't answered my question," he said huskily, and steered his dick further into my hinterlands. "How does that feel?"

At last, I got my head turned so that I wasn't inhaling tastefully designed cotton.

"Actually," I said, "it doesn't feel bad at all."

"It doesn't feel bad at all?" he repeated, and his voice rose, and for a moment, he sounded like my old Timmy, about to launch into some operatic declamation of hurt feelings and wounded pride.

Then, "How about *this?*" he growled—really, he was growling more tonight than he had in our whole relationship—and he stepped on the gas and drove his hot rod into the middle of my camp. "How does *that* feel?"

I considered his question. Actually, it felt pretty good. His bush was scraping against my buttocks, so I knew that he was all the way in. His prick, a little longer and a little wider than standard size, was in me as far as it could go. I was being stretched and spread out, and it felt good.

"It feels good," I told him.

It was as if my words pressed down on the gas pedal of his lust. "And *this*—and *this*—and *this?*" he asked. In quick succession, he pistoned again and again, withdrawing and then crashing into me— and crashing in, it seemed, farther and farther. Each time I thought that he was completely inside me, and each time he propelled himself a greater distance into my interior. "And *this*—and *this*—and *this?*"

I would have answered, but all I could respond was "Uh—uh— uh" as he kept hitting new boundaries. My whole body was bouncing into the bed—boing! boing! boing!

Oh, it felt good! His motor of passion was heating me up, and a glow spread from my asshole up into my pelvis and through my cock and balls and into my belly and into my chest. I was hot all over, and the furnace inciting this flurry of fire was his dick, bamming and blamming into me—bam! bam! blam!

And then he stopped. In the middle of a bam or a blam, he stopped.

"Well?" I asked the sheet.

"Well?" he echoed. "Well, what?"

"Well," I said, "are you going to finish what you've begun?"

"What do you want me to do?"

"You know what I want you to do."

"Ask me."

"Ask you?" I said. Unfortunately, I squeaked again. "*Ask you?*"
Conversing in italics was exhausting.

"All right," I said, "continue."

"What?"

"Go on."

"What?"

"Don't stop, damn it!"

"You know what I want to hear."

"No, I *don't* know what you want to hear."

"Think about it."

I thought about it.

"Oh, no," I sighed.

"Oh, yes," he said. It was funny how two short words could convey such satisfaction.

"No," I said.

There was a silence.

"No."

Silence.

"All right," I said. "All right. Fuck me, you big hunky stud."

He did.

He fucked me up and down and sideways, left and right and through the center aisle. He fucked me high and low. He fucked me fast and he fucked me slow. He fucked me tender and fucked me true; he fucked me black and blue.

"*Ah!—ah!—ah!*" I said. And "*Oh—oh!—oh!*" I said. And then I said, "Um—um—ummmm."

And still he fucked. His pile-driver cock bored into my ass.

He turned me on my back, and he leered over me, incisors sparkling, and he fucked me.

He made me kneel, and he mounted me and rode me until I was wringing wet.

"Tighten that ass!" he shouted. "Tighten that ass!"

"Who the hell do you think you are?" I said. "Jeff Stryker?"

And he propelled me back down on the bed so that my nose was again buried in Laura Ashley flowers, and he planted his hands on both sides of my head for leverage, and he fucked me, he screwed me, he impaled me, he lanced me, he lacerated me, he ripped and roared, no longer a car, now a train steaming down my hills and into my valleys.

The bedsprings squealed, and I squealed—I admit it—and I said to the bedclothes, "Give me your cock! Use my wet eager ass! Big slab of meat! Give me your beef—your joint, your tool! Yeah, man! Yeah, yeah, yeah!"

Above me, Timmy began to whinny like a horse nearing the finish line at the Kentucky Derby.

I shouted monosyllabically into the bed.

The noise was almost deafening—the bedsprings were screeching, and Timmy was snorting, and I was yelping, and flesh was slapping against flesh like tympani.

Timmy's cock sliced me up and cut me down and split me and bound me. He bounced on top of me with such vigor that I thought that surely the bed beneath us would collapse and thud into the apartment below and into the next apartment and down and down, just as he was thudding down and down and yet farther down into me, into my very foundation.

His whinnying was ear-splitting, and my shouting was loud enough to wake people half a continent away, and his dick was piercing me, and the bedsprings were screaming, and heat rose all the way from the tips of my toes, up calves and thighs and bucking hips into my whole body and centered at the base of my cock and burned along its length and across its width and spurted out onto the bed, feeding the Laura Ashley flowers, bathing my stomach in its sticky warmth—

—and at the same time, Timmy hit a note high enough to shatter light bulbs, and he pounded into me, and he shot, shot so hard and so richly that this torrent surged and bubbled through me and filled me and overflowed through my pulsing dick out onto bed and belly.

Together, in harmony, we cried, "Aaaaaaaaah!"

Timmy collapsed on top of me. His head was over my shoulder and beside mine on the bed. I spat out the cotton chrysanthemum that I had clenched between my teeth and weakly swiveled my head so that I was looking directly into his eyes.

Did he smile enigmatically? I thought so, but I may have been wrong, because at that instant, I slipped into an exhausted sleep.

When I awoke, Timmy was sitting up and leaning against the headboard. The expression on his face was one of supreme smugness.

"What the hell," I said weakly, "was that?"

He smiled. "You just met Timothy."

"Timothy?"

"Timothy. Davy met Timothy. Usually, Timmy is with David, but last night, Davy was with Timothy."

"Excuse me?" I said blankly.

"Think about it," he said.

I thought about it.

"Oh," I said. "*Oh!*"

"Exactly," said he.

"Hmm," I wittily replied. "Timothy was definitely a surprise."

"Did you like the surprise?"

I thought about *that*. My ass ached pleasurably, and my stomach was stuck to Laura Ashley.

"Yes," I said. "I did like it."

"How much?" he asked, and his left eyebrow ascended nearly to his hairline.

I winced. I knew what he wanted to hear. Could I utter the odious word, one of Timmy's favorite expressions?

"It was," I said, "it was—awesome."

His right eyebrow joined its companion. "Wow," he said.

"Wow," I agreed. "Is there a possibility that I'll see Timothy more than once?"

He opened his mouth in a circle of surprise and elation. With his mouth agape and his eyebrows arched, he looked like a smiley face.

"Maybe," he said. "You never know when he'll show up."

"I hope that we'll meet again," I said, and, unexpectedly, I did hope so. Who would have thought that having the tables turned on me, being flipped like a frying, sizzling egg by the spatula of Timmy's cock, would be so filling and so fulfilling?

"I'll give him your message," said Timmy. He slid down the bed and turned over.

The globes of his ass shone. What a perfect ass he has—and sometimes is. How luxuriously lovely are the peaks of carnal promise, how voluptuous, how enticing, how alluring. How many enchantments hide within his deepest recesses, waiting to be caressed and aroused by my explorer dick.

His eyes twinkled.

"Fuck me, you big hunky stud," he said.

And I did.

DEVON

MARK WILDYR

MY FATHER ROLLED DOWN THE DODGE PICKUP'S WINDOW, admitting the heat and dust as we left our quarter-section and drove across town to the old Jones place early Monday morning.

"Are you looking forward to your summer, Patrick?"

I brushed a blond cowlick out of my eyes and nodded. "Guess so. As much as a fellow can look forward to stretching fence. But thanks for offering to pay me."

"Only right," he answered. Then he read my mind, as he usually did. "Up till now it was just chores, really, but this'll keep you hopping full-time till you go off to college in the fall. Got a corral and shed to build after the fencing's done if I'm gonna run cattle on that land."

"Yeah. I'll get it done, Pop."

"I know you will. You with me asking the Hartshorn boy to give you a hand?"

I paused before answering. Everyone talked about Devon Hartshorn, but nobody ever said anything about him, if you know what I mean. His family was new to town when some drunk plowed into their car out on Highway 55. Killed everybody except the Hartshorn boy, who was never the same afterward. The kids at school claimed he was feeble-minded or worse. The thought of working with a blithering idiot raised the hair on my neck.

But that wasn't all of it. Nobody was left to take care of the kid after the family was killed, so they put him in a public home. When he turned eighteen, the man who ran the place took him to live at his house. Everybody thought that was mighty Christian of Mr. Jones until the ugly rumors started. He was *abusing* the kid, people said. Abuse to me was a walloping that wasn't earned, but the kids in the know whispered about another kind. Some guys claimed Mr. Jones was . . . well, screwing the kid. The outraged locals ran the man out of town, and now Devon lived alone in the old Jones house out on the west side.

Dad spoke into my silence. "Devon's a good boy despite all that's happened to him. He's a good worker, even if he is kinda soft in the head. Do you know him, son?"

"Seen him around town, but that's all. And, yeah. I'm OK with working with him," I said as we turned into the dirt drive beside a white clapboard, cross-gabled house.

I'd never seen Devon up close and don't know what I expected, but it wasn't what I got. A handsome, fit young man with coffee-colored hair and deep brown eyes tripped down the steps and grasped my dad's hand.

"Morning, Devon," Dad said. "You know my boy, Patrick? You're gonna be working for him this summer. You two are gonna fence part of the old Mills place for me."

"Yes, sir, Mr. Holt. Hello, Patrick," he said, solemnly greeting me with a firm handshake. "Did Mr. Mills say it's OK?"

"Mr. Mills is dead, Devon," my old man explained. "I bought his land, and that's what you and Patrick are going to fence. Understand?"

"Yes, sir. I'll work good for you, Patrick."

"Uh . . . OK," I said in a daze. Dad explained things to Devon like he was a ten-year-old, but the guy was built like an adult—although he looked younger than me. And that couldn't be; Mr. Jones got chased out of town four years ago. If the kid was eighteen then, he'd be twenty-two now at least.

"You sure you're OK with this?" my father asked when Devon hopped in the truck bed and we started for the house. "He's a good kid, Patrick," he went on when I nodded. "You treat him decent, you hear. Everybody acts like he's different—and he is, I guess—but they're either condescending as hell or else they treat him like a mindless animal. I know you won't do that."

Devon and I loaded a posthole digger, fence posts, wire, cutters, and the come-along jack from the barn and headed for the job, fortified by two fat sack lunches and a big cooler of water. Neither Devon nor I said a thing on the six-mile drive to the Mills place. I was too nervous, and he apparently had nothing to contribute.

I quickly learned if I carefully explained what was expected, Devon performed perfectly. If I assumed he understood something, it led to disaster. When we broke for lunch, I tried to initiate a conversation.

"You're a good worker," I started and immediately realized that condescension thing had reared its ugly head.

"Thanks, Patrick. Mr. Jones said that was what everybody expects out of a fellow."

The casual mention of his abuser threw me off stride. "I'm surprised you even mention that son-of-a-bitch's name. Uh . . . him treating you that way and all."

His reaction was astounding. "Don't go saying bad things about Mr. Jones! He was good to me. Till he up and left me all by myself. Why did he do that? I thought he liked me. Said he loved me. What does love mean?" Devon asked, throwing me a curve.

Stunned, I looked at the incredibly handsome boy . . . man . . . sitting beside me on the Dodge's tailgate, chewing his sandwich placidly. "Uh, that's when you like somebody really well."

"Oh, then I guess I love you, Patrick."

"No, no!" I sputtered. "I mean like when a man and a woman want to get married. Or how a fellow feels about his father or mother."

He frowned in concentration. "Can a man love a man?"

"Sure. Like brothers, you know. Otherwise, they're just buddies."

"Buddies. Is that what we are, Patrick? I had a buddy once," he went on in his childlike way. "Mr. Jones was my buddy. He loved me." The frown came again. "But he went away."

"You don't know why he went away? Be damned, you don't have any idea, do you?" I muttered when those big, liquid, clueless eyes turned on me. "How could you like a man like Jones?"

"He was a good man," Devon said seriously. "He treated me real good. Took care of me when nobody else wanted me."

That made sense—put up with the abuse in payment for the care. My curiosity got the better of me. "Didn't you resent what he . . . did to you?"

"He didn't do nothing to me," came the sincere reply, making me wonder if a great injustice had been done in the heat of the chase.

"He didn't . . . do things to you? You know, personal things."

A confused frown revealed Devon's lack of comprehension. "He did good things to me."

I backed off. "Well, if it'll make you feel any better, he didn't want to leave you. He got . . . uh, he had to leave, and they wouldn't let him take you with him."

"I know. That's what he told me. Said he couldn't even write to me."

"Great," I muttered, crawling to my feet.

When I took Devon home after work and paid him for the day as my dad had instructed me, he promised to be ready bright and early the next morning. We were both filthy from the day's work, and I wondered if he'd have enough sense to clean his clothes.

I had time to clean up before Mom put supper on the table but decided I was too tired to go into town and find my girl, Sara Sue Crowley. I settled for talking to her on the telephone for fifteen minutes instead.

◆

DEVON WAS WAITING ON THE FRONT PORCH when I pulled up early the next morning. My fears were unfounded; he and his clothes were clean—except for his fingernails. He probably didn't have a manicure case, so I resolved to bring my spare set the next day. Work went well that Tuesday, so I decided to take a longer lunch break in the shade of a big cottonwood near a small brook. That surface water was one reason Dad bought the pasturage. I sat with my legs spread out in front of me, enjoying the cool shade and the heady aroma of the summer grass. The only audible noises—aside from our own—were the drone of crickets and an occasional buzzing insect. Dev, as I'd taken to calling him, startled me when he spoke.

"Bet you've got a big one. You know, a big thing."

I was so stunned I forgot to get mad. "Why the hell would you say something like that?"

"Well, it pooches out a lot, so I guess it's big. See, like now."

I looked down at myself. There was a definite lump behind my fly. I drew up my legs defensively.

"Don't do that," he protested. "I like to look at it. I look at it all the time when we're working."

"Don't talk like that, Dev!"

"Mr. Jones said you couldn't talk like that to nobody but real good friends. I thought you and me was friends, Patrick."

I flushed. "We are, Dev, but you still can't talk to me like that."

"Sorry." He was quiet for a few minutes. "Don't guess I can see it, then."

"See it! You want to see my cock?" My voice went up an octave, abandoning its manly timbre. "Hell, no, you can't see it!"

"Cock. I like that. Mr. Jones always called it a dick. Mostly, I just call it a thing."

"It's a penis," I snapped.

He snickered. "Peanuts!"

"No, penis," I corrected, and then started laughing with him. He actually clutched his stomach and rolled on his side. His glee was infectious; we roared with laughter.

When we went to work again, I caught him staring at my crotch. What the hell! No skin off my nose.

"It's OK. You can look, Dev, but only when there's nobody around."

"Thank you, Patrick," he said, grinning happily and giving my basket an extra-hard stare. "But can I see it for real?"

"No!" I said shortly and sent him a hundred yards down the fence line to stretch barbed wire with the come-along. Then I stapled the strand to posts we'd already set in the ground. By the time I delivered him home that evening, my fly was the most studied place on the planet. I'll swear he could recognize me solely by the bulge in my britches.

That night I made it into town in time to pick up Sara Sue from the town's drugstore, where she work behind the soda fountain. She laughed a hello, calling me by my last name—Holt—the way she always does. Despite working all day, she smelled good. Looked good, too. Wish she'd take an interest in my groin like Dev. Well, on occasion, she did, except I was the one doing the begging then. We ate a burger, had a shake, and talked a bunch, but all I got was a long, deep goodnight kiss in front of her house instead of her tiny little hand exploring my privates.

◆

THE NEXT MORNING, I TOSSED A SMALL KIT IN DEV'S LAP as he got into the cab. "Here. You can keep your nails clean with these."

"Is that for me?" he asked. "A present for me? Thank you, Patrick. Will you show me how to use it?"

As we drove to work, I explained the use of each of the little instruments and got a kick out of the excited way he started digging dirt out from under his fingernails. By now I was getting a handle on Devon Hartshorn. He wasn't an idiot or anything like that; I'm not even sure he was retarded. He was just slow, and at times it showed up more than others. Mostly he acted almost normal, although sometimes you had to baby him along. But he could take care of himself and do good work and make halfway decent conversation. I decided I liked him.

By Friday morning, we'd worked our way to a corner of the property and made a turn. A stand of trees off to our right told me the brook was close, so we piled into the truck and drove over to have our lunch. The trees overhung a spot where the stream pooled, making a sheltered area and providing relief from the heat. Dev was delighted with it.

31

A little antsy over my intention, I got up and shucked my shirt after we ate. "Come on, let's cool off in the water."

His reaction surprised me. "Oh, no! Mr. Jones always said to wait thirty minutes after I eat before going swimming."

"It's OK, Dev. The water's not deep enough to swim. We're just going to cool off."

"Oh. I guess that's all right then. You're awful smart, Patrick. And real pretty."

I'm sure I blushed—*flushed;* girls blush. "Boys aren't pretty, Dev. They're . . . handsome, I guess."

"Mr. Jones always said I was pretty. Pretty as a girl, he'd say."

"How'd that make you feel?" I asked, hopping around on one foot while I tugged the boot off the other.

"Real good, 'cause he meant it to be nice. And so did I, Patrick. You know, when I said you was pretty . . . uh, handsome."

"Shut up, Dev," I said, removing the last bit of my clothing.

"Oh, good! I get to see your thing."

"Guess you do," I agreed, wading into the thigh-deep water and turning to face him. The stream was cold despite the day's heat. Oh, well, that would be a good excuse when my prick wasn't as big as he thought it ought to be.

I'll admit I examined him with some curiosity as he walked down the grassy slope with his eyes fastened on my pecker. Somehow it didn't seem right. Flawed goods ought to *look* flawed, but Devon was built like a high school quarterback and was better looking than the king of the senior prom. He was also better hung than my dad's Appaloosa stud.

"Look, it's different!" he exclaimed in amazement, pointing at my crotch. Startled, I looked down to see if it had fallen off or something, but everything looked normal except I'd stiffened up a little.

"What's different?"

"Our things," he said, grabbing his penis between two fingers. I was about to protest that the cold water had shrunk me when he skinned himself back. "I got a hood on mine, see. You don't have one. What happened to the skin on the end of your thing, Patrick?"

"I'm circumcised, Dev. Most guys are nowadays."

"Cir . . . cir . . ."

"Circumcised. Cut. They cut the foreskin off."

"Cut!" He was horrified. "They cut your thing? Who did? Was it a accident?"

"No, it wasn't an accident. The doctor did it after I was born."

"How come?"

"Hygiene, I guess. Supposed to be easier to keep clean."

Worry clawed at his face. "Do I have to do it?"

"No. You just have to be careful to clean behind the foreskin," I said, noticing with alarm that he was still skinning himself back and forth and growing alarmingly. "Stop that!" I demanded, abruptly sitting down in the water. He continued to stand beside me in the stream.

"Can I feel it?" he asked. "I never felt a cut one before."

"No, you can't feel it!" I responded, and then went fishing. "Wasn't Mr. Jones cut like me?"

"No. He had one like mine, except not as big as yours and mine. And he showed me how to clean up so I don't smell bad."

"Did you touch his thing . . . uh, cock?"

Dev nodded vigorously. "He let me touch it whenever I wanted to."

"Did he touch you?"

"Sure. That's what you do when someone touches you. You touch him back."

"Wouldn't you rather touch a girl?"

The shock on his face was genuine. "Oh, no, Patrick! Girls are good and pure, and you don't do things like that to them."

"Who told you that? Mr. Jones?"

33

"No. My grandmother told me you don't do bad things to girls. They're too pure. At least, I think it was my grandmother," he added with a puzzled frown. "I can't hardly remember. But I remember for sure my mom saying that, too. Before she went away." An idea apparently occurred; a connection was made. "Did . . . did Mr. Jones have a accident too? Is that why he had to go away?"

"No, he had to go away because people thought he was taking advantage of you."

The expression on his face alarmed me. "What do you mean?"

"Well," I said hesitantly, "they thought he was abusing you. You know, touching your thing and . . . uh, you know."

It was as if Devon Hartshorn shut down. His face closed up, and he sank wordlessly into the cold water until the current pressed against his broad chest. Frankly, it scared the hell out of me. I wondered if I'd unleashed a monster or something. Finally, he spoke.

"He went away because of me."

I felt like a real shit, so I spent the next fifteen minutes trying to change the subject. At last, he began to respond to my questions, and I learned Dev could read and write and do the rudiments of arithmetic, simple addition and subtraction and the multiplication tables up to the fives. He finally came out of his funk when I began teaching him the sixes. My cock had shrunk and my balls were blue by the time we crawled out of the water and dressed, but at least he was acting OK again.

It was almost quitting time before he paused in his work and leveled those big eyes at me. "Was it my fault, Patrick? Did I do something to get Mr. Jones in trouble?"

I got a little sad listening to his slow, deliberate voice. Realizing that my answer was terribly important, I paused before answering. "No, Dev, I don't think so. Did you ever tell anybody about Mr. Jones touching your thing?"

"No, he always said it was something that was just for us. We didn't share."

"Did you ever touch anybody else like that?"

He was momentarily outraged. "No! Not while Mr. Jones was with me."

My eyes widened. "You touched somebody after that?"

He shook his head and dropped his gaze. "No, but I wanted to. I wanted to touch you, Patrick. It's been a long time since I got to touch anybody, and I wanted to touch you."

Shit! Hoist on my own petard! "All right, Dev, if you promise you won't ever tell anybody, you can touch me."

Pure joy radiated from him as he pressed his hand against my crotch. For a long moment his fingers caressed my flaccid cock through the denim of my jeans before I moved away.

"Can I feel it for real?" he asked immediately.

"Maybe," I hedged. "If we go in the water again, maybe you can."

All the way to the Jones place I wondered what the hell I'd gotten myself into, but at least he wasn't sad any longer. He sat across the seat from me grinning like a frog with a dragonfly.

◆

FRIDAY AND SATURDAY NIGHTS DID NOT GO AS PLANNED. I got snockered—really, really snockered—with a couple of buddies at a roadhouse on the highway that winked at the law and let kids in. Sara Sue and I didn't really have a date Friday, but she'd expected to at least hear from me, and I didn't even think of it until I was sitting on the milking stool Saturday morning all sick and hungover. I think Dad knew what ailed me, but he held his tongue. Mom was damned suspicious.

As you can imagine, Saturday night was nothing to shout about. I took Sara Sue to the movies, but all I got out of it was the pleasure of spending twenty dollars on her and enduring a five-minute lecture and a three-hour frost. Shit! I'd have had more fun with Devon Hartshorn! Where the hell did that thought come from?

◆

AS SOON AS DEV SLAMMED THE TRUCK DOOR BEHIND HIM Monday morning, he turned to me eagerly. "Are we going swimming today, Patrick?"

Damnation! Had he spent the whole weekend thinking about my cock? Probably.

Dev pitched in as though noon would come around quicker if he worked harder. When we drove to the little grove sheltering the pool, he ate only half his lunch and then sat staring at me until I gave up.

"OK, let's go," I said. By the time I was stripped, he was buck naked and dancing from one foot to the other in excitement.

"Can I now? Can I? Please, Patrick?"

"Go ahead," I said, opening my stance and planting my fists on my hips.

Timidly, he put a finger to the head of my dick. When I didn't react, he grew bolder, placing his palm flat against me. Damned if my pecker didn't stir a little. Then he grasped it in his fingers and fiddled for a minute. I was about to brush his hand away when he spoke.

"How come the hair on your head's yellow, but the hair down there's kinda brown?"

"That's the way blonds are, I guess."

"Blonds. Is that what you are, Patrick?" Without waiting for an answer, he added, "It's a nice one. I like it. I like it a lot, but I don't know how to do it!"

That stumped me. "Do what?"

"Well," he said slowly, "I just pull mine back and push it up again. You don't have nothing to push and pull."

Realizing he was speaking of my lack of a foreskin, I brushed his hand aside. "I said you could touch it, Dev. I didn't say you could jack me off."

"But can you do it? Can you make it spit up? You know, like when it feels so good that the stuff comes out . . . not pee-pee, but the white stuff."

"I know what you mean," I answered, turning away and marching into the water before he saw I was getting hard. "And yes, it can spit up. It can spit up real good!"

"I'll bet it can. Can I see?"

"No!"

"Please! I don't see how it can since you don't have—"

"It can!" I snapped and sank to the gravel bottom of the brook. He splashed in and sat beside me.

"Patrick, are you mad at me? Please don't be mad at me."

"I'm . . . not," I said, realizing I had a full-blown erection. Shit! I hoped he couldn't see it through the water.

Angry at myself for reacting, mad at Sara Sue for acting shitty just because I got drunk and ignored her, and frustrated at dealing with this simple, good-looking fucker, I lay back in the water. Unfortunately, I didn't take into account its buoyancy, and my middle floated to the top for a moment. I didn't intend for that to happen . . . I don't think.

"Patrick!" I heard his excited yelp. "It's big. It's hard and sticking up like you want to feel good. Can I make you feel good?"

Without answering, I stood and followed my erection back up the embankment. Dev trailed along behind me. I sopped away the water with one of the towels I'd brought and tossed the other one to him. Dev was too excited to dry himself, he just stood in front of me, wide eyes fastened to my hard cock, his own beginning to swell impressively.

We stood examining each other for a long minute before I sprawled on the blanket we used for a picnic cloth. He sat beside me, pressing me flat on my back with a broad hand on my chest. I knew what would happen next but was helpless to prevent it.

Dev's work-hardened hand clasped me in a gentle grip. "Oh, Patrick! It's beautiful!"

The thought of a cock as beautiful wouldn't scan, but it sure did feel beautiful when he ran his fist up and down it. His other hand gently cupped my balls. I closed my eyes and surrendered.

Before long, he gave a snort of frustration. "I can't do it right, Patrick, 'cause it don't have a skin to slide up and down. Oh, I know!"

My verbal assurance that he was doing just fine died in my throat as his lips closed over me. I lost what little power of resistance remained as he sucked my cock, fondled my balls, and played with my chest and belly. Nobody had ever done that for me before, and it provoked unimagined sensations and rewards. His mouth and tongue were infinitely better than his fingers. Hell, they were better than Sara Sue's little fist.

Dev bobbed up and down on me in a steady rhythm. Occasionally, his lips reached all the way to the root and his nose rested in my cock hair for a moment. I opened my eyes and watched him, getting an additional rush from seeing that handsome head swallow my rigid pole.

"Dev, I'm gonna come! You hear? I'm gonna shoot my wad!" He paid no attention, keeping to the very effective rhythm he had established. "Oh, man! Oh, man!" I wailed. My ass clenched, my balls drew up, and I unloaded in his mouth. He paused then, struggling to take all of my come, slowly working up and down the length of my convulsing cock until I stopped shooting. Finally, I put a hand on his head to stop him.

He looked up at me with innocent brown eyes. "Did I do it good, Patrick?"

"Gr . . . great," I panted, expecting revulsion, disgust, dismay—at the very least, shame. Instead I felt sated, satisfied, and lazy. I didn't mind him stroking my chest and thighs lightly. "What do you get out of doing that?" I asked.

"You mean why do I like to do that with my mouth? It makes me feel good to make you feel good, Patrick. And you did! I could tell you felt real good when you shot your stuff in my mouth."

"Yeah, I did," I admitted. "Dev, you can't tell *anyone* what we did, not anyone!"

"Oh, I won't, Patrick!" He laid a finger across his lips like a child pledging a secret. "Not nobody. Mr. Jones says that's real personal and you don't tell people real personal things. You don't ever talk about it with nobody else. But I really did like it. Thank you, Patrick. Thank you a whole bunch." He hesitated. "I guess I love you now, Patrick. It feels good to love somebody."

Having no response, I lay back and closed my eyes. "I'm going to take a nap."

"Me, too. That's a real good idea," he responded, lying down beside me. He was quiet for a moment and then said, "Patrick, will you hold me? Haven't had nobody to hold me in a long time."

"Sure . . . I guess," I said, stretching my arm out. He snuggled his trim body against me. Finding it not objectionable, I sort of curled into him, throwing a leg over his thigh and an arm across that broad, smooth chest. "This feel OK?"

"It feels real good, Patrick. Thank you."

When I woke, Dev was spooned against me. My flaccid cock rested against his crack. I stretched languidly, grinding my groin against him.

"Oh, that feels good, Patrick. Do it again," he whispered, startling me. I'd thought him asleep.

Damned if I didn't start to get hard as my semi-erect cock rode his ass a second time. He sighed again. Not quite believing what I was contemplating, I rubbed my erection up and down his cleft. He pulled his cheeks apart and thrust his butt at me. I centered and lunged. He gasped at my rough entry.

"That's all right, Patrick," he said. "It'll be all right when you get it inside me. You're awful big, you know."

"Yeah," I panted as I shoved again, "about half the size of yours."

He pushed his ass against me, driving the rest of my rod up his butt. "It's all in now, Patrick. Do it to me real good, will you please?"

So I did it to him. I did it to him for half an hour. I fucked him on his side for a while and then rolled him on his stomach and fucked some more. I speared him like our bull screwed Bessie, like Dad's stud covering a mare. He took it all and asked for more. He rose to meet me as I plunged into him. He cried with joy when I went especially deep.

The small seed of anger hiding inside me at doing this thing evaporated. I shoved his legs wider with my knees and found a rhythm. I fucked steadily and was surprised to realize I was doing it as much for him as for me. Just before I slid over the edge, his voice startled me.

"Oh, Patrick! I'm gonna spit up! Oh . . . oh . . . ooooh! I got stuff all over your blanket!"

The most amazing thing happened. His spasming ass massaged my cock, his channel sucked me over the top, and I blew an ejaculation I didn't even know existed. I plunged, I stabbed, I came, I convulsed, I groaned, I cried, I fucked!

When the whirlwind was past, I lay panting atop his sweat-drenched body. My lips rested on his smooth cheek. "That was something, Dev. Did you like it?"

"Oh, yes, Patrick! I been wanting for you to do that forever. Did I do good for you?"

40

"You bet! Terrific."

"Are we gonna do it again?"

"Oh, yeah, Dev. We're gonna do it again."

He twisted around, giving me a look at his handsome profile. "I love you, Patrick."

"You know what, sport? I think I'm beginning to understand."

BUSINESS WITH PLEASURE

GAVIN ATLAS

I FELT CERTAIN IT WAS A BAD IDEA for me to get naked at another of Jeremy's parties, especially considering my position as a financial advisor at Wesley-Shields Limited. But as I rode in the taxi to his apartment, it was obvious that I couldn't resist.

On the way there, I had the paranoid sensation that everyone knew what I was about to do. The guy at the wine shop, the taxi driver, pedestrians on the street, and even Jeremy's doorman all gave me little smiles that made me feel that they'd heard about me.

In the elevator I tried to focus on the good mood I'd been in all day since Mr. Wesley, the owner of the company I work for, had spoken to me this morning. He knew we advisors were all having an awful time because of how badly Wall Street has been doing, but he just patted me on the back and said, "Hang in there." I wondered how he'd feel if he knew I wanted him.

I took a deep breath as I reached Jeremy's floor. What had I gotten myself into? Though nothing had been said aloud, I knew these guys were going to strip me down in the living room, maybe as soon as I arrived. Part of me felt submissive and extremely turned on, but it was at war with the part that felt nervous and ashamed. My body was decent, but not porn star quality. I didn't imagine most people would be eager to see me get fucked, but these guys apparently were into it.

I had arrived a bit late, and I nodded shyly at the group while Jeremy took my coat. Before the door was closed, I'd already been handed a double vodka tonic.

"Drink up," Jeremy said, with his eyebrows raised.

For about forty-five minutes we made idle chatter, until I noticed Jeremy winking at Kurt while handing me a fresh cocktail. Then Kurt unbuttoned my shirt and another guy, Eugene, began massaging my back and crotch. I drank carefully, pretending to be drunker than I was. If they thought I was inebriated, I imagined I wouldn't feel as embarrassed later for letting this happen. Also, it definitely encouraged them to take liberties with my clothing. However, I wanted to have my wits about me if things started to get out of hand.

The phone rang, and Jeremy looked at the caller ID. He picked up and said, "Yes, Jeff, our party bottom made it tonight." Jeremy grinned at me, a bit sloshed himself. "Describe him? He's twenty-five and about five foot eight. Kind of a black-Irish look. Dark hair with blue eyes. Muscular. Perfect ass. Get here quick or it might be over."

"Why do you . . . have to keep calling me a party bottom?" I said, deliberately hitching my speech to sound wasted. "It's embarrassing. I've only done this once before."

"Uh, because you love it?" Jeremy said.

"Humph," I said, sipping my drink, "I'm a good boy."

"That's very true," said Eugene, reaching down to undo the button on my jeans.

I sat on Jeremy's carpet, looking out the window at his sweeping view of the East River and Queens. Jeremy and the friends he had invited sat around me on the sectional sofa. I felt like their pet, sitting beneath my masters on the floor.

"I'm just curious about something," Eugene said, as he came down from the sofa to work me out of my pants. He may have been a nerdy Chinese guy with thick glasses, but he'd been the most aggressive of all that evening. He slid my jeans down to my knees and stretched my white briefs to reveal my bare hip.

"Mm-hmm," Eugene said. "You do tan nude. I thought so."

"You made that observation last time," Jeremy said, getting up to answer the door. It was Jeff.

"Damn, that was fast," Jeremy told him. "You must have been practically downstairs when you called."

I'd never seen Jeff before. He was tall and well-built, with mischievous brown eyes that seemed to dance with light. Even though he was very attractive, he looked only a couple of years older than me, which made him too young to be my usual type. Still, I was intrigued when I heard he'd be here just for me.

"So what exactly happened last time?" Jeff said, grabbing a beer from a cooler and sitting down.

"These guys helped me move in," Jeremy said, "and I fixed them spaghetti when we were done. I accidentally spilled sauce all over Rory."

"That was no accident," I said, pointing a finger at Jeremy.

"I had no clothes to lend him because they were still packed," Jeremy continued. "I gave him a towel—"

"—which Rory couldn't figure out how to tie, so it kept falling off," Eugene added.

"Or maybe I could tie it just fine, but you guys kept pulling it off," I protested. Jeff let out a deep laugh.

"He hadn't worn underwear, so we all got to see Rory nude," Jeremy said, giving me a hungry look. "And after a bit of that, I couldn't help myself, and I nailed him right here on the carpet."

My dick had started to stiffen when Jeremy began telling Jeff what happened, and now I had a full hard-on. Eugene noticed.

"For some reason, Rory wore underwear tonight," Eugene said, fingering my waistband.

"Yeah, well, who knows what you guys might spill on me this time." I decided it was time to put on my straight frat boy act. "God, am I drunk," I said, holding my head.

"Let's fix this underwear situation," Eugene said, slipping my white briefs down to where he had my jeans. Then Jeremy helped Eugene take them both completely off.

"You guys!" I protested meekly and falsely.

Jeff whistled. "Hot little body," he said. "I can see why everyone wanted a repeat performance."

My face felt hot. I still battled nerves, but I wanted Jeff badly. And I wanted everyone to watch.

Jeff knelt down in front of me and gave me a gentle kiss. "Can I be the first inside you?" He put his hand between my legs and softly groped my ass and balls. "I've actually seen you out before. I've wanted you for a long time."

I felt a little dizzy. Maybe it was Jeff's words, or maybe I hadn't done a good job of watching my alcohol intake after all. Or maybe so much blood had rushed to my groin that my brain didn't have enough. "Oh . . . gosh," I said, "do you promise not to tell anyone, you guys?"

"Of course," Jeff said, and there were other murmurs of agreement. *I shouldn't. I shouldn't. I shouldn't.*

I must.

I lay back and lifted my legs. Jeremy produced lube and condoms from behind the couch. Jeff didn't strip all the way, just lowering his pants enough to get busy. That felt a bit unfair because I would have loved to see him undressed, but I was too horny to complain. I closed my eyes while Jeff lubed me with firm, eager fingers.

"Mmm, you're kinda tight," Jeff purred as he lined up his dick to enter me. "From the way these guys talked, I didn't think you would be."

As Jeff began to thrust in and out, I looked from face to face, feeling my stomach tighten in a combination of shame and ecstasy. Why was there nothing better than getting screwed in front of an audience?

Jeff's cock wasn't huge, but he knew how to use it. He ground his hips in a circular motion for a while and struck my prostate in a steady rhythm.

"Look at me," he said, putting his hand on my face. "I want you to know that it's me who's fucking you." I moaned at this, aware of how silent and still the men around us were.

Then Eugene moved to pull my legs back farther, and I saw how enraptured he was with what was happening to me. He swallowed hard, his expression practically one of pain as he stared at Jeff's dick going in and out of my hole.

"My God, what a sweet ass," Jeff said. His breathing became labored, and he grunted over and over as he began to come inside me. His thrusts were the deepest yet, forcing me to cry out. I pinched off my dick, trying my best not to come in case I had to take more cocks. But my body was out of control, and I shot forcefully into my own hand.

"Ooh, Rory," Jeff said, as his breath returned to normal. "I really hope these parties become a habit."

I grinned and blushed. I wanted to say, "No, I can't do this again. I'm really not a slut," but from my state of dreamy afterglow, no one would begin to believe me.

Monday morning I sat in my cubicle feeling uncomfortable in my suit. My ass was still sore from the weekend. I had told them that one guy was my limit for the evening, but they talked me into taking a second dick. Kurt's. And then a third for which they blindfolded me, so I wouldn't know who was inside me. I thought I smelled Eugene's cologne as I was fucked so urgently and ferociously that it felt like a bolt of anger behind each thrust of lust.

Then on Sunday, Jeff called at 2 a.m. and asked to come over. I felt kind of thrilled that such a hot guy wanted me again and wondered if possibly he desired more than sex. But after an hour of rough dicking during which he came twice, he said he had to get back to his girlfriend.

"She thinks I went to get cigarettes," he'd said with a guilty laugh.

I found myself feeling angry but realized that was ridiculous. If he thought of me as just an easy piece of ass to fuck, whose fault was that?

So today my butt was still paying the price, making it difficult to concentrate. It was just my luck that Mr. Wesley would choose this morning to say hello to me again while I could barely function.

"Young Mr. Caulfield," he said, still wearing his gray wool overcoat and hat. "How are things going for you down here on floor twelve?"

I stuttered something unintelligible, and he said, "Fine, fine," clapping me on the shoulder. "Keep up the good work."

Great. I'm sure I'd made a swell impression. Speaking intelligently to superiors had never been my forte, but I'm certain a big part of the problem just then was my huge, futile crush. Mr. Wesley was the epitome of the silver fox—tall with a healthy build covered by immaculate five-thousand-dollar suits. The deep timbre of his voice always made me shiver, and he walked with a confident stride that said, "I am the most powerful man in the room."

I couldn't help but wonder what had made Mr. Wesley stop on my floor. The distraction of his presence made the flurry of phone calls even more difficult for me.

"Yes, Mrs. Willoughby, I understand that you're upset I didn't recommend the same options to you that I did for your grandson. But you see, his time horizon is much longer, so it's not too risky for him to invest in an aggressive growth fund . . . Yes, of course you can talk to my supervisor. One moment." I sighed. I tried very hard to be good at my job, but I wasn't cut out for it. Other than Mr. Wesley, temperaments were testy around here, and I felt like I was always an inch away from termination. In this economy, every day was a bad day.

An hour later, I'd forced myself through the various financial newspapers we were required to read and handled several more calls from clients disgusted with the performance of their portfolios. The throbbing in my butt and my lack of sleep made me hazily believe that each caller was screwing me. I realized at that moment that my true vocation should be getting fucked for a living. Too bad it was illegal.

The intercom on my desk buzzed, and I was called into the office of my boss's boss. My dick, which had been semi-hard at my fantasies of becoming a call boy, went soft. I barely communicated with Mr. Barnes. This couldn't be good.

This was only the second time I'd been up to the twenty-eighth floor, the highest at Wesley-Shields that I'd visited. The halls were dark and cool. Instead of busy clatter, there was an imposing quiet. Large, probably famous, paintings covered the walls, and every corner was festooned with massive flower arrangements. I wasn't happy to be in all this luxury. My last visit resulted from an incident that led to the firing of ten people. I was nearly included, until it became clear I had nothing to do with the problem at hand.

I knocked on Mr. Barnes's half-open door. I saw him sitting with a man I didn't know. Mr. Barnes reminded me of a college professor who never gave good grades. He was tall and had a stern countenance. I'd heard he'd been a football player in college, and even though that must have been thirty years ago, he still had the build.

"Rory, come in. Do you know Peter Cowell, the new director of human resources?"

Oh, God. I really am being fired.

"Uh, no. If this is about Mrs. Willoughby's call, I really thought —"

"No, this is an entirely different matter," said Mr. Barnes. "Sit down." He motioned to a third chair in close proximity to theirs. "Peter here played racquetball yesterday with an associate of yours named Eugene Choi."

I felt my stomach lurch. "Um, really?"

"Yes," said Mr. Cowell, "and I'm afraid he mentioned your indiscretions over the weekend."

I felt stunned. Why would Eugene do that? I'd suspected from the way I'd been fucked last time that Eugene had it in for me. "Oh, my God. I am so sorry," I stammered.

Mr. Cowell leaned forward and looked me in the eye. "From your apology it's apparent you know that it can't become public knowledge that Wesley-Shields employees engage in such activities as the party Mr. Choi described in detail."

"Y-yes. I'll clear my desk out immediately."

"That's one possibility," Mr. Cowell said, arching an eyebrow. "There is a potential alternative." I noticed his hair for the first time. He wore it a bit long and rakishly styled for a Wesley-Shields executive. He had a bit of a regal bearing and the eyes of a hunter. It felt as if he were looking at me as prey.

"First, we need you to sign this confidentiality agreement," said Mr. Barnes, handing me a two-page document. "Any infraction of the agreement could lead to severe penalties, including, but not limited to, a lawsuit and possible jail time for divulging company secrets."

"And I guess if I don't sign, I'll lose my job?" My question was met with grim expressions. "Well, then . . ." I took a pen from Mr. Barnes and signed.

Mr. Barnes gave me a significant look. "This is very serious. Utter and complete silence on this matter. Are we understood? Utter and complete."

"Yes, of course."

"Good," said Mr. Barnes. He steepled his fingers. "Now we are free to inform you that the firm has need of a young man with your proclivities."

"My proclivities?"

"How do I put this delicately?" said Mr. Cowell, as he ran his hand through his hair. "You provide certain services in a semi-public environment."

I felt my eyes widen in surprise. Once again, my dick began to harden. "I'm sure I'm interpreting this incorrectly."

"Then let's make sure there's no room for miscommunication," said Mr. Barnes. "You let guys fuck your ass at parties. From now on, your job at Wesley-Shields is just that. To get your ass fucked."

"What!" I looked at them in disbelief. My breath was suddenly very shallow, and I became conscious of the throbbing in my hole again.

"Yes," continued Mr. Cowell, "frequently. And sometimes at social functions. The company has a few important clients at different firms who will want to pump those buns of yours regularly."

"Oh . . . my . . . God," I whispered. A wet spot formed in my briefs.

"Of course, there will be some other light duties," said Mr. Barnes with a small nod, as if this were a normal conversation. "Answering phones, perhaps some typing."

"A receptionist job? But I have a professional degree! In fact, I won't even be treated with the respect a receptionist receives if I have to give up my ass all day long!"

Mr. Barnes nodded as if he sympathized. "True, but we'll compensate you for the respect you lose by doubling your salary."

Whoa.

Mr. Cowell leaned forward and grabbed my thigh. "You know, Rory, it's a very tough job market out there."

"True," I said, gulping, as he started massaging my leg, his hand inching closer to my crotch.

"And you went to that insignificant Briggs State," added Mr. Barnes, grabbing my other thigh. "These days, if firms are hiring anyone at all, it's graduates of Wharton or Harvard."

"Not to mention that when the word spreads about what you like to do in your private time, you won't have a snowball's chance in Hell."

I wanted to say, "You can stop with the blackmail. I'm into it," but their veiled threats were turning me on as much as their hands. I wasn't stupid enough to think I'd be the one going to jail for this kind of proposal, but I certainly had no intention of squealing. They had a firm grip on my thighs now and parted my legs.

"So, you're saying either I lose my ass to you two or I'll be flipping burgers?"

"Precisely."

"I . . . I guess I have no choice. My ass is yours."

"Excellent." With deft motions, Mr. Cowell unfastened my belt and unzipped me. "Of course, we'll have to give you a test drive to make sure you're right for the position." He yanked my dress pants down around my butt and revealed my erection. "Stand up," he commanded. "That will make stripping you easier."

I stood obediently as Mr. Cowell and Mr. Barnes took everything off me but my tie, which remained loosely around my neck. Then with a firm hand, Mr. Barnes pushed me down on all fours. He unzipped himself and began poking his large, stiff dick in my face. Out of the corner of my eye, I saw Mr. Cowell produce a condom and a tiny bottle of lube from his jacket pocket.

"Show me your skills," Mr. Barnes purred as I took him in my mouth, tasting salt and sweat. I nearly choked at his first thrust, but it struck me as appropriate. Of course a powerful man would have a powerful dick, and naturally it was my lot to kneel before it. I would have gladly run my lips up and down his shaft, but he held my head steady so he could push in and out at leisure.

"You know, this ass would look amazing framed in a jockstrap," Mr. Cowell observed as he lubed me up. Then I felt his dick graze my crack as he covered it in the condom. He guided himself inside me on the first try. "Mmmm, nice," he said, running his hands up my back. I shivered with pleasure.

They fucked me from both ends, each with their own animal rhythm. Mr. Cowell felt about as big as Mr. Barnes, but much more ruthless. His motions pushed me forward, forcing me to take more of Mr. Barnes down my throat. I moaned and grunted, doing my best to please both men.

"Oh, God, this is heaven," said Mr. Barnes, his head tilted up in ecstasy.

"Eugene . . . said . . . you had an incredible ass," Mr. Cowell said, his voice ragged, "but that's an understatement." The compliment made my stomach flutter, and I arched my back to allow him even deeper access. "That's it, boy," Mr. Cowell said with a growl.

Mr. Barnes's breathing sped up, and so did the pace of his strokes. "Oh, Jesus," he whispered. He grunted loudly and then jerked his dick roughly out of my mouth in time to shoot his come all over my face and shoulder. He bent over me in exhaustion, pressing his strong hands on my back and kneading my muscles. "Ohh, I needed that."

"Me too," Mr. Cowell replied, gasping. "I can't believe I get to nail this ass every day now."

Every day? Oh my God, what have I got myself into? Again, I tried to pinch off my dick so I wouldn't come, but I let out a keening moan and shot white gobs all over my stomach and the carpet.

Mr. Cowell shouted three times as I felt his come flood the condom. His last thrusts were so forceful I would have fallen over if Mr. Barnes hadn't been holding me up.

"Excellent," said Mr. Cowell again, his rough fingers pulling on my hair. "Your body will suit our purposes perfectly."

After their "test drive," I was allowed to clean out my desk and go home. The next morning I still felt sore as I made my way to the twenty-eighth floor, but I had never been so eager to get to work in my life. I practically ran to Mr. Barnes's office.

"Good morning, Rory. This isn't where you're working today," Mr. Barnes said to me, "but this is where you'll leave your suit. You do have your jockstrap on?"

I nodded and undressed. Mr. Barnes unlocked a door in his office and led me through a hallway I didn't know existed. He used the same key to open an elevator. There were no floor buttons listed.

"When you arrive, face the window, lie back on the desk, and put your legs in the air. Unless told otherwise, that's what you will do every morning."

As I stepped out of the elevator, I realized that the entire floor was one office. The huge windows overlooked Central Park. I heard footsteps on the other side of the room. I scrambled to get on the huge mahogany desk just as I heard a door unlock.

There was Mr. Wesley! I immediately dismounted from the desk and apologized profusely. This was certainly a prank, and I'd been a complete fool.

"No, no. As you were, Rory Caulfield," Mr. Wesley said. He walked in and gave me a simmering look.

"R-really?"

"Oh, yes. You are as beautiful as they said," he murmured. "If I'd only known what you liked to do earlier, you could have had this much sooner."

He reached over and delicately touched my face. "I'd like to call you 'darling,' but from what I've heard, you're the kind that would rather be called 'a pussy boy party bottom.' Which is it, truly?"

I moaned. "I . . . I'm too embarrassed to say . . ."

"Don't be. We never get what we want if we don't ask." His fingers grazed the inside of my left thigh.

"Yes, sir," I said, spreading my legs wider. I felt such disbelief at what was happening that I kept forgetting to breathe and then had to gasp in shock. My dick was so hard that it throbbed.

"I've waited so long for a young man like you to come along." He gave me a feral smile. "A pussy boy party bottom," he said, his hand moving to my hole, "is just what I need."

"Oh, yes, sir!" I said, as he ran his hand over my dick, which strained against my jock.

Mr. Wesley hit an intercom button. "Barnes, it's time to mix business with pleasure. Send up my two guests. They're in for the treat of a lifetime."

I closed my eyes and moaned. I imagined I'd never have a bad day at work again.

RECONNECTED
KEN O'NEILL

I FEEL CERTAIN THE DAY WILL COME when I'll look back on this moment—me, lying on my bed, in the fetal position, clasping my laptop tightly to my chest while singing the theme from *Ice Castles*—and I will recall it as the instant I realized I was in the depths of a nervous collapse. I like to think of it as a collapse rather than a breakdown—it sounds less serious, somehow. Like I have a touch of the vapors. Perhaps all I need is a bit of rest on the veranda. Maybe I should take the waters. Probably I just need some air.

No. Air is not going to do the trick. What I need is for the cable guy to show up and get me reconnected to the Internet. He was due here between 10:00 and 5:00. From my balled-up pose on the bed, I peer over the top of my Power Book at the alarm clock on my side table: it's 4:57. I've had no service for over two days. Two days—more than that—since the modem died. I have things I need to do. I have ... I have a routine. A way the day is ordered. For example, I need to read and respond to my Craigslist M4M personals. It's vital that I find out what the men are up to in, say, Miami, Boston, Chicago, Austin, Dallas, Santa Fe, Las Vegas, L.A., San Francisco, Portland, and Seattle. That takes up a lot of my day.

I do, however, save a great deal of time by eliminating New York City (not to mention the states of New Jersey and Connecticut). I live in Manhattan. I find the tri-state area postings a little close to home for my taste. I could actually meet one of those guys. Be expected to ... This ... This thing I do, it's not about meeting anyone. I never do that. That's not my goal. What I do is infinitely more magical than that. It's about romance. Fantasy. There's the tantalizing beginning when we exchange photos. Followed by a sharing of secrets and desires. My time online with these men is about hope, possibilities, and dreams. *Yes,* dreams. True, my dreams are left unfulfilled, but they're also untarnished by the ugliness of reality.

I've been unable to check my inbox for fifty-four hours—the need to do so is overwhelming. I look at my watch; it matches the time on my alarm clock: 5:01. We have now passed the window I was guaranteed for his arrival. The cable guy never showed today. I have no way to get online. I feel the urge to segue from *Through the Eyes of Love* straight into *Don't Cry Out Loud,* even though I know it won't make me feel any better.

I'm panicked. Breaking a sweat. My heart is pounding so loudly it's like someone is knocking on my chest. Oh, wait. It is knocking. Somebody's at the door!

I leap from my bed, put my computer back on my desk, and run

out through the living room and microscopic vestibule. "You're late,"
I snap the instant I fling the door open.

The technician who's just witnessed my Mildred Pierce imitation is
at least six inches taller than I am. He's wearing what should be an
unflattering, oversized, navy short-sleeve shirt and slacks. The outfit
is boxy and shapeless. It looks like something Chairman Mao would
have donated to Goodwill. The uniform has been designed to flatter
no one. This man, however, looks great in it. His shoulders are so
broad, chest so pumped, biceps so bulged, that even this blue-collar
muumuu can't hide his perfection.

But enough about that: He's late. I detest tardiness. My ex, Calvin,
was always late. For everything. There's no reason for it. I find it in-
excusable. I glance pointedly at my wristwatch. I tap my right foot
impatiently. I've chosen to include the toe-tapping gesture just in case
my exasperated tone of voice and the exaggerated stare at my watch
were signs too subtle to convey my annoyance.

"I'm not late. It's 4:59." He too is staring at his watch.

"It's 5:03."

"Your watch is fast," he says with finality. Apparently Time Warner
Cable has given him not one iota of training in the ways of customer
service.

"I'm not fast. You're slow!" The shrillness I hear in my voice is
painful even to me. I sound ridiculous. Out of control. I've gone two
days without the Web, and it's turned me into Frank Sinatra in *The
Man with the Golden Arm*.

"I've been accused of many things," the brawny repairman says.
"*Slow* has never been one of them." He's grinning at me now. His
smile is dazzling. (Not that I care. Not that I'll be placated by a tow-
ering hunk with perfectly straight teeth.) "Shall we continue to de-
bate my punctuality and the accuracy of my Timex, or would you
prefer that I get you back online? It's entirely up to you."

His audacity is shocking. Does he really think I'll tolerate such surliness just because he's tall, hunky, and has a perfect smile and glorious violet eyes? Lord have mercy—his eyes! How did I not notice those eyes before now?

I'm finding it hard to stay mad at him. "Please come in," I say, too demurely. I can't help myself. He may be ill-mannered, but he's unbelievably captivating. In my enthusiasm to welcome him into my apartment, I catch myself starting to move into a bow, as if the initials H.R.H. preceded cable guy's name. I force myself to stop mid-bend. This makes me look as if my back has gone into spasm.

"Ouch," he says, as if he's feeling my pain. "Sacroiliac? I'm a big believer in Eastern medicine. Did you know lower back pain signifies repressed anger and sexual frustration?"

"I'M NOT . . ." I don't bother finishing the sentence because the two words I managed to utter made me sound exactly like Donald Trump screaming, "You're fired!" So, really, what would be the point in continuing with my I'm-not-angry-or-sexually-frustrated argument?

I step aside and let him pass. He walks into the living room. I follow. I see him looking around—taking it all in. I'm proud of the room. I decorated it myself. It's light, springy, fun. New York can be so dingy and severe. It's a hard place to live. In my domicile I try to remain serene. A celebratory jolt of color really helps.

He looks back at me. I'm prepared to accept his compliments on my good taste and tell him where I bought the sofa and the pillows (the former at ABC Carpet, the latter at Jonathon Adler). But he offers no accolades. Instead, he grumbles, "Where's the computer?"

Oh, right. I knew there was a reason he came over. "It's in the bedroom. Right this way." I extend my arm in the direction of the room, as if I'm Vanna White about to reveal a vowel.

I can't remember the last time I entered my bedroom with a strange man. A stranger, rather. This man is not strange. He's just obnoxious, arrogant, rude, and the first real live person to make me hard in about three years.

I lead him to my desk, and he stands right behind me. Closer than is considered appropriate in polite society. But of course, this man is not polite. He places a hand on my shoulder, casually. As if we're posing for a snapshot, or he's about to offer me a bit of sage advice.

"Just by looking," he says, "I can pretty much guess what your problem is."

He's still standing behind me, so I don't know what he's looking at. I've been wondering if he was staring at my ass. If that's in fact the case, what does he think my problem is?

"How old's that modem? Seven, eight years?"

It's been almost eight years since Calvin left me, so I guess it's over seven since I got that modem. Of course I don't explain that my life is divided into B.C. (before Calvin) and A.D. (after that dick left me). "Nearly eight," I say.

"I'll replace it. Should do the trick. Don't worry," he says. He gives my shoulder a squeeze. "I'll take care of you." One more squeeze.

What does that mean: He'll take care of me?

"Could you um . . ."

"Yes?" I'm truly panicked. Still, I can't help but notice how flirty I sound.

"Could you do me a favor?"

"Of course." Less panicked. More flirty.

"Could you move?"

"What?"

"Please. I need to get to your desk."

I feel rejected, though I can't explain why. He is here to fix my computer, after all. I go and flop across my bed, but I worry this pose makes me look too come-hither, so I opt for a more conservative posture. I sit up perfectly straight. I'm as close to the edge of the bed as is possible without falling off. My legs are crossed tightly at the ankles; my hands rest primly atop my knees. Just add a mantilla and a pair of Mary Janes, and I'd be all set for my first Holy Communion.

He turns; sees me perched. "Comfortable?" he asks. Again, he shines his magnificent smile on me. The smile that I fear will be my undoing.

"OK, so let's see if this thing works." He hands over my old, dust-covered modem. (The time spent devoted to cyber-correspondence has begun to take precedence over more domestic chores. Note to self: hire housekeeper.) On my desk, in place of the old one, a much tinier, brand-new model sits. It's maybe a third the size of my old modem. I'm struck how, in every way, the world keeps getting smaller, less consequential.

"Why don't you log onto your e-mail account? Sometimes things need to be reset; I can take care of that for you."

I hadn't considered this. I remain frozen in my Catholic schoolgirl pose. I don't want to sign on in front of him. I'm not sure what's on my computer. I think there are a bunch of cock shots sent to me by a charming gentleman from Tucson I've been "seeing" lately.

"Relax, buddy," he says with eerie omniscience. "I do this all day long. I doubt you've got anything on there that's gonna shock me. I'm not gonna faint at the sight of your downloaded pussy porn."

Pussy porn?

That's got to be a joke, right? Has he not seen my apartment? Not noticed the meticulous color coordination? There are nine throw pillows in the living room alone. Exactly how many men have a multitude of throw pillows on their couch while simultaneously having an extensive collection of *pussy porn* on their computer? I'm going to hazard a guess and say: ZERO.

He's growing impatient with me. He taps the seat of my desk chair, beckoning me to it. I don't really see that I have a choice, so I obey him. I'm relieved that he doesn't say, "Good boy," when I take my seat.

I turn the computer on, sign into my account, and see that I have 119 unread e-mails.

"My, my. Somebody's popular," he growls.

Shit. This can't be my regular account. This must be my Craigslist screen name. And right now I notice at the top of the home page: "Welcome, ASSLOVER."

I stand so I can block his view of the screen. The second I do, I feel his hand on the seat of my pants.

"Ass lover, huh? I don't think so. I've got you pegged as a sweet little bottom boy."

"Excuse me?" I turn to face him, even though it means he's no longer palming my butt, which I must confess I was quite enjoying. "I will have you know, I'm a total top!" I don't like confrontation; it makes me nervous. And my anxiety has registered in my voice. My speech has affected a quality decidedly coloratura.

The repairman is laughing at me. I don't mean chuckling or tittering. His eyes are watering. He can't catch his breath. He drops to the floor, holding his sides as he convulses. Generally, such extreme bursts of laughter can only be heard emanating from the mouths of potheads or the criminally insane.

For the second time in about twenty minutes, I'm tapping my foot to demonstrate my extreme irritation.

He's gasping away, trying to speak, but he still can't. Finally he says, "Can I give you a piece of advice?" But before he does, he goes off on one more jag of laughter. "Next time you want to pass yourself off as a total top"—because he's obviously so clever he's made quotation fingers around the words "total top"—"you might want to think about hiding the throw pillows. They don't really support your total top argument."

"*Really?*" I say in an attempt to buy myself a little time in which to come up with a more cutting and clever retort.

"You know what I think you should do?" he says.

"*What?*" I'm still trying to think of something cutting and clever.

"Get down on your knees and start sucking my juicy, nine-inch dick." His hands are back on my shoulders, and he's pressing down.

"Stop." I push his hands away. "I will admit that you have a certain Neanderthal appeal. But I think you should know I'm completely celibate."

Now it's his turn to say, "*Really?*" He walks to my computer and opens up my inbox. "I find that a little hard to believe, ASSLOVER." He's reading my mail, which I believe is a federal offense. I stare at the subject lines as he opens each missive: "RE: NAIL ME; Pound Me, Sir; Drill Me, Please," and the equally poetic and socially responsible, "IF YOU WRAP IT, YOU CAN TAP IT," are all on display.

"You want me to believe that *you* are celibate?" He grabs my arm.

"Listen," I say, freeing myself from his grasp once again, "you're very hot, but I can't do this. I'm a sex addict."

"I thought you said you were celibate. Are you celibate, or are you a sex addict?"

"I'm celibate and I'm a sex addict."

"How does that work?"

"It doesn't, really."

"So all those guys waiting for you to nail, pound, drill, and tap them?"

"Never going to happen."

He looks at me. He wears a sweet but muddled expression. He does not know what to make of my behavior. But of course, I don't really know what to make of my behavior either, so on this point we're on the same page. "Hey," he says. His eyebrows have lifted; he's having a thought. If this were a cartoon there'd be a light bulb burning above his head. "I don't think you're addicted to having sex. You're addicted to *not* having sex. Maybe if you spent some time really doing it, you wouldn't have the compulsion to spend so much time not doing it. Doesn't that make sense?"

I ponder this; I can see the logic.

His hands are back on my shoulders, but now they're barely touching me. He's not pushing at all. Nevertheless, I find myself falling onto my knees. I unzip him with my teeth, which might be something I saw once in a movie, but I've certainly never done it in real life before. I unbutton the top button of his pants, pull them down over his hips, and let them land around his ankles. He's in boxers. His dick has broken free. He's already totally hard, which flatters me. It's a beautiful cock. Thick, perfectly straight, topped with a tasty-looking mushroom head. It's flawless, but it's not nine inches.

"Sorry for saying I had nine inches before. Figured if I said ten and a half, I'd scare you off." Which, of course, he would have. Which makes me think, *Oh my God, we're strangers and yet he knows me so well.*

I start licking his shaft, not sure I'll be able to manage more than that. I can feel him bucking his hips against my lips. He wants in. I open wide and discover, thankfully, that fellatio is just like riding a bike. I still know how to do it. My mouth is around him. I hear him moaning. I've got more than half his monster dick down my throat, and I'm not even gagging. Tomorrow I may discover that I've developed TMJ, but for right now this feels better than anything I've ever done before.

"Oh, that's so good," he's repeating over and over. "Oh, God, I want to fuck you."

I want him to fuck me. That comes as a surprise to me because he's not exactly what you'd consider "trial size." Or as my grandmother always liked to say, "You can't pour a gallon of milk into a quart-size jug." There's another reason I won't be able to let him fuck me: I don't have any condoms. I have a bigger-than-average dick myself, but it isn't actually long enough to penetrate any of the men in Portland I so avidly pursue, so I haven't had need of rubbers.

I pry my lips from his cock just long enough to say, "Sorry. We can't. No condoms." I feel more disappointment than relief.

He grabs for his pants, still balled around his ankles. From a pocket he fishes a Magnum XL and a couple of individual-use lube packets. (I didn't even know they made those.) "I used to be a Boy Scout," he says, pulling my shirt over my head. I don't know how he removes my pants, but it happens instantly. It's as if he's Samantha from *Bewitched*. I mean, if Samantha were six foot three and two hundred pounds of pure muscle and had a dick bigger than the two Darrens combined.

He lifts me up and carries me over to my bed. I think about asking him to remove the bedspread first, because it was handmade in Florence and cost a fortune, but I don't want to break the mood. He places me down ever so softly, gently on my back. I'm glad he's put me in this position because all I want to do is look at his face, his smile, those unbelievable eyes. Oh, and also, lying on my back makes my stomach look really flat, which, trust me, it wouldn't if I were up on all fours.

Flat-looking stomach or not, I instinctively clench my gut to make it look even tighter. I look great. Unfortunately, I'm unable to breathe.

"Try and relax," he says.

"I am." I allow myself one quick gasp of breath to keep from passing out. But then I'm right back to tummy tightening.

"You're not breathing." He places his mouth over mine. I let my tongue slide between his lips. How have I gone so long without so much as a kiss? He pulls his mouth from mine. "Not yet. Just breathe with me." And his lips are once again pressed to mine. I feel his lungs expand and then the warmth of his exhalation floats into me. I take the gift, expanding my lungs as I do. I receive the full stream of his air until he has no more to give. Now I send it back to him. I feel the weight of him against me. He's perfectly still except for the breathing. In. Out. Slowly we exchange oxygen and energy. He seems prepared to do this for as long as I need. Forever.

Now I feel his tongue and we kiss. His lips are soft, tender, like ice cream is on those rare occasions when I'm patient enough to let it sit on the counter for ten minutes to soften before I eat it. The movement of his tongue is deliberate, fluid, and achingly slow. He is unhurried in his exploration of every centimeter of my mouth. I don't know who this man is, but he's not the rude, gruff repairman who arrived at my door, seemingly just to annoy and torment me. That man is gone, and in his place I find some kind of pure, Tantric love god.

I have some awareness of his hands ripping open the lube and condom packages, but there is no break in our action, no awkwardness or fumbling. There is only his mouth, now on my nipples, and my moans.

I try to return the favor and move to lick his glorious nipples, but he stops me. "Let's make today all about you."

He rolls me to my side and spoons me. I feel him behind me. Every inch of me is being touched by some part of him. His arms wrap around me. He's kissing me, letting his lips roam from my jaw line up to my ear. I feel his engorged nipples press against my upper back. His hard stomach aligns with my sacrum. His cock divides the crack of my ass.

"You're in control," he says. I want to tell him that on every level I am totally out of control. I merely smile, and his tongue brushes along my exposed teeth. "You're in control," he whispers again. "We can stay just as we are. Or, you can press yourself against me. Take me inside you. Fuck me."

As amazing as this feels—this intimacy—I do not want to just stay as we are. I press my hips against him. His hot breath is in my ear. I feel safe with him; it's a wonderful and foreign feeling. Suddenly I'm aware of my own strength and power. I take him. All of him. Even though it's his dick in my ass, I am the one fucking him.

Drops of water are hitting my chest. They're tears that have rolled down my cheek and tumbled onto my torso. I'm not in pain; that's not why I'm crying. The feeling of him inside me is euphoric. I'm not sure why I'm having this show of emotion. I guess it's because I'm remembering what vulnerability feels like.

His tongue traces the path of my tears. His mouth, a basin, catches them. "I never moved a man to tears before." His mouth moves to my ear. "You're beautiful," he whispers. I resist the urge to shout, "*Am not!*" Right now I could easily begin making a mental list of all my flaws—physical and otherwise. I could blurt out something totally self-deprecating, to deflect my attention away from what he's just said to me. But I don't. I stop myself. I silence all the chatter in my head. I allow myself to be held, to be nurtured, to be filled, to take in his words.

I've never considered myself an exhibitionist, but right now I'm really praying Melissa Manchester has broken into my apartment, made her way to the bedroom, and is watching us do it. Because, if she hasn't, it must be me I hear singing, *Please don't let this feeling end/It might not come again/And I want to remember . . .*

If there's any doubt as to the true identity of the chanteuse, the question is settled when I hear him laugh. Really, it's just one short, sweet chuckle. "I need you to make a choice," he says. "Either my cock up your ass, or you keep singing that song. No way we're gonna have both."

My decision takes no time at all.

I feel him picking up his pace, thrusting into me as his hand travels to my dick. His fingers dance along my shaft. I know I won't last much longer, and I begin fiercely bucking against his cock. Our tongues are touching. I feel an electric current come through him. He's close, too.

"Breathe again with me," he says, and I do. He's leading, teaching me. Our breathing is staccato, shallow. We're like a gay porn version of a Lamaze class.

The sensation starts in my toes and fingertips. A pulsing tremor. I want to look at my hands to see what's happening, but I don't. I keep my eyes closed; my mouth locked against his as we breathe. The pulsing shoots down my arms and up my legs. It's in my cock and balls, my ass, too. But it's not there—in those obvious places—with any more intensity than it is any place else. My whole body is giving me pleasure. I think my eyelids are orgasming. I feel the flutter of my lashes as they brush against each other. I can't take it anymore. I add a moan, now a scream, to my breathing. He moans and screams, too. I'm shooting now; I can tell from his shuddering body that he is too. My cum is everywhere. This bedspread is dry clean only, and I don't care. Only a celibate, cybersex addict would have dry-clean-only bedding. And that's not who I am anymore.

Before I can get a clear image of this new me, I remember the old me—the sobbing me, as Calvin walked out the door. The instant my Tantric love god pulls out of me, I'm visited by despair. In my mind I've already left this sacred moment and rushed to what I fear will lie ahead. I know what will happen. He'll get up. Get dressed. Say, "That was fun." I'll never see him again. And where will that leave me? Despite its many shortcomings, I always know where my computer is.

Maybe I should get up first. Signal that I know this was just a hookup, nothing more. This guy walks around town with single-serve lube packages in his pocket. Obviously he's done this before. I'm not special to him. I start to get up.

"Don't move," he says. "Stay with me."

I fall back into his arms. Though I still fear that we're just prolonging the inevitable. "This was kind of amazing," he says.

I turn to look at him. I don't speak. I'm waiting for him to add the "but."

"I'm gonna have to leave pretty soon," he says.

Of course he is.

"I don't want to. I have to sign out at work. Return the van."

Oh? That's a good excuse. That makes sense. I hadn't thought of that. "You want my e-mail address?" I say.

He flashes the smile I'm growing to love. "No. I don't think that's a good idea." Thank God I'm still lying down. I feel certain I'm about to collapse.

"Under the circumstances," he says, staring at my computer, eyeing the 119 e-mails, "Perhaps we should correspond by telephone. Hey. I don't even know your first name. The service call invoice just said 'Mr. Gray.'"

I almost say "Todd." It's a habit. "Todd" is my online name. "Tom," I say.

"Tom," he repeats, pulling me tighter into his arms, giving my sticky dick a gentle squeeze. "I'd very much like to see you again. And again. And again. And again."

"Yeah? I'd like that, too."

"Good. But now I have to fly."

He's up. Pulling on his boxy blue uniform. I write down my number for him. Hand it to him. He kisses me and starts to leave.

"Wait," I say. "I don't know your name, either."

"Gosh. I'm sorry. I'm Craig. No relation to the list guy." He pulls out piece of paper and a pen and gives me his number. "Hope you aren't one of those guys who does the forty-eight-hour waiting thing. I'll be home at 8:00. Call me. Oh, and I don't know . . . Maybe . . .

You might want to think about unplugging that," he says, snarling at my Mac as if it's his rival. As if they're both my suitors, and he might challenge it to a duel.

After he leaves, I go over to my desk. So much mail. With one stroke, it's all deleted. It wasn't so hard to do, actually.

I lower my computer's lid; watch as it goes to sleep.

BABYCAKES
RYAN FIELD

NATE WAS A MAN who had missed out on a lot of fun, is how he would have described himself. After college he went straight to law school; after that he went back to his dreary hometown to open a small law office and take care of his aging mother. He lived in Martha Falls, Maryland, a small, square hamlet about fifty miles outside Baltimore, and a million miles away from any hint of a gay lifestyle. He'd settled there into the banal, uninspired existence of caregiver and didn't bother to leave again until a week after her funeral.

He was thirty-five years old by then but looked more like twenty-five. An only child who had been left with the responsibility of dealing with Alzheimer's. He could have put her in a nursing home. But he didn't.

Though many of his nights were spent rubbing the clenched fists of his mother's bony hands and softly explaining to her there was no need to rant about being lost and afraid, there had also been plenty of free time to work out with weights in the basement and run endless miles on the treadmill in his childhood bedroom. While saving his sanity with exercise, Nate developed strong, solid legs that led upward to a lean, tight waist. His hard chest muscles popped like upside-down coffee cups after bench presses; when he squeezed his arms across his chest a thin line of muscle cleavage made his dick grow long and hard. It wasn't unusual for him to masturbate, in front of the faded workout mirror against the dusty cinder-block wall, two or three times a week.

He wasn't a virgin; he'd been with other men. Two or three times a year he'd make sure his mother was slightly over-medicated and sleeping soundly, and then he'd sneak off to a highway rest stop for a little safe action. The married men on the down low liked to tug his soft blond hair when he knelt on the pavement and blew them in public; the way the closeted young guys in college were always in such a hurry to pull his pants down and bend him over the hood of a car made him smile when he was alone in bed at night. He liked spreading his legs and submitting to them; the exhibitionist in him couldn't resist their hungry stares and heavy breathing. Many of them asked if he was a professional male stripper. In the summer months he sometimes undressed, got out of his car, and walked slowly into the woods, knowing all too well the guys who had been sitting alone in parked cars couldn't resist following him. All this was safe: Nate never went there without a handful of condoms.

A week after his mother died, he booked a trip to the most tropical, exotic place he could find on the map: Cairns, in the heart of North Queensland, which is Australia's primary gateway to the Great Barrier Reef Islands. There were tropical dreamlands there with names like Lizard Island and Green Island. He was so tired of jerking off in the mirror; he was bored with the frustrating routine at the rest stop (on a good night, two or three guys would nail him; but most of the time he sat there alone in the darkness waiting for dick that never came). Cairns looked like the kind of vibrant, eclectic city he needed to visit in order to stay sane. Oh, he'd been dreaming about a trip like this for some time. His heart raced at the thought of walking the reef island beaches at twilight in nothing but a skimpy Speedo while other men stared at his smooth legs and round ass; his cock pitched a tent when he imagined all those hot, hairy-legged Australian men in rowing shorts. The thought of traveling to such a far-off paradise not only stimulated his intellect but also stirred his starved libido.

The day he arrived in Cairn, the sun was bright and a balmy breeze blew the lush, green palms toward the bluest sky he'd ever seen. But more than that, the young man who escorted him up to his room was dark and beefy and hairy. He wore white shorts, and you could see the outline of his dick, a thick portion of meat pressed to the right. Just the sort of guy Nate preferred, the complete opposite of his blond, smooth body. "Are you a native?" Nate asked.

"Oh, yes, I am that," said the young man. "An authentic island boy, I am." His accent was unmistakably aboriginal English. It was very similar to Australian English, but distinct in certain ways. No mention of the "h" sound, and when the young man said "that" it sounded more like "dot."

Nate smiled. He didn't care how the little island cutie sounded. "Can you recommend some of the local attractions?" The guy was so hot, Nate had to bite his bottom lip and turn toward the window.

"Oh, yes, sir. You must sign up for the four-wheel-drive day trip to the Daintree Forest. It is magical." He became animated, his voice rising with a lilt. "The temperature there is always around eighty-five degrees, and it's never too hot because all the greens create a canopy of shade."

Nate smiled. "How do I do that?"

"Ah, well, this is your lucky day, man," he said. His dark brown eyes were wide; he began to wave his hand in the air and a bicep jumped from his upper arm. "Two of my friends and me, we just started our own very nice tour of the forest. You can be one of the first good customers."

Nate laughed. The cute little guy couldn't have been more than twenty-five years old, but he had all the moxie of a fifty-year-old. "How much does this cost?"

"Very cheap: two hundred American dollars," he said. "And, my friends and me, we know how to take real good care of good-looking, blond, American men."

Nate's eyes bugged out, and he smiled so wide you could see his upper gums. The young man had just paid him a rather blunt compliment. "I see. Where should I meet you, and what time?"

"Nine o'clock tomorrow morning," he said. "We will be waiting in front of the hotel for you."

Later that night while resting in bed, Nate had second thoughts about all this four-wheel-drive business. He'd said yes so impulsively, just because he liked the way the dark little guy looked in shorts. What if these guys took him out to some remote rain forest, robbed him, and left him there to die? What if they stole his wallet and wristwatch and stabbed him to death? What if he disappeared and no one heard from him again? But he eventually fell into a deep, heavy sleep, and when he woke the next morning he decided he'd had a whole lifetime of "what ifs" and now he only wanted to know "what's next."

So he put on a skimpy black mesh tank top to show off his chest, a tight pair of white shorts to show off his ass, and heavy black boots just in case there was any walking to do. Then he pulled six bottles of cold water from the hotel minibar and dropped them into his knapsack; he snapped a baseball cap onto the shoulder strap. The only money he brought was the fee for the tour; everything else of value he shoved into the hotel safe.

As promised, the little guy was leaning against an ancient four-wheel-drive vehicle outside the hotel entrance with his arms folded and his legs crossed. Nate wanted to get down on his knees there in the driveway and start licking his ankles. A tall, dark man sat behind the steering wheel on the right side of the front seat, and someone Nate couldn't see because the rear windows were tinted was sitting in the back seat. When the little guy saw Nate, he jumped forward and opened the back door immediately.

Nate lowered his eyebrows and stared at the boxy SUV. There were dents in the fenders, the off-white paint was faded and chipped, and the right side of the rear end sloped downward. The tires were massive; you had to jump up on the running board and climb inside. "Are you sure this thing is safe?" Nate asked.

"This is so safe; drives like a dream, man," his new friend said. He motioned for Nate to get into the car, adding, "My name is Abim; it means ghost. You have the two hundred bucks, yes?"

Nate struggled to reach into his tight shorts to pull out the money. He noticed Abim staring at his hairless legs; the young guy's eyes were wide, and he puckered his lips as though he were about to whistle. "My name is Nate," he said, and then handed Abim the cash.

"Nice short pants, Nate," he said. "Most Americans don't look so good in them."

Nate laughed. "Oh, really." He was glad he'd shaved his entire body that morning.

"We better get going," Abim said. "Get ready for the tour of your lifetime, Nate."

Nate climbed into the backseat, and Abim closed the door. As Abim walked around the back of the truck to get into the passenger seat up front, the driver started the engine and the tall young man in the back seat whipped out a huge dick and said, "You like banana?"

Nate's eyes popped. "Ah, well . . ." The man's dick was long; its head was covered by a foreskin.

Abim was in the car by then and shouted, "Put that thing away. You'll scare him!" Then he shook his head and looked back at Nate; when he said "thing" it sounded like "ding." "I'm so sorry, man. He's new with this tour. He means no harm. His name is Bambra, which means mushroom."

Nate wanted to say, "That's OK, I like banana a lot," but he simply smiled and nodded at Bambra. His name suited him well: when he pulled the foreskin back, the head of his cock reminded Nate of a nice fresh mushroom top.

Abrim sighed and then motioned the driver to get moving. "And this is Keli, which means dog. He will be our driver today. He's very strong and very good; he knows the tropical rain forest with his eyes closed."

Nate looked at the driver. He certainly was a large man; his head nearly hit the ceiling of the SUV. And his skin was ebony and smooth. "It's nice to meet you, Keli."

Keli nodded. Clearly, he wasn't much of a talker.

But then no one really had much of an opportunity to speak with Abim in the car. He spoke endlessly, explaining the town of Cairn, how to get to the Great Barrier Reef, and how to avoid being eaten by a croc. His voice went high, with run-on sentences, and the more he spoke, the more he left behind the aboriginal English accent. Nate wondered how anyone could speak so much without taking a breath.

While Abim rambled on about how the rain forest was over 135 million years old and 430 species of birds lived among the trees, Bambra whipped out his dick again and started to jerk it with slow, steady motions. Nate pretended to stare out the window, as though he hadn't noticed anything unusual, but it was awfully difficult to keep his eyes off the nine-inch cock of a good-looking young guy who was practically waving it in his face.

A few minutes later, Abim said, "I think Bambra likes you, Nate. I think he wants to play."

Bambra smiled. "You like banana, Nate?" He spread his dark hairy legs wider and leaned back in the seat; his dick stuck out of his shorts like a flagstaff.

Keli, the driver, covered his mouth and laughed.

Nate hesitated, but Abim said, "Go ahead."

That's when Nate leaned to his left, rested his body against the wide backseat, and said, "Oh yeah, I like banana." And as they entered the Daintree Rain Forest, Nate began to suck the sweet brown banana. Bambra hadn't showered that morning, and his cock tasted a bit cheesy, but that didn't stop Nate from slurping the entire shaft all the way down his throat. His lips rubbed against the young man's wiry pubic hair; he could smell the watered-down vinegar aroma of his balls. When they passed another group of tourists taking photos of a magnificent waterfall that was set back in an alcove of lush green palms, the only thing Nate saw was the head of Bambra's dick oozing with pre-come. When he licked a drop with the tip of his tongue, it occurred to him that he probably wouldn't see much of the Daintree Forest at all that day.

Abim leaned over the front seat to watch Nate sucking off Bambra. Then he poked Keli and said, "I think our friend Nate might like some more banana."

Keli laughed when Abim climbed into the back and knelt down on the floor. Without looking up from sucking Bambra's dick, Nate reached around and grabbed Abim's crotch. Abim smiled and unzipped his shorts; he spread his hairy legs and put his hands on his hips while Nate reached into the young man's pants and wrapped his hand around Abim's erection. It wasn't as long as Bambra's dick, but it was also uncut and thick: it reminded Nate of the last time he drank beer from a can.

The driver made a quick left turn and drove down a dark, unpaved, one-lane road. He drove well, avoiding bumps and holes. Nate looked up from sucking Bambra and asked, "Where are we going?" His lips were puffy now; his chin was wet with his own saliva.

"I have a friend who has a small villa here in the rain forest," Abim said. "We can park there and no one will bother us." Then he reached forward, grabbed Nate by the back of the head, and pushed Nate's puffy lips to his cock. "See if you like my banana, too."

Nate had to open his mouth as wide as it would go in order to take Abim's cock through his lips and down his throat. He closed his eyes and started to moan when Abim's shaft rested on his tongue; his cheekbones indented and his lips went soft and spongy. While he sucked he grabbed Bambra's cock with his left hand and started to jerk it off; he placed his right palm on Abim's hairy thigh for support.

When the truck came to a stop Abim grabbed the back of Nate's head. Nate looked up with innocent blue eyes. "Let me help you take off your clothes, Nate," Abim urged him.

Nate sat up and looked around to see where they were parked. His blond hair was sticking up in the back, and there were beads of sweat dripping down from his temples. The truck faced a magnificent wall of exotic green shrubs: bushes with spiked palms, tall trees with wide symmetrical leaves, and a prickly, round-leaved ground cover layered the edges of the driveway. Every so often a hint of red or yellow or purple popped from the green. When he looked out the back window of the truck, he saw a small wooden villa that reminded him of a tree house, set up higher on several layers of carefully placed rocks. A natural waterfall, with perfectly placed rocks, ran downhill along the left side of the villa; Abim rolled down his window and Nate could hear the water rush down the slope.

"Don't worry; no one is here," Abim said. "This place is totally private."

Anyone who knew Nate would have thought he'd just won the lottery. He raised his eyebrows and smiled so wide you could see every tooth in his mouth. Abim laughed while he pulled off Nate's black mesh shirt and slid the short pants down his legs; he wasn't wearing underwear. Then Nate pulled off his heavy black boots and white socks. Keli, who was watching the strip show from the front seat, rubbed his hands together and licked his lips. When Nate was completely naked, Bambra ran his wide palm up Nate's smooth thigh. Bambra's brown eyes were now as wide as Nate's; he was fascinated by all that smooth, fair skin. Abim slipped his hand up Nate's other thigh and rested it on the small of Nate's back. It occurred to Nate that neither of the young men were reaching for his dick, that he was surrounded by dominant types who were only interested in his ass.

So he spread his pretty legs for the guys, arched his shapely back so his ass would be in the air, and leaned over the front seat. Keli's uncut dick was hanging out of his jeans by then. Nate bent all the way over the seat and slipped it down his throat. It was as long as Bambra's and about as wide as Abim's, with a slight curve. It tasted salty, as though he'd wrapped a slice of bacon around the shaft. When he started to suck Keli, both Abim and Bambra leaned forward and began to play with the backs of his legs and his ass. Bambra licked and nibbled; Abim turned his large hand sideways, pressed his fingers together, and shoved the pinky side of his hand up the crack of Nate's ass length-wise. Nate spread his legs wider; his toes curled against the back seat.

He continued to gulp and suck while Keli held the back of his head and Abim's hand pressed against his ass crack.

When Abim removed his hand, both he and Bambra began to spread Nate's ass cheeks wider. Bambra licked the pink hole first; Nate moaned when the young man's rough stubble brushed against his tender skin. Then Abim took his turn: he buried his face between Nate's ass cheeks and shoved the tip of his tongue in. A moment later Bambra placed both palms on Nate's ass and spread his cheeks as wide as they would go, while Abim shoved his middle finger all the way up Nate's wet ass.

Nate stopped sucking and gripped the steering wheel. His eyes began to roll and his mouth fell open. When Abim saw how well Nate was reacting to the finger fuck, he looked at Bambra, shrugged his shoulders as if to say, "This bitch wants extra," and stuck two more fingers up Nate's sweet ass.

"Ah, yes, deeper, guys," Nate whispered.

"You like?" Abim asked. He was biting his bottom lip and watching his own fingers probe Nate's hole like a dirty old man watching porn.

"Can we go outside, guys?" Nate asked. He wanted them to take turns on him against the rocks in the stream; he wanted to get nailed hard and fast in this tropical paradise.

"Ah, well, but not too far," Abim said. "We can go out, but not too far from the truck. You never know if the tourists will be walking around. This is private property, but they don't always care."

Nate nodded yes, and then he climbed into the back seat while Abim opened the rear door.

Abim got out first. "Here, let me help you." Though he was short, his strength was amazing. He reached up into the truck, grabbed Nate by the waist, and lifted him down gently on the dirt driveway. Nate held on to his wide shoulders for support; his legs were a bit wobbly from being spread wishbone-style for so long. "There you go, baby-cakes. You're never going to forget this tour." He lowered his hands from Nate's waist and placed them on the middle of Nate's ass.

Bambra and Keli got out of the truck and stood on either side of Abim. Nate was the only one completely naked; the others were still fully clothed, but their dicks were sticking out of their pants. These guys were ready to pounce: their dark pupils were dilated, their legs were spread wide, and they bounced on the balls of their feet.

"We don't get too many good-looking American blond boys like you," Abim said. "I think Bambra and Keli want to have a go at you first."

Nate smiled; he knew what these boys wanted. "Just let me get some condoms from my bag in the truck."

He bent over slowly so they could stare at his ass, pulled three condoms from his backpack, and then handed one to each young man. While they opened the small packets, Nate slowly walked to a grassy area about thirty feet from the truck and stretched his arms all the way in the air. Keli walked up from behind, grabbed him by the waist and pulled him down slowly. When Nate was on his hands and knees, he spread his legs and arched his back again. Keli spit down on his dick and pressed the tip to Nate's hole. Keli was awkward and his dick was large. As he shoved it into Nate's ass, there was a moment of shooting pain. But only a moment: Nate took a deep breath, sighed, and then started to back into Keli's cock. Abim and Bambra stood beside them and watched, holding their condom-covered erections, while Keli started to buck and pound Nate into the grass; it didn't take long before Nate was flat on his stomach. Keli was a strong boy; he nailed Nate to the damp green carpet. He fucked hard and fast, and he blew a full load of seed into the tip of the condom quickly.

Nate clutched a rock with his right hand and spread his legs wider when Keli pulled out. Ah, he'd liked that: it was the perfect fuck. Keli was the horny top guy, interested only in pounding his sweet ass and getting off without any foreplay nonsense. Of course, Nate was paying for the tour, but he knew these guys were having a good time, too. He didn't want them to forget this particular tour either.

Bambra was next; he didn't need any lube to get inside. Nate's hole was already open and ready for action. He fucked with a distinct rhythm, as though he were pounding away to the minute waltz. One, two, three . . . bam, was how it went. Nate opened his mouth and bent his legs up. His toes curled and his eyes rolled. Bambra's fucking caused Nate's dick to rub against the grass. Keli had been so silent: when he came he simply grunted and bucked faster. But when Bambra reached orgasm, he started to shout, "Ah . . . Ah . . . yes . . . here goes." Nate felt the cotton fabric of Bambra's shorts rub against the backs of his thighs. Bambra went deep and shouted: "Fuuuuck!"

He didn't pull out right away. Bambra fell on top of Nate's naked body and whispered, "Ah, that's nice, man. You're so soft inside I could stay forever." And then he slowly began to buck so he could squeeze out the last few drops of cum.

But Abim kicked Bambra in the leg. "Get off now. It's my turn, man. You've been in there long enough."

Bambra pulled out and Nate smiled. What more could a nice-looking lawyer from Martha Falls, Maryland, want? Two hot young boys with aboriginal accents fighting for a turn to fuck him?

Abim shoved Bambra out of the way and gave him a nasty look. Then he went down on the grass, ran his hand across Nate's ass, and guided his cock to the opening. By then Nate's hole was like a vacuum ready to suck up anything long and hard. But when Abim's extra-thick dick entered the pink tunnel, Nate thought he saw a white light. Though the other two men had been good fucks, Abim clearly had the advantage with his girth. The sensation of fullness began at the lips of

Nate's hole and spread all the way up his ass to that special spot where his orgasms usually began.

"Ah, Abim," Nate said, "go deeper, man, please."

Abim smiled. "I saved the best for last, babycakes. I know what I'm doing."

He fucked Nate slowly and sporadically at first. He'd pull all the way out, shove it in deeply, and then repeat that two or three times. And just when Nate was ready for another plunge, Abim would bury his cock all the way in and hammer his pelvis against Nate's ass cheeks.

But Abim was just like the other guys. He wanted to come fast, too. And when he started to really pummel away, it wasn't like Bambra's waltz-fuck. His rhythm was more like the beat of a disco drum, and it looked as though he were doing push-ups in fast-forward motion. The harder he fucked, the closer Nate came to blowing his own load. Abim's hands were on either side of his head by then. Nate leaned to the left and began to suck one of Abim's thick fingers while the young guy continued to smash him into the grass.

"Ah, Abim," Nate said, "I'm so close. Harder, yes!"

The other two guys were still watching, but they'd already shoved their dicks back into their pants. Keli was tapping his foot and looking at his watch.

Abim didn't say a word. He started to grunt; a drop of sweat fell from his temple onto Nate's back. The ass thumping grew more intense.

"Ah, yes," Nate shouted. His head was bouncing, and he expanded his arms as far as they would go.

Abim gave one hard stab and they both came together. Nate could actually feel Abim's chunky dick head swell and blow through the latex condom; Abim felt Nate's hole constrict and twitch when his ass exploded into an orgasm.

A moment later the young man rested his body against Nate's back and sighed. His dirty black boot brushed against Nate's leg, and he whispered, "How was that, man?"

Nate clamped down on his dick and held it tightly. "Can I make you my official tropical tour guide for as long as I'm here?"

"We'll take you anywhere you want to go, mate," Abim said. Then he laughed.

Though he was still nailed to the grass and a big dick was still buried up his ass, Nate noticed that Abim's accent had all but disappeared by then. He sounded Australian, but not at all aboriginal. "Hey, Abim," Nate whispered. "What happened to your island boy accent?"

Abim smiled and then reached around and grabbed a handful of Nate's chest muscle. "That's for the tourists. My real name is Bobby, and I was born in Sydney. And Bambra is Mike, and Keli is really Tommy. The Americans and English love it, all the stereotypes. And they really don't know whether the accent is Jamaican or aborigine. Sometimes I'm not sure myself. I hope you're not disappointed, babycakes."

Nate smiled. "Not at all, Bobby. I can't wait to see where we're going tomorrow."

"One of the reef islands, where we can take turns on you on the beach," Abim said.

THE RV OF WINDOWS

REX LANDRY

MY JOB REQUIRES ME to ride the open lonely highways. It was mid-morning, and the sun was baking down on the asphalt. There had not been another vehicle in sight for almost an hour when I came upon a large motor home. I adjusted my speed so I could enjoy the company of other people, even if they hadn't noticed me and were in another vehicle.

I had been coasting behind the giant RV for about ten minutes when I noticed the curtains and blinds of large picture window facing me had been opened. Seconds later a hunky young lad, who appeared to be barely legal, stood facing me, looking out the window. He proceeded to do a slow erotic striptease for my benefit. Damn, this twink was hot. He had bleached-blond hair, a firm, tight body, gorgeous, perfectly round glutes, and an impressive thick cock that jutted up to his flat stomach.

My young hottie pressed his dick against the window and rubbed it against the glass as he kissed the window. My hands found their way inside my pants, and I stroked my manhood as he began to play with his balls and cock. He placed two fingers in his mouth and sucked on them. He then turned around and inserted them both inside his hot ass and pushed them completely inside. My pants were down to my knees. I found driving next to impossible, but I'd be damned if I was going to let the young man out of my sight.

Just when I thought I was going to bust my nuts, another young stud equally as beautiful as the first (only he was stockier and had curly black hair) came up to the naked stud and kissed him tenderly on the mouth. They kissed passionately as I tried to maintain some level of control. The blond stud helped the second lad remove his clothes and then immediately dropped to his knees and began nursing his long cock. To say the dark-haired lad was blessed is an understatement. How the first was able to suck on him was truly a miracle. His cock was not only long but had one of the largest glans I have ever seen. These guys were hot for each other.

Just when I thought it couldn't get hotter, the dark-haired beauty lifted the young blond stud up. The blond embraced the brunette and slowly lowered his firm ass down on his friend's giant pole. Within seconds he was riding his friend the way one might ride a wild bronco. I found myself flushed, my cock hard, and my hands pumping like crazy.

My cock erupted, sending my spunk on the steering wheel and the windshield. My new young friends both puckered their lips and blew me kisses. My own ass twitched just thinking about the abuse the blond was receiving. He was insatiable. He ground his ass onto his friend's cock, taking the entire length into his hot canal. I took my fingers and wiped my come from the window and licked them clean. This seemed to please my young friends, who gave me two thumbs up. Apparently the dark-haired lad climaxed inside the blond. The blond hopped down from the pole he had been riding and bent over so I could see the come flow from his open, swollen hole. The dark-haired man dropped to his knees and began to lick his friend's ass clean of his own come. When he had licked him dry, he turned him around and began sucking on his cock. It didn't take long before he was enjoying a load of fresh, hot sperm. He lapped it up and sucked him dry. They kissed passionately again and then took a bow.

I reached to the floorboard and lifted the blue strobe light. I placed it on the dash and turned on the siren. The large RV pulled off the deserted highway. A third young man opened the door, wearing only a necklace and small white cotton shorts that barely covered him.

"Is something wrong?" he nervously asked.

"I just witnessed an unlawful entry, and I need to inspect to see if there is any damage."

I opened the door to the motor home: standing before me were the two naked young men. Before I could open my mouth, the blond placed his hands on my shoulders and pushed me to my knees. The two of them took turns feeding me their cocks. The driver was now nude and unbuttoning my shirt. The three of them had me naked in no time.

"Officer, how can it be unlawful entry when I impaled myself on John's cock?" the blond asked and winked at me.

"It has to be unlawful. No one would willingly take that monster up his ass."

"We both do it all the time," the driver responded. "I bet you could take it up yours if you weren't such a tight ass."

"Yeah, let's loosen him up and let John show him the time of his life," the blond said.

"Ram two of your fingers up his ass, Tony," John ordered the blond.

I was about to protest when I noticed Tony had locked my right wrist in my handcuffs and had looped the cuffs around a pole before locking the other cuff to my left hand. I was defenseless and loving every moment. While Tony pried my tight ass open with his large fingers, the driver placed his hooded tool on my lips.

"Go ahead and get me hard. I want to fuck that hairy ass of yours."

"Go ahead and suck on Dave's nasty cock. He never bathes, and I'm sure he's pretty rank by now," John ordered.

He was right. Dave's cock downright stank, but that didn't stop me from enjoying his beautiful dick. I pulled back his hood and licked him clean. Dave slowly pushed his cock in my mouth and Tony worked his two fingers up to his knuckles. John dropped to the floor and took my cock in his mouth. My head was swimming from excitement. These three young men were at their prime, and damn if they weren't hot.

Tony worked my hole until I was loose. He pulled out his fingers and replaced them with a large plastic object. I couldn't see it but assumed it was a large dildo. I squirmed as Tony pushed more and more inside my burning gut. I opened my mouth wider to scream but Dave took the opportunity to slide more of his nasty cock in my mouth. All the while John toyed with my low-hanging balls as he sucked on my cock. Man, could that boy suck. It felt like he was going to not only drain my balls dry but suck all the blood from me. My cock was engorged with blood, leaving very little to reach my brain. The effect these guys were having on me was unbelievable.

Tony managed to get the full length of the plastic dick inside me. He reamed me good and hard. My prostate reacted violently. I jerked back but couldn't move too far because of the cuffs around my wrists. Tony firmly held the plastic dick in place, keeping the dildo from being expelled from my ass. Just as my body adjusted to its invader, Tony pulled the toy out and then rammed me once again. The feeling was fantastic. Tony repeated the thrusting until I began bucking back in rhythm with his thrusts.

Dave traded places with Tony. As I began sucking on Tony's cock, Dave placed his nasty rod against my open asshole and slowly inched his way inside. The warmth of his dick was much better than the cold hard plastic, though I don't think he was any softer than the dildo. He plowed my ass as John continued to suck on one ball and then the next. Occasionally, he would lick the length of my penis and suck on the head. He was careful to bring me to the edge and then back away.

I've never been the center of attention. Hell, the closest I've been to an orgy was being kissed by my former lover while another friend sucked on his cock. Tony tasted great. I lapped up his leaking sperm, hoping he would give me a full load. He placed his hands on the back of my head and used my face as a receptacle for his hot piston. I could barely breathe. Tony was in full control of my mouth, just as Dave was in total control of my ass. If I even moaned as if I wanted to get away, John would bite down on my balls.

Just when I thought I was going to explode, Dave thrust even harder into my ass, and I felt him release a large load of goo deep inside my guts. He stayed inside me and told Tony to choke me with his sperm. Right on command, Tony began spurting inside my mouth. I tried to swallow his entire tasty load, but it was more than I've ever had before and some escaped down my chin. He used his hands to milk himself dry inside my mouth, and then he used his fingers to wipe my chin clean. He ordered me to lick his fingers clean. I gladly obeyed.

My ass was sore and I felt a little drained. I didn't notice that Tony had unlocked my cuffs and repositioned my hands around the pole before relocking them. The three strapping lads flipped me over on my back. Tony and Dave took my legs in their hands and raised my legs high in the air so my ass was perfectly displayed. John positioned a hand mirror so I could see my still open pucker-hole dripping with Dave's sperm. John leaned down and began licking and sucking on my anus until I was squeaky clean. His tongue felt great against my hot flesh. But instead of cooling off, I felt even more on fire with the desire to have John invade my ass with his mighty pole.

"Man, fuck me with that huge cock of yours," I heard myself say.

"Not so fast, lawman. I think Tony would like a little of your ass first."

"I just drained him. He can't have anything left, and besides, he won't be hard for hours," I responded.

I was wrong. Tony let go of my leg and changed places with John. It was unbelievable; he was rock hard and penetrating my ass before I could blink. He was about the same size as Dave. He worked my ass like nothing I've ever experienced before. He was loving and gentle, then rough and fast. He alternated his routine. He was a Jekyll and Hyde. When he blasted his load in my ass, it was as large as the one he deposited in my mouth. And then he leaned forward and tenderly kissed me. I was melting in his strong arms.

It was Dave's turn to lick my ass clean. These young men sure loved to eat sperm and didn't let one drop go to waste. While Dave ate my ass, John placed his swollen cock on my lips.

"Are you ready for some real action, lawman?" he taunted me.

I responded by opening my mouth and sucking on his huge head. I knew I couldn't take much of it in my mouth. I don't see how Tony took so much of him in his. All I knew was I was going to get fucked by his massive meat, and I began to get scared.

"That's it. Suck on me like a good little pig," John said.

As I sucked a little more of him into my mouth, Dave began paddling me with a thick oak paddle. It hurt like hell. I opened my mouth wider to scream, and John took the opportunity to push a little more of his massive rod inside my mouth. Over and over the two did their routine, until my ass was beet red and seven inches of John's cock were in my mouth. Tony came over and whispered in my ear.

"I think you need to be cooled off."

Tony rammed a frozen Popsicle inside my ass. I must admit the sensation was exhilarating.

"That's it, you pig. Take my Popsicle too," John ordered.

John pulled out. Before he could ram back inside my mouth, I blurted out, "Fuck me already. Split my ass wide open with your monster, John, I want you now!"

Tony laughed, pulled the Popsicle from my ass, and inserted it in my mouth. I could taste my ass mixed with the flavors of Tony's and Dave's deposits on the melting sweet treat. Who would ever have dreamed a Popsicle could taste so good?

Tony and Dave once again held my legs high in place as John quickly licked my sticky cheeks clean. John positioned his tool at the entrance to my bowels and fell on top of me, driving his cock slowly inside me as he did. I was amazed how my ass opened up for him. Tears flooded down my cheeks when his large balls began bouncing on my ass. He was fully inside and I was completely full. He was gentle at first, but then the animal in John came out. He leaned over and nibbled on my teats as he humped my ass. He kissed his way up my chest until his lips were firmly placed on mine and sucked on my lower lip, then my tongue. He pumped me hard and fast. My loins were on fire from the friction. He bit down on my lower lip as he fucked the shit out of me and sucked the blood as he drilled me harder. I was being split in two and loving every second.

John fucked me for twenty minutes before he groaned in ecstasy. He released his load in my ass, the third such deposit of the day. He pulled out and quickly placed his mushroom head on my lips. Knowing the routine, I opened my mouth and licked him clean as Tony and Dave pumped the last few drops of come out of John's cock onto my tongue. When they were satisfied his balls were empty, they dove down to my ass and licked me clean.

With all the action, I had forgotten I hadn't released another load of my own. I looked down, and my cock was rock hard and stood straight up like a rocket ready to launch. Tony came up for air and noticed my cock. He swung around and placed his ass on my face and ordered me to rim him. I happily obeyed. Dave and John each took one of my aching balls in their mouths and began to lightly suck. Tony stood up, positioned his perfect ass over my cock, and lowered his can onto my throbbing meat. He rode me for less than five minutes before I exploded inside his hot ass. He got up and lowered his sopping ass back onto my lips and ordered me to clean him up. I did so as Dave and John licked my pole clean.

Dave unlocked the cuffs, and we all crawled up on the bed and slept for an hour.

"He's a pretty nice pig, don't you think?" John asked the others.

"He's pretty damn hot," Tony replied.

"Yeah, he's hot all right," Dave said. "But I really like for my pigs to squeal. You think we can get him to squeal, boys?"

"Yeah, let's get him to squeal," Tony said.

"I'm game," I replied, thinking of what was to come.

SLAMMING THE POET

NEIL PLAKCY

MY FRIEND GUNTER ISN'T THE TYPE OF GUY you associate with literature, so when he asked me if I wanted to go to a poetry slam with him, I thought it had something to do with punk music—you know, where people in leather, chains, and bad hair crowd into a pit and slam into each other.

Turns out that while being a totally uncloseted homosexual, Gunter was a closet poet, attending a poetry workshop once a week at the Atherton Y on University Avenue, up by the University of Hawaii campus. The things you don't know about somebody, even after you've sucked his dick.

"I'm going to read a poem out loud for the first time in front of a crowd," he said. "Kimo, I need you there for moral support."

Gunter's been there for me more than a few times, so despite my total lack of interest in poetry, slammed, spammed, or otherwise, I went along. We got there early so Gunter could sign up for the open mic part of the evening, which was to be followed by a performance from a mainland poet named Ricardo White, winner of a couple of slam events in New York and Chicago.

It was funny seeing Gunter outside his natural element. He's tall and skinny but muscular, with close-cropped blond hair and an eyebrow ring. When we cruise the gay bars of Waikiki, he wears close-fitting muscle shirts and tight shorts that show off his sexy ass. This evening, though, he was wearing a polo shirt and khakis, and he could pass for a graduate student at the university.

It was a young crowd, with a smattering of older sandal-and-serape types. One Hawaiian woman looked like she was dressed for a hula contest, her full breasts popping out of her bikini top. She was wearing so many leis she could have opened her own floral shop.

Gunter was third on the roster, and the small auditorium settled into an expectant hush as he made his way to the podium. "We strip our clothes off in a frenzy of mutual desire," his poem began, and my interest was piqued. Had he written a poem about me?

"You bend me over, stick your tongue up my ass," he continued, reciting from memory, making eye contact with his audience. "You curl the tip up like a miniature dick and start to fuck me, lubing up my hole for the assault of your monster cock."

Well, maybe it wasn't about me.

The poem went on, a three-minute ode to the joys of ass fucking, and by the end, when Gunter's lover jammed his cock in one last time and spasmed in glorious ejaculation, I could see a few guys shifting uneasily in their seats. There was a polite spattering of applause as Gunter left the stage and made his way back to me.

"We never read poetry like that in English lit class," I whispered to him as he sat down. "Maybe I would have paid attention if we had."

I was an English major in college, before I spent a year on the North Shore surfing, before I went to the police academy and patrolled the streets of Honolulu, before I made detective, and before I became one of Honolulu's most photographed homosexuals.

The rest of the slam poets were nowhere near as interesting—until Ricardo White took the stage. He was a big, burly, black guy, his hair in short dreads around his face. His poetry read like the lyrics to rap music. There were a lot of references to "the man" and "the system," as if he wanted us to believe he'd come to Honolulu fresh from gang action in San Quentin.

He dressed like a rapper with baggy pants, oversized T-shirt, ball cap, and gold chains. And though I was in my off-duty surfer dude clothes—aloha shirt, board shorts, and sneakers—he kept making eye contact with me, as if he knew I was a cop and he was daring me to arrest him—perhaps for breaking the laws of rhythm or meter.

After his performance, he announced his picks for the top slammers of the evening. To my surprise, Gunter took first place. "Totally chillin', dude," White said to Gunter while handing him a tiny trophy, one of those generic Greeks in a loincloth holding his arms up in victory.

Gunter was so excited he wrapped his arms around Ricardo White and nearly levitated him off the floor. There was wine and cheese afterward, and because Gunter was the big winner, we had to stick around. I stood in the back against the wall, sipping a cheap white wine and munching on Swiss cheese chunks, waiting while Gunter bashfully explained his theory of poetics to some aged hippie with a gray handlebar mustache. Then Ricardo saw me and disengaged himself from the crowd around him.

"Dude, your boyfriend's awesome," he said, coming over to me.

"He's not my boyfriend," I said. Trying to see if I could shock him, I said, "Just a fuck buddy."

"And do you think he'd mind if I fucked his buddy?" He leered at me, and I was ready to tell him exactly who he could fuck when I happened to look down. There, silhouetted against his baggy pants, was the dick of death. Long and thick, with an uncircumcised knob that was already leaking pre-come into the fabric at his crotch.

I reevaluated my position and decided I wanted to have Ricardo White's dick in my mouth and up my ass. "Why don't you ask his buddy directly?"

"Does that door over there lead to the street?"

"Let's find out." I caught Gunter's eye and winked, then headed for the door, Ricardo White hot on my heels. The door led to an alley behind the Y, lit only by a single light at the far end. Ricardo followed me outside, then grabbed my hand as the door swung shut behind him.

"Come here, you," he said.

I leaned back against the wall, and Ricardo was on me like a puppy going for chow. He pressed his big body against mine, forcing me back against the brick wall, his tongue in my mouth and his big fat prick pressing up against my stomach. I hadn't found him that attractive when he was reading, but out there in the alley he unleashed a kind of animal passion inside me, and I was clawing at his shirt, sucking his lips, and grinding my dick against him like I'd just been released from a year in solitary confinement.

It was hot and humid out there, without even a hint of a breeze, and there was just enough light to see the sweat on Ricardo's face glistening.

Suddenly, the alley door popped open and Gunter stood there, silhouetted in the light from the bar. "You guys gonna be long?" he asked. "Cause we drove here in your truck, remember? I need a ride home."

Ricardo White pulled away from me, and I discovered my heart was beating faster than a hot rod on the H1. "I want to fuck your buddy here long and hard," White said to Gunter. "How about if Nemo and I take you home and then we find ourselves some place a little more private than a back alley?"

"Kimo," I said. "Not Nemo. And that works for me."

It was tough pulling away from Ricardo White, repositioning my throbbing hard-on in my pants, and buttoning up my aloha shirt where it had somehow come open. But I managed. I put Ricardo's roll-aboard suitcase in the back, and we jammed into the front seat of my truck, Ricardo in the middle, one hand in my lap and one in Gunter's, and it was a struggle to drive safely back to Waikiki.

Ricardo's touch was light but sure as he stroked my dick and Gunter's. While he did so, he recited a poem to us, what he called his ode to oral sex. I was afraid I'd come right there in my shorts, but he stopped just in time. By the time I pulled up in the driveway of the little house Gunter shared with a roommate, I was starting to get a serious case of blue balls.

"I feel like a celebration," Gunter said, opening the door to get out. "I've got a bottle of champagne in the fridge, but my roommate's home tonight. I could grab the champagne and come over to your place with you guys."

Knowing Gunter, I knew the invitation was for more than just champagne. He'd had his eye on Ricardo's sexy ass from the moment we arrived at the slam. The question was, did I want to share?

Hell, Gunter was my best friend. And that's what friends do, right? Share?

I said, "Fine by me."

Ricardo White said, "Now that's the aloha spirit I keep hearing about."

While Gunter went inside, Ricardo and I played a little tonsil hockey. Man, the guy could kiss. I felt myself in serious danger of getting lost in his throat.

Gunter was back with the cold bottle a moment later, and Ricardo and I pulled apart. Fortunately, it was only a short drive to my apartment. Ricardo and I started making out in the living room while Gunter stepped over to my galley kitchen to open the champagne, and by the time he found and filled three glasses, I was sitting on Ricardo's lap with my legs around him, working on swallowing his tonsils. "Damn, I keep feeling like I'm interrupting you," Gunter said.

Ricardo unbuttoned his shirt and offered up one luscious caramel-colored tit to Gunter, who drizzled some champagne on it and began licking and sucking. I peeled Ricardo's shirt off and did the same with his other tit, my hands working on opening his baggy black trousers. He wore white boxer briefs underneath, and there was already a wet spot by the mushroom-shaped cap of his dick. I drizzled more champagne on his dick and began sucking him through the white fabric.

Ricardo guzzled his glass of champagne and began deep-throating Gunter as I sucked his thick, coffee-colored dick. There aren't that many black guys in Honolulu, so Ricardo was a novelty for me, and I was thoroughly enjoying the experience. It was fun to share it with Gunter, too. He was always a vocal and enthusiastic partner whenever we hooked up.

"You are one hot brother," he said to Ricardo. He put his finger to his mouth, then touched Ricardo's silky thigh and made hissing steam sounds.

I loved the taste of the champagne combined with the feel of Ricardo's nipple in my mouth. I licked it and gently nibbled at it, and he arched his back in response. He began reciting a poem about nipple worship, in which the word "tits" rhymed with every other line. It wasn't great poetry, but it was sexy as hell.

"Let me see that sweet ass of yours," Ricardo said, but when I looked up he was talking to Gunter, who quickly stripped. Ricardo slid down on the sofa, me still sucking his dick through his briefs, and Gunter positioned his naked ass above the poet's face and proceeded to get his butt hole slammed with a long, thick tongue.

I pulled down Ricardo's white shorts, freeing his impressive trouser snake, purple-brown and stiff. The head glistened with pre-come, and I was fascinated by how much darker it was than the rest of his skin. His balls were equally dark, small globes pulled up close to his dick. I wondered if they would loosen up if I sucked them.

I stripped off my aloha shirt, kicked off my deck shoes, and then dropped my shorts and boxers. My own dick sprang free, having gone through a half-dozen cycles of hard and soft since the first moment I saw the visiting poet. My body is pretty hot, toned by lots of exercise, and because my skin is smooth and the only places you'll find any hair is under my arms and around my crotch, the muscles tend to stand out.

"Mmm, mmm, baby," Ricardo said. "Come here and give me some of that."

Gunter took my place at Ricardo's dick, sheathing it in a condom, slathering some lube on it, and then lowering his skinny white ass onto it. I moved to the other end of the sofa, positioned my ass above the slam poet's mouth, and got my own tongue fucking.

Maybe it was all that reciting he did, but the man knew how to use his mouth. I felt his tongue licking and slurping and probing every corner of my butt hole, and the experience made me shiver and shake and long to have that tongue replaced by his big juicy dick.

While he was going at me, I felt him spasming and saw that he'd shot a load up Gunter's ass. "Damn," I said, "I thought you were saving that for me."

"Don't worry, baby, there's a lot more where that came from," Ricardo said.

I only have a studio apartment, albeit a large one with a window that looks down Lili'uokalani Street toward the ocean, so it was a quick jump from the sofa to my king-size bed. All three of us were naked, cuddling together, a jumble of dicks, asses, and mouths, constantly moving and exploring each other.

I'd fooled around with Gunter many times by then, but his combination of desire and athleticism always turned me on. He was a security guard at a fancy condo in Waikiki, and he filled his down time with exercises, clenching and unclenching his ass, practicing squats, so he'd built up his stamina and was able to contort his long, skinny body in a dozen different ways.

I'm just your garden variety sexual enthusiast—I like to suck dick, get fucked, and make out with cute guys, but Gunter has the passion and body of a gymnast. He was above us, below us, to the left and to the right, thoroughly impressing our guest poet, whose dick was quickly back up to full force.

I sat back against the pillows with my legs open. Ricardo lifted them above his shoulders, scooting me farther back, and then, his dick sheathed and spit-moistened, pushed past my entry gate and deep into me. The assault hurt at first, but quickly he picked up a smooth rhythm that lulled all the pain away. He stared deeply into my eyes, and then Gunter snaked his head between us to take me into his mouth.

It was a complete assault on the senses. Ricardo White recited another one of his poems as he fucked me, to the accompaniment of loud sucking from Gunter. Through the open window, a sea breeze blew in a touch of salt air, which mingled with the smell of sweat and come rising from all three of our bodies. In the far distance, some-body was playing slack-key guitar music, and somebody else was revving a motorcycle.

I realized I was starving, having only eaten a couple of cheese cubes at the poetry slam, but there was no time to eat now. Ricardo's dick was silky smooth, pulsing in and out of me in a rhythm punctuated by his verses, and the hot wetness of Gunter's mouth was driving my dick to distraction. The contrast of Gunter's close-cropped blond head against Ricardo's dark brown, nearly hairless chest was a pho-tograph waiting to be snapped, my own olive skin the perfect shade halfway between them. Every time I licked my lips or swallowed, I tasted again the sweet funkiness of Ricardo's dick, the salty tang of his pre-come.

I came quickly in Gunter's mouth, my body tightening, then ex-ploding with the relief that had been denied to it for so long. My dick was so tender then, and I wanted to pull it out of Gunter's mouth and curl up somewhere, but he wouldn't let go, and Ricardo kept on fuck-ing me, pounding his rod into my ass long beyond pleasure and pain, into some rarefied dimension where all I could focus on was the sen-sation of his dick in me, sliding and pounding until I was almost senseless.

By the time I finally felt him stiffen and then shoot into the reser-voir at the condom's tip, my body had turned to jelly and I'd lost all feeling in my toes and fingers. He pulled back from me and rolled to the side, and I was able to relax my clenched butt muscles and let my legs drop to the sheets. "That's the way we do it ghetto-style, baby," Ricardo said.

Gunter burst out laughing. "You grew up in the suburbs of Okla-homa City," he said. "I read your bio. And you have a master's degree in poetry."

"It's a metaphorical ghetto," Ricardo said, and I started laughing too.

"I don't care what it is," I said. "But it felt damn good."

Ricardo and I sat back against the headboard, and Gunter stood before us, naked, declaiming another of his poems, this one about the glory of the penis. His own dick swelled as he recited the poem, and we both clapped politely when he was finished.

"How about you, Kimo?" Ricardo asked. "You got a poem in you that's dying to get out?"

"I express my poetic voice through my body," I said. "Can you hear what it's saying?"

"It sure as hell ain't iambic pentameter," Ricardo said, grabbing my dick, which had started to harden up again during Gunter's reading. He went down on me, and Gunter started tickling his bare ass, his fingers dancing down the hairy stretch that led to the poet's butt hole.

I figured we were all ready for another go at making physical poetry, and I dived into the fray.

Ricardo had an early flight the next morning, and I awoke bleary-eyed around six to find him padding around my apartment picking up various pieces of clothing. Gunter was sprawled next to me, snoring lightly.

"I called a cab," Ricardo said. "Thanks for showing me some real Hawaiian-style hospitality."

"We aim to please," I said. "The tourist office will be sending you a satisfaction survey."

"I'll be sure to let them know how well you treated me," he said. He looked out my window. "There's my cab. You tell your friend to keep on writing his poetry. He's got a voice."

"I will." I got up to lock the door behind Ricardo, used the bathroom, and then cuddled back up against Gunter, who shifted against me so that my stiffening dick rested in the crack of his ass.

When we both finally woke up a few hours later, sore in all kinds of places that reminded us of the fun the night before, I found a copy of Ricardo's poems on the kitchen table, which he'd autographed to both of us—Gerhard and Nemo. "Pleasure getting slammed by you," he wrote.

"The pleasure was all ours," Gunter said. Then he yawned and motioned me back to the bed.

CROSSING OVER

R. KRAMER BUSSEL

I NEVER WOULD HAVE PEGGED JEFF as the bondage type, let alone a total top. Then again, did any of the suited-up men in the room at the after-work professional gay mixer look kinky to me? Maybe I was just naïve back then—and it really wasn't that long ago, maybe three months—and all of them had secret dungeons in their suburban basements. Or maybe that was just Jeff; I don't know because I've been with him ever since, making up for lost time.

But I'm getting too far ahead of myself. I was sipping a vodka soda, sweating into my suit that April evening at some gay bar that had just opened in Midtown—the name doesn't matter because it closed soon thereafter. Every month since I'd moved to New York a year ago, I went to these things, hoping to meet someone, but not that many men seemed interested in me. I wasn't sure if it was because I was a teacher, albeit at a tony private high school, while everyone else was a fundraiser or owned his own business or was a curator or doctor or lawyer. Something respectable and lucrative. Or maybe it was obvious that I had only been with three guys in my life, though I'd have thought my inexperience was a plus. I always came off as too straight or too nervous or too *something,* and even though it wasn't specifically a dating event, plenty of other men were getting numbers, and even getting busy, all around me. I stared for a few seconds too long at a couple making out right next to me before Jeff walked over.

He looked me up and down, and when his eyes returned to my face, I wasn't sure whether he approved. He just stared, unnervingly, but he was really hot. He was a few inches taller than my five ten, bald, and, I learned later, had a symbol in another language tattooed on his shoulder. But even in a shirt and slacks, he didn't look completely corporate, or if he did, he was in a new category, like business hot. Even with the shaved head, he looked as if he *might* shove me against the wall and talk dirty, but nowhere near as dirty as things wound up getting between us that first night. But again, I'm getting ahead of myself. There I was, with his eyes raking my body while I just stood there, forgotten glass held uselessly between my fingers. I couldn't take more than fifteen seconds of silence, so I stuck out my hand and said, "Hi, I'm Scott."

"Hi, Scott," he said. Something about the tone of his voice, a slight uplift and perhaps an echoing of my speech, made it seem like he was making fun of me, but not in a cruel way—in a way that made my cock hard. He stepped closer, encircling me, trapping me against the bar. I liked it. "I'm Jeff," he whispered in my ear, deftly slipping my

drink from my hand, putting it down, then pinning my arm behind
me. He did it so fast, so subtly, like this was a normal greeting among
men, that I didn't say a word. Besides, my heart was pounding too
loudly for me to speak over it. He moved closer, so his whole body
was pressing against mine, pushing my back into the bar. "I think you
should come home with me tonight, Scott." He used his feet to nudge
mine apart. I didn't know this man at all, yet right then, I wanted him
to know me. All of me. I wanted to tilt my head back and let him do
whatever he wanted with me. And that's exactly what I did, except
we left the bar right away; we had no more use for it. I had no one to
say good-bye to, but as we made our way through the crowd, Jeff
was greeted with numerous "See you later's and "Hey man's" and a
few comments about me that made me blush.

"I'm just down the street," he said, marching forward, expecting
me to follow. And follow I did. Follow was suddenly all I wanted to
do. I wanted Jeff to order me around. I wanted him to tie me up and
do naughty things to me. I wanted to leave the specifics up to him. I
was no longer surprised that he was the dominant type, and I knew
right away that I liked it.

He was different from my other lovers, who'd all been close to my
age and as close to virgin as I was. We'd fucked each other and sucked
each other's cocks, and—don't get me wrong—it was hot as hell, but
nothing like this. With Jeff, I knew he was going to show me something I'd been waiting for my whole life, reintroduce me to sex, and
make me long for him until I'd offer him anything to get him to touch
me. I wanted to trust him with my body, even if putting my trust in
him left me more than a tad nervous. Before we reached his place, he
turned around, and I stopped too, right there on the sidewalk. He just
looked at me, up and then all the way down, very slowly, his eyes
seeming to read my every kinky thought. Finally, I looked down at
the ground, the blush rising to my cheeks as he made me his, just like

that, with his eyes. I really felt like a virgin all over again when he pinched my cheek between his fingers, hard enough to let me know that he was telling me something more than just that he thought I was cute. He wanted me to be his, in every way. And just like that, I was.

We walked the rest of the way in silence, until we approached his apartment, which was, appropriately, below ground. I say that because as soon as we walked in and he'd locked the door, he led me straight to the back. Not to his bedroom, which we passed along the way, and from the quick glimpse I got looked fairly average, but to the dungeon, a room painted all in black that optimized the small space. A cross was set up in a far corner, and one wall was lined with paddles, handcuffs, knives, and other implements that made me breathe hard. Coils of rope lay on the floor, and a spanking bench also adorned the room.

"You belong in here, Scott, don't you?" he asked, walking toward me.

"Yes, I do," I said, trembling as I spoke. I was nervous, but not about what he might do to me. I was suddenly nervous that I might not please him, that he might dismiss me before I was done, that he wouldn't like the boy he saw once I stripped off my clothes. Suddenly, more than anything else, I wanted him to want me, to approve, to keep me around.

He pinched my cheek again, harder than the last time, while simultaneously pinching one of my nipples. The pain was secondary to the look on his face, one traced with annoyance and filled with power. "Yes, what, Scott?" he asked, twisting my nipple as I whimpered and my cock stiffened.

"Yes, sir," I said, in a louder voice than the whisper I wanted to deliver. I knew a whisper would just prompt him to demand a better answer.

"Very good. That's how you're to address me, but only when I speak to you. Now strip," he ordered me, standing right in front of me while I got down to my birthday suit, leaving my more pricey suit crumpled on the ground. Jeff kicked my clothing into a corner, and I watched it mingle with dustballs. My dick was pointing straight up, but I didn't do anything to try to change that. I'm proud of my cock, and actually consider it my best feature, though I work out enough to know that the rest of me isn't bad either. But to my slight dismay, Jeff ignored my cock; he had more important things to show me.

"Over here," he ordered, his voice booming through the room, much louder than it needed to be. He had me line up with the T of the cross, facing away from him, my dick practically forgotten as I eased into place. You'd think having your arms shackled above your head would be uncomfortable, but immediately, I liked it. I liked the feeling of surrender, the way he tenderly strapped me in with padded leather cuffs. I felt that I'd come home. A flood of warmth rushed through me, calming the last of my nerves. "Whose ass is this?" Jeff asked as he grabbed my cheeks, pulling them apart.

I forgot about the fact that we'd met less than an hour ago, that I didn't know his last name, that none of my friends had a clue where I was. If I hadn't trusted him, I'd never have let him bind me to the cross, and although I have my flaws, I'm an excellent judge of character. Jeff had a paternal way about him, and without explicitly saying so, I knew he knew what he was doing, that he wanted to show me all the pleasure I could get if I just gave myself over to him. So when I answered, "Yours, sir, that ass is yours," I wasn't just parroting something he wanted me to say. It was true, and I had the hard cock and buzzing brain to prove it.

"That's right," he said, and with a fierce whack, he spanked me. I let out a sob of delight as he did it again and again, until I could barely tell which cheek he was hitting. I shut my eyes and focused on the sensations racing through my body. My ankles and wrists were snug in their cuffs, leaving me to focus on my ass and then my back. Jeff had moved on to a flogger and was pounding my back with it, giving me the kinkiest backrub I could imagine. Each thud reverberated through my body, pressing me deeper against the cross, then seemed to loop back, leaving me lighter, freer. I'm a fast learner, and I quickly realized that that was the real paradox of bondage: by being bound, I could be free. If I were left to my own devices, I'd want to twitch, turn, and squirm; I'd find a way to talk myself, and Jeff, out of going further in the name of safety or cautiousness. I'd convince myself I'd had enough when really, I could never get enough.

Jeff pushed me well past the point of comfort. His strikes hurt, not just my skin, but on a deeper level. The pain seemed to settle into my muscles, staying there, lying in wait, and not being able to move much of my body, save for my head and ass and futile tugs at my bonds, exacerbated the sensations. "How are you feeling, boy?" he asked me at one point when he'd seemingly sliced and diced my back and bottom until they'd be permanently red. The heat reminded me of a bad sunburn, one whose sizzle lingers long after I've gotten out of the sun.

"Good, sir. Very good," I said. It was true, even though I was sore. I was sore *for him*, for my new master, at least, I hoped that's who he was. I was sore because he'd chosen to make me sore, and I was also so turned on I kept expecting to spontaneously come. I wasn't sure how long he'd been striking me; time had stopped being important once I'd stepped into my cuffs. That's how I already thought of them, and the cross, as mine. Jeff ran his hands up and down my body, teasing me by lingering on my balls, nipping at my neck. I could feel his erection against my back.

"I'm glad to hear that, because I'm taking you down now," he said, and I felt a momentary shudder of disappointment. Had I wanted to stay tied up forever? Yes, a part of me did, but I knew that wasn't possible. What Jeff did after he untied me, though, surprised me more than anything up until that point. I moved aside and he stood to re-place me, shucking his pants and presenting me with a monster erec-tion. Facing outward, he assumed the position, and ordered me to strap him in.

"You want me to beat you, sir?" I asked tentatively. I would do anything for him, clearly, but that would be asking a little too much.

"No, of course not. I want you to suck my cock. In fact, I don't just want it, I demand it." In a flash, I got it, as I fastened the leather bind-ings around his wrists and ankles. He wanted that feeling of being un-able to escape, of push-pull, of having nowhere he could go except right there, with his dick in my mouth. I hurried, and soon I was down on my knees, with my mouth straining to suck him off, to swal-low his entire length. He was the biggest guy I'd been with, and I was grateful he couldn't thrust forward too much, though he did tell me when he wanted me to go faster or suck harder. Even though he was now tied up, I was still under his command. I reached forward, fondling his bound leg as I sucked him, while my other hand wrapped around the base of his cock. I knew that the cross, the rope, the en-tire room, were going to be my new lovers, along with Jeff. They were a package deal, and as Jeff came, releasing a hot, salty load down my throat, I was so grateful he'd picked me as his new plaything. I'd crossed over to the other side, and not only would I never need to at-tend a kinky mixer again, I had so much more to learn, and the per-fect teacher to do it.

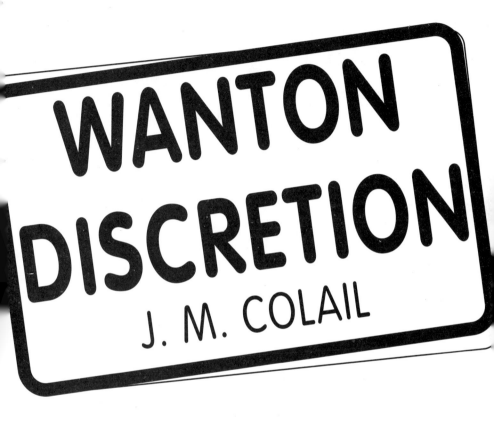

WANTON DISCRETION

J. M. COLAIL

THE CHAMPAGNE WAS CHOICE, accompanied by an assortment of fresh fruits that only the wealthiest aristocrats were able to import at this time of year. I surveyed the elegant ballroom, decorated with the finest curios currently in vogue. The orchestral octet sat in the corner while the city's loveliest, eligible ladies twirled around in their most luxurious ball gowns.

I was still a bachelor at twenty-four, a rarity in this day and age, and heir to my family's company. I was a slab of meat put to auction before these well-to-do maidens who discussed my social and financial status with squeals and giggles, comparing me to other bachelors in the room. I sipped my champagne and glanced at my pocket watch. Only half an hour longer and I could leave without insulting the grand Countess who sponsored this gala event. I was bored out of my mind.

I engaged in small talk with the other gentlemen, who discussed market fluctuations and the endowments of the several young women who smiled and batted their lashes at them. And by endowments, I mean their family background—nothing so risqué as fleshy preferences. No, this was the spawning ground of political and professional marriages, where nothing as trite as personality mattered, only the compatibility of one's family profile.

I stole a glimpse at my watch again and sighed. I had waited to engage a lady in a dance until the last possible moment, and that time was nearing. Their incessant yapping and feigned shyness drove me to distraction, and I wished to put off my growing headache for as long as possible. I was sipping my champagne as slowly as I could manage when a young man with silky brown hair, deep green eyes, and full lips set in a masculine jaw genuinely piqued my interest. He had a slim waist and broad shoulders and a charming bulge in his perfectly tailored trousers. I gulped the rest of my champagne and approached him with a smile.

"Evening. How are you tonight?" I said, extending my hand.

"Very good. And yourself?" he responded, with a handsome, wholesome smile that made my nether regions twitter in reaction. He shook my hand firmly, letting his hand linger in mine for a moment.

"Good, good. My name's Robert Stoichkov. And yours?"

"Thomas Kitner. It's a pleasure."

"Indeed," I answered, noticing his eyes summarizing my form in a glance. "So why aren't you out there sweeping some young thing off her feet?"

"For the same reason you aren't," he answered with a smirk. He took a sip of his champagne and surveyed the dance floor. "These girls have two sets of eyes, one in their faces and one on my wallet."

"Too true," I agreed, laughing and nodding at his accurate characterization. He was smart and pretty—a lascivious combination. "But I'm sure if you paid a little attention to a girl here, she'd let you between her thighs without a second thought," I said, taking a chance to glimpse his slender frame again. He blushed adorably, and I felt a fire ignite within my belly.

"Come now," he began timidly, then looked in my eyes with a devilish grin. "If you merely asked a girl to dance, I'm sure she'd have to change her drawers before the next song."

I laughed, enjoying Thomas's sense of humor, which was a close match to my own. I took another glass of champagne and admired his slim figure, which I nearly had undressed in my mind, when the Countess approached and curtsied.

The Countess was draped in an elegant pink gown with a tight bodice that lifted her ample bosom to an avalanche of cleavage. She fancied herself as something of a matchmaker and hosted these elaborate galas once a week. After pointing out a few young ladies and extolling their virtuous and moral qualities, she excused herself and greeted another guest and immediately delved into the favorable attributes of several aristocratic debutantes.

I finished the rest of my champagne in one gulp and sighed deeply. "I could really go for a strong, stiff drink," I murmured, staring into the empty champagne flute.

"Me too," Thomas said and cocked his head to the side. "Would you care to join me?"

I happily agreed, glad that he took my suggestion quickly. We decided to meet by the coatroom after the next song. I had to dance with at least one girl, or my mother would hear about it from the Countess. Nor did I want to insult the Countess, a long-time family friend, by not participating in her famed event.

I approached a girl at random and invited her to dance. She giggled and accepted, blushing when she took my hand. I led her to the dance floor and pulled her into my arms. As I swept her across the expensive tiled floor, she inquired about my financial and social status. She swooned when I told her that my family owned an international financial conglomerate. She was the only daughter of a construction tycoon who was looking to expand his business. She prattled on about one thing or another, and I looked over her shoulder to see Thomas twirling a beautiful girl in his arms. Our eyes met and the fire in my belly burned hotter; I had to look away, or the struggle within my trousers would have offended my dance partner.

The song ended and I thanked the girl for the dance. She begged me to stay, but I let her down gently and met Thomas at the coatroom. A maidservant retrieved our hats and coats and we stepped into the cold winter evening. It had begun snowing; a fresh layer of white covered the landscape. We took a carriage to a pub, conveniently located within walking distance of my house. Once inside the dimly lit establishment, we ordered a shot of whiskey to warm ourselves, followed by continuous pints of ale.

"Women have it so easy these days," Thomas said, taking a long drink. "They have maids to clean up after them, cooks to prepare meals, and nannies to raise their children!"

I laughed and agreed. "But it's not *all* women, just the well-to-do debutantes," I qualified, when the barmaid approached. "Not *real* women, who work for a living," I explained as the woman set down two more pints.

"True enough," Thomas agreed, finishing off his glass and picking up his fresh replacement. "But, if it were in vogue, I'm sure they'd hire prostitutes to take care of their husbands' desires!"

"That might not be a bad idea," I agreed. "Those women probably wouldn't know their pussies from a hole in the ground!"

"No pun intended," Thomas added, sending us into a raucous laughing fit.

As time passed and we lost track of how many pints were served, we finally decided it was time to leave. We bundled up, preparing for the winter attack on our inebriated senses, and stepped into a foot of snow. I was thankful Mother Nature was blessing me with such good luck.

"My, it's certainly piled up!" I said, glancing at Thomas's handsome face. Large snowflakes stuck to his eyelashes and his moist lips were irresistible. "You know, I don't live too far from here . . . within walking distance. It may be safer for you to stay the night rather than risk a carriage ride home," I suggested, carefully gauging his reaction.

Thomas thought for a moment, then smiled handsomely. "I hope I'm not imposing by accepting your offer," he answered.

"Of course not. I invited you! Now, let's be on our way before we catch our deaths," I said, leading the way to my house. I was very glad I gave my maid the evening off since I didn't know when I'd be getting home. Or if someone would be with me.

We arrived at my front door after a short walk. I took his hat and coat and gave him a quick tour of my house. I showed him the guest room he could use and where the bathroom was.

"Well, then, if there's anything you need, please let me know. I'm sure you'd like to wash up before retiring," I said, smiling gently.

Thomas thanked me, and I went to my room, right next to the guest room. I waited patiently, taking off my jacket, shirt, and belt. I listened for Thomas to head to the bathroom and then waited a moment before following him.

"Oh! I apologize, I didn't think you were still in here," I said, holding the door wide open.

Thomas stood in front of the sink with his handsome profile reflected in the mirror. "It's quite all right. I'm almost done in here," he answered nonchalantly, though with a subtle smile on his lips.

I stepped forward, my body tingling with anticipation, and laid my hands on his shoulders. His muscles tensed, then relaxed, and I felt my erection rise in response to the warmth of his body.

"I had a really good time tonight," I whispered, pushing myself closer and rubbing his shoulders. There was no doubt he could feel my stiff prick against his lower back.

He looked at me over his shoulder, his green eyes staring into mine, and smiled seductively. "As did I," he answered quietly and closed his eyes when I leaned forward to kiss him.

His lips were warm and moist and his tongue was strong and demanding. My cock throbbed and I slid my hand down to the front of his trousers. His firm organ greeted my hand with a pulsating welcome, but Thomas stopped me and pulled away from my kiss.

"Where's your bedroom?"

I felt myself grow stiffer yet and led him to my bedroom, where I continued to feel up his crotch and unzip his trousers. He put his hands on my shoulders as I got down on my knees. I pulled down his pants and underwear and marveled at the engorged, veined member before me. My mouth watered. I licked the shaft, opened my mouth, and swallowed the large tip with a heady desire. I took him as deep as my throat would allow, and his hands gripped my shoulders as moans rolled off his tongue. I sucked and slurped and massaged his balls until I felt him tremble as his crisis drew near. I doubled my efforts and he erupted in my mouth and down my throat.

He gasped for breath and smiled when I looked up at him. I felt pre-come soaking through my underpants. He helped me to my feet and kissed me, appreciatively at first, then wantonly. He pushed me back on the bed and stepped out of his trousers. His pressed, tailored shirt hung wrinkled on his slender frame as he leaned down and kissed me again. While he covered my face with kisses and caresses, his hands unzipped my trousers and then he sat back to look over my stiff, tingling shaft.

"I've been hard for you since the minute I saw you," I told him.

My body trembled when he touched me. He kneaded the tip and bent his head down, licking the shaft tenderly. I felt his hot breath and pushed my hips up to greet his velvety mouth. He swallowed as much of me as he could, bobbing his head and squeezing my balls.

"Ohh . . . wait . . ." I whispered, lifting his head to look at me. His brows furrowed, wondering why I asked him to stop. "Come around this way," I instructed, rubbing my hand over his hip and backside, turning him around until his cock rested on my lips. I could imagine the smile on his face as his fleshy organ grew to its limit. I raised my head and licked the slit adoringly as he thankfully returned his tongue and mouth to my prick. I sucked hard, trying to bring him to a crisis equal to my own, but I came quickly, eager for the sweet release. He mouthed my balls while I licked and slurped his delicious member and introduced my fingertip to his tight ring of muscle. He moaned with the intruder's persistence, releasing my balls as he wriggled on top of me. He climaxed beautifully, arching his back and pushing himself as deep into my mouth as he could. He collapsed on top of me, his lovely weapon pressed against my cheek and his own face nestled between my thighs.

"Oh, God . . . Robert," he panted.

His body heat emanated into me and quickly rekindled the fire in my loins. I pushed him off me and flipped him onto his stomach, caressing his firm, round rump and parting the cheeks to glimpse the ring of flesh that pulsed so invitingly. I plunged my tongue into the warm hole, closing my eyes to focus my senses. I was blessed with a long, limber tongue and Thomas showed his gratitude by squirming and moaning beneath me.

I withdrew my tongue and introduced two fingers into his charming hole while I reached for a small tub of cold cream from the nightstand. Thomas peeked at me over his shoulder; he pushed his hips back and parted his legs even more. I grinned with his eager compliance, placed my distended weapon at the delicious entrance, and pressed gently. Thomas moaned uneasily as I persisted, the lips of the charming orifice stretching to accommodate the lusty intruder. His quiet suffering abated and he pushed back against me until I was swallowed to the hilt. He bucked his hips and tightened his muscles, and feeling the sweet, warm pressure of his sheath around my inflamed sword, I slid my hand around front and gripped his stiff prick. Thomas met my thrusts desperately, his moans becoming pleas. I gripped his waist and pulled him back on my weapon with desirous fervor each time I pumped forward. My climax neared, as did Thomas's, and I rammed him as deep as I could, overflowing his hungry orifice with my hot, white come.

We took a short break to gather our senses and then continued our delicious couplings well into the night. Truly, I fucked the boy raw.

He was a delightful bedfellow, willing to try any position I suggested. His passion was great and we agreed to eliminate "no" and "stop" from our vocabularies. Eventually, we fell asleep; he snuggled close to me with his head on my chest and my arm wrapped around his shoulders.

In the morning, the sun sparkled on the newly fallen snow. My maid woke us up with two cups of coffee. Thomas blushed lightly, but remained in my embrace while my maid set down the mugs on the bedside table. She stepped back and held the tray to her chest.

"What would you like for breakfast, sir?" she asked, glancing at Thomas quickly.

I knew her expressions, and I smiled in spite of myself. Rosalie, my maid, was a good-hearted girl, sweet and kind, with unlimited discretion.

"Is there anything in particular you want?" I asked Thomas. He shook his head and his soft hair tickled my flesh. "The usual, then," I told Rosalie. "And if you could bring it up when it's ready."

"Yes, of course, sir," she answered with a timid smile, then bowed and left the room.

Thomas looked at me. I rested my head on the pillow, smiling. He was so handsome; I felt myself responding to the warmth of his closeness.

"I take it you've done this before," Thomas said, with a hint of disappointment in his voice.

"Whatever do you mean?" I asked, feeling it necessary to tease him a bit.

"Your maid . . . she didn't seem surprised to find another man in your bed."

"Oh, well, I suppose not. But . . . I assume you've done this before too," I returned, glancing at his beautiful face with a grin curling my lips.

"Now, whatever do you mean?" Thomas asked, mocking me playfully.

"You were much too . . . talented for it to have been your first time."

"Are you disappointed?" he asked, propping himself up on his elbows.

"No, no . . . but it would've been quite an honor to have been your first man," I said truthfully, leaning forward and kissing his forehead.

"Just a kiss on the forehead?" he asked sulkily.

I kissed him ravenously and guided his hand to my erect prick. "Would you kiss me here?" I asked.

Thomas smiled. "But your maid will be back with breakfast soon —"

"So?" I responded simply.

Thomas slipped his hand beneath the sheet and began to frig me gently. He pulled back the sheet and kissed the tip tenderly, just as I had asked. Then he began to lick the shaft and play with the delightful appendages.

I held out for as long as I could. I wanted to see Thomas's expression when Rosalie walked in. He was so talented with his strong tongue that it was difficult, but I somehow managed to prolong my climax until Rosalie opened the door. Thomas withdrew his mouth and I shot on his face. He turned bright red, while I chuckled and wiped his cheek clean. Rosalie set down a tray with toast, grapefruits, and coffee, then excused herself with blushing cheeks and a whisper of a smile. I handed Thomas a plate with two slices of toast.

After breakfast, Thomas got dressed, much to my dismay. He insisted that he must go home, even though I had planned to keep him in my bed all day. At last, I dressed too and walked him to the front door.

"Can I see you again?" I asked.

"Absolutely," he answered with a smile.

"Will you come tonight?"

"That depends on you," he said, turning his smile into an impish grin. "If you're as good as you were last night, I'll be coming over and over."

I laughed and kissed him once more. He was a remarkable man: handsome, intelligent, funny, and excellent in bed. He left with a promise to visit this evening.

VODKA DICK

SHANE ALLISON

THEY KEEP MY DICK HARD the way they prance around campus with their shirts off, teasing me by wearing next to fucking nothing, sweat glazing off of lithe torsos, nipples all pink and pert. Spend most of the day playing Frisbee football, guzzling beer like it was Kool-Aid. So oblivious to their beauty. I want them so much it makes my gums ache. With all those guys living under one roof, some fucking has gotta be going down, dicks being worshiped under a cloak of secrecy from their fellow brothers.

I was going to pledge during rush week, but the morning of, I took one look at myself in the medicine cabinet mirror and knew that I wasn't fraternity material. Leas' not until I met Sam. He was this guy from my playwriting class I had been crushing on all semester. He had skater boy looks, thin, arms and legs decorated with tatts of roses and ancient symbols. He had dark hair, brown eyes, and an earring in the fleshy part of his eyebrow. Playwriting was the only class I had that was two hours long. Thank damn god it met only once a week. Our instructor was some granola-munching T.A. from Mormon country Utah. He had balls the size of bed knobs when he told us that he didn't give out A's. Might as well say we weren't worthy enough for anything higher than a B. The class was made up of girls, mostly. Me, Sam, and a few other guys made up the rest.

I would always pick Sam to play gay characters in my plays. We would hang out after class. Seems like everybody on campus knew him. It was always "Hey, Sam" and "What's up, Sam?" I was envious of his popularity.

One day as we were on our way to the food court to grab something to eat, I asked him, "How do you know all these people?"

"Just friends that I've met at bars and keggers." Sam got the meatball hoagie and I got a broiled chicken wrap. It was all I could afford.

"I got an invite to a kegger at the Phi Eta Sigma House. You should come with me. They throw badass parties, man. They'll be a lot of pussy there and a whole lotta dick for you."

I like guys that are a little fucked up, and Sam fit the bill. Just didn't give a fuck what people thought and would say what was on his mind. All he talked about was girls. If he wasn't going on about pussy, he was talking about smoking pot. Sam knew how much I was into him.

"Sorry, man. I like pussy too much," he would say. "It's hard for me to imagine a hairy ass in my face." I busted out with laughter when he said that. Shit was funny as hell.

"I don't know. I gotta shitload of stuff to do. I gotta finish up this paper for my German Cinema class, and I wanna get started on this play Keene assigned," I told him.

"C'mon, man. That shit ain't due until next week. You got plenty of time." Sam's teeth were like perfect white Chiclets when he smiled. I would often wonder how his lips would feel pressed against my own, his tongue tasting like Camel Lights in my mouth.

"I'll think about it," I told him.

"Well, in case you change your mind . . ." He took a pen that was stuck in the spiral binding of his theme book and jotted down the address of the frat house on a napkin. I looked at what he had written, ink pressed gently into the delicate white paper.

"Is this the same frat that's been in the paper?" I asked. "Some shit about a girl getting raped?"

"That was just some chick trying to get back at her boyfriend. The guy that's excused is in my Chaucer class, and he said she made the shit up."

I knew it was more than what Sam was telling me. Shit was enough that it made the local news, but there was no proof that anything had gone down, so the school didn't bother to shut the frat down.

I sat in my dorm room that night, alone with a bowl of cold, half-eaten, shrimp-flavored Ramen noodles. Desk was strewn with used novels, books, and poems in progress. I had the place all to myself that semester after my roommate moved off campus into a one-bed-room apartment on Tharpe Street. I was having a shitty case of writer's block and couldn't concentrate. I looked at the napkin that Sam had written the fraternity's address on.

"Fuck it," I said, and grabbed my jacket. I kept changing my mind, thinking that I wouldn't fit into that world of the spoiled and privileged. When I got there, people were spilling out of the mouth of the Sigma house, laughing, shooting the shit over nothing while drinking booze out of red and blue Dixie cups. They didn't pay much attention to me as I walked up the brick steps to the entrance. The place looked like some plantation house out of *Roots*. More preppy types packed themselves inside. It reeked of booze and cigarettes. I could count twenty guys that all looked the same with their hats turned backward, cargo shorts hanging off their asses, teasing me. The sorority bimbos all resembled contestants from beauty pageants. I found Sam in another part of the frat house at the end of a tube while some idiot flushed beer down his throat. The red Dixie cups were marked with a "B" that I guess stood for beer, and the blue ones were marked with a "V." I tapped someone on the shoulder and asked, "What does the "V" mean?"

"Vodka," he said. It was my favorite liquor to get fucked up on. I grabbed a blue cup and nursed the hard booze as I made my way through the house.

The night trundled on. People kept pushing their way inside, squeezing themselves into every corner and crevice of the frat house. By midnight, I had had several cups of vodka. Wasn't long before I was seeing double, feeling sick. I broke away from the drunken crowd and headed upstairs. I walked down a hall with doors attached to bedrooms. Most of them were locked, full with couples copulating behind them. "Occupied." "Someone's in here." "Fuck off," they would yell. The door to the last bedroom on the right was ajar. I nudged it open a little to find someone lying down. It was Sam.

"I knew your ass wasn't going to last long the way you were downing the beer downstairs," I grinned.

He wasn't moving. I walked toward him. His shirt was hiked slightly over his stomach that was overgrown with belly hair. Booze was spilled on the sheets.

"Hey, man, you all right?" I asked. He didn't come to. Sam was passed out and shit-faced. I noticed that his jeans were undone at the clasp, exposing green and white underwear. Figured he was trying to make it to the bathroom, but passed out. So helpless, vulnerable. I closed the door and locked it so we wouldn't be disturbed. I went to the bathroom first to pee. The bathroom was colder than a dead crack whore. Piss plopped loudly in the toilet water. The rim of the sink was fussy with bottles of aftershave, a tube of mint-flavored tooth-paste. The room reeked of spilled beer. I started to toy with Sam's zipper, pulled at his waistline, smearing Sam at the foot end of the bed. He couldn't have weighed no more than a buck fifty. His tat-tooed legs slung off the end. I unzipped my pants and tugged my dick out of the panel of my underwear past the teeth of my zipper. It got hard fast. Sam's pubes were black like soda. Fished his dick out of the green cotton. It was just as I imagined it: hung with a pretty head. I dropped to my knees between his legs, took it into my mouth. I was scared he would wake up to my advances, but he didn't budge. I fin-gered his balls, sucked him deep without gagging. Pubes tickled my lips.

"Anyone in there?" The sudden voice scared the shit out of me.

"Fuck off!" I yelled. I pulled Sam's shorts down around his ass. I turned him over, ran my fingers along his ass crack. I licked his core; it was tart on my tongue. I lubed my dick with spit, but it dried up after only a few strokes. I went to the bathroom in search of some-thing slick. There was shaving cream, pills for pain relief, an as-sortment of colognes and hair gel, which was the closest thing to lubricant. I grabbed it and headed back to Sam. I unscrewed the lid off the hair dressing, dipped in two fingers, and slathered the pink grease on my dick. I applied more up Sam's ass. His hole was hot on my fin-ger. I searched the room for some rubbers. I don't fuck no man's ass without protection. I knew whichever room it was, there was some jimmy-hats somewhere. I found a few strewn about in one of the nightstand drawers. I tore along the perforated edge, pulled it from its cocoon of cellophane, and rolled the latex down on my dick.

I pried Sam's ass cheeks apart. My dick slid in nicely. I fucked him gently. I was sure he was faking it, pretending. How could he not feel a dick as big as mine up his ass? Yet I played along.

It wasn't how I wanted Sam: punch drunk and passed out on some stranger's bed. I knew I would never get a chance to get in his pants if he was upright, sober. It was tough for me to come due to all the vodka. I pulled out when I felt myself close. I jacked off and came. Cum discharged across Sam's ass, on his back in fat white drops. Pearls of it dropped on the maroon carpet under us. The guilt of what I had done washed over me immediately. I felt like an animal. I rose up off my knees and pulled up my pants. I gently unrolled the rubber off my dick, dropped it in the toilet, and flushed. I unfurled a few tongues of toilet paper and dappled my forehead dry from the sweat that had formed. I searched for where my cum had landed on the bedroom floor. I wiped the carpet clean as well as Sam. I was careful with his junk as I tucked it back into his underwear.

"Wake yo' ass up. I know you fakin'," I said, standing over him.

"Sam!" I yelled, "Come on, man, get up." I tried to shake him awake.

"Get up!" I hollered as I thrashed him across the face. I put my finger under his nose to check to see if he was breathing.

"Oh shit, oh fuck. Sam, wake up!" I panicked, not sure what to do. I thought of getting help but decided against it. A nigger in a white fraternity house would surely raise questions, prick up the ears of campus cops. I couldn't get arrested. I would lose my scholarship. I'm the first in my family to attend college. I looked around to make sure that everything was the way I found it. I wiped the bathroom sink and flushed the tissues.

"Sam, man, I'm sorry," I said. I sneaked out the side door of the bedroom that led out into the backyard of the frat house. I peered around the corner where some students were steadily drinking, carousing about outside, and walked in the opposite direction, careful not to be seen. Back in my dorm, the room smelled faintly of shrimp flavoring. I tossed and turned all night, thinking about Sam, wondered if someone had found his body. That next day, I didn't bother to go to my morning classes. Kept my eyes glued to the news in hopes of hearing reports about a guy being found dead at the Sigma House. Tried to get my mind off what went down by hammering out a few pages of my play, but I couldn't concentrate.

I grabbed my backpack and took off. It wasn't helping me to stay cooped up. The front yard of the frat house was peppered with the blue and red cups, empty keggers on the porch. I didn't see any cop cars, no crime scene tape wrapped around the frat's perimeter. I went on to Drama Technique with only two pages of my play written. My classmates started to come in one, two at a time. My palms were sweaty. The back of my throat salty. After Peter, our T.A., took roll, he asked us who would like to volunteer first to put on their play. That's when the door creaked open. It was Sam. I thought my heart was going to drop into my sneakers. Sam was alive. I couldn't have been more relieved. I stared at him the entire time in class. Sam didn't give me much eye contact. We didn't speak until after.

"Hey, you OK?" I asked.

"Yeah, why do you ask?"

"You didn't look too good at the party."

"Dude, I was drunk off my ass."

"What time did you leave?" I asked.

"I don't remember too much. I woke up with a bitchin' hangover, practically having coffee poured down my throat by my friend, Kyle."

It was just my luck that he couldn't remember anything. He didn't know what I had done.

"I'm starving," Sam said. "You wanna go get something to eat?"

All that worrying had worked up my appetite.

"Yeah, let's go," I said. We spoke over chicken sandwiches about the frat party. I picked his brain to find out just how much he remembered. It wasn't much. Bits and pieces of that night. My secret was safe.

REVENGE VISITS VEGAS

FRED TOWERS

HAVE YOU EVER HAD A BOYFRIEND BREAK YOUR HEART? Did you want revenge? Well, then, let me tell you a story.

As usual, we ate dinner at an expensive restaurant I could never afford. It was always obvious in the way the staff treated me as invisible but worshiped my boyfriend, Scott.

"Mr. Tanner, your table is ready. This way, sir." Scott nodded, before he followed the host wearing a tuxedo. I tagged along behind them. The host pulled his chair out and asked if he needed anything else.

I learned early in the relationship not to wait to be seated because it wouldn't happen. I'd be left standing like an idiot. Once I scooted my chair up to the elegant table, the waiter approached the table. Before I had even glanced at the menu, Scott ordered for us. Silence engulfed us then.

As we ate dinner, Scott gulped down most of a bottle of wine. "Mike, we need to talk." He licked his thin lips and sighed as if speaking were a chore. "I need to tell you something." He stared past me as he continued to speak. "I'm not happy, and I think we should go our separate ways."

I should've known there was trouble when I saw him lick his lips. He only did that when he was nervous. I pushed ahead anyway. "But, Scott, why? What happened?" I reached across the table for his hands, but he yanked them out of my reach. "I thought we were happy."

Scott sighed. "I'm not attracted to you anymore." He met my eyes for the first time that evening. "You've let yourself go."

As I stared at the man I thought I knew, he waved for the waiter and paid him with a hundred-dollar bill. "Keep the change."

"You're the one who always wants to go out to eat." I heard my voice rise into queen octaves, but I didn't care. "Just because you can eat everything from éclairs to cock and still be a skinny rail."

Scott's eyes danced around the room, before shooting me a look. "Mike, don't act like this." He threw his napkin onto the table as he stood. "We can still be friends."

After the crying period ended, I laughed at those last words. Who was he kidding anyway? So, this is where the story gets really interesting.

About a year later, he called. "Mike? Is that you?"

I pulled the phone away from my ear and stared at it. I recognized the area code for Las Vegas because I've always wanted to go there. Did I mention I'm obsessed with the Southwest? I pretended not to recognize his voice. "Yeah, who's this?" At times, I can be such a bitch.

"It's Scott." His deep voice shook as if he were unsure of himself, which was quite a thrilling contrast for me to his usual self-assured demeanor. "Don't hang up, please." He sighed. "I wanted to see if you'd like to come for a visit."

"Visit you?" I sighed to drag out my response.

He jumped into the pause with a vengeance. "I'll pay for everything. The plane ticket. Everything. You won't want for anything while you're here. What do you say?"

I could imagine him biting his lip as he waited for my response. Even though I knew the answer, I asked, "Where at?"

"Vegas." His voice perked up. "I know how you love the Southwest. We can go see the desert, take a boat tour of Lake Mead, gamble, or lie around the pool." He paused to breathe. "Whatever you want."

Listening to him ramble on, I admired my new slim, muscular body in the full-length mirror. I flexed to watch my pecs dance. "Sure. Sounds great." I forced my voice to sound bored, even though I was ecstatic. After I hung up the phone, I laughed because I knew he'd be shocked to see me. I wanted to rub it in his face that he let me get away. Like I said, I can be such a bitch.

Well, it wasn't long before I boarded the plane and found my seat in first class. I enjoyed the roomy seat. The last time I flew, I weighed more and felt claustrophobic in coach. Of course, I couldn't afford any better, so I suffered through it.

At the airport in Vegas, when I saw a man in a uniform holding a sign with my name on it, my jaw dropped. I held my hand out to the gentleman and smiled. "I'm Michael Chasnn."

"Hello, Mr. Chasnn. I'm your limo driver today." He looked at the bag slung over my shoulder and held out his hand. "May I take your bag, sir?"

When the man smiled, my heart melted, and my cock reminded me that it hadn't received any attention in a couple of days. While I was in a daze over his lusciousness, he removed my bag from my shoulder, brushing his hand against my arm. Goose bumps sprouted across my arm from his touch. I followed him out to the car with my mouth hanging open, trying to walk with my cock swollen to the hilt against my pants.

"Here you go, sir." He held the door open and waved me into the back. "If you need anything, let me know." While he put my bag into the trunk, I loosened my belt and unzipped my pants. Crawling into the driver's seat, he glanced into the rearview mirror. "Uh, sir, do you want to raise the window for privacy?"

When I saw him staring at my crotch, I nodded and smiled. "No, thank you. I'd like an audience." I pulled my cock out of my white briefs and stroked it. "If you don't mind?"

"Uh, no, sir. Not at all. It'd be my pleasure." He gulped as if he wanted to say more, but stopped himself.

I slouched in the seat and proceeded to pump my cock faster. He drove with one eye on the road and the other on me. At a stoplight, we'd lock eyes in the mirror, and he'd forget to go on the green. Every time I moaned, I'd hear him, too. I watched him lick his lips and thought about them circling my cock's head. That thought put me over the edge. I exploded onto my dress shirt with a deep, satisfied sigh. I heard the driver grunt and bite his lip in response.

After a few moments, the driver said, "Uh, sir, I missed our turn. I'm sorry to keep your friend, Mr. Tanner, waiting."

"No problem." I smiled and removed my shirt. "He can wait." I chuckled as I slid my shriveling cock back into my briefs.

The driver nodded. "Sir, I'm going to raise the privacy window, now, so I can concentrate on my driving." The tinted glass slowly separated our visual embrace.

Boy, he had beautiful emerald eyes. I still think about them making love to me through the rearview mirror.

At the Plaza Hotel in downtown Vegas, he opened my door. "Sir, we're here." He assisted me out of the car and trailed his eyes over my bare chest. "He'll show you the way." He handed my bag off to someone.

"I left you a souvenir." I nodded toward the backseat, and he blushed. It was my most expensive shirt, but I figured Scott could buy me a new one. He owed me after all he put me through.

"Thank you, sir. I'll treasure it." He smiled. "I hope you enjoy your visit."

"If the rest of it is this good, I will."

As the bellhop escorted me to the penthouse, I noticed eyes following me from the people at the tables and the slots. During the elevator ride, the bellboy trailed his eyes over my body. He waved me out first, and I jumped when he grabbed my ass. When I glanced over my shoulder at him, he stared straight ahead past me as if nothing happened.

In the penthouse suite, he escorted me in and placed my bag on the bed in the guest bedroom. "Sir, your friend has arrived," he said through the closed bathroom door. "Do you need anything else?" After a muffled response from Scott, he exited, nodding at me. "Have a nice stay."

I grabbed a beer out of the fridge and plopped onto an overstuffed sofa in the suite's luxurious living room, while I waited for Scott.

"Mike, you here?"

"Yeah, what are you doing?" I answered, but I didn't get up. I figured he could come to me for a change because I was no longer his overly appreciative puppy.

"Just out of the shower." He shuffled through drawers for a moment in the bedroom. "Let me get dressed. Then we'll go do something." When he stepped into the living room and saw me, he halted in mid-step with his mouth hanging open.

I stood up and smiled. "Hello, Scott."

"Mike?" He swallowed and stumbled toward me. "Boy, you've changed. I almost didn't recognize you." He stared at my chest as he spoke.

I flexed my pecs nonchalantly, while he admired them. "You look the same." I didn't mean it as an insult or a compliment, but he glanced down at his crisply ironed shirt tucked into his stylish pleated shorts. I saw his bony knees peeking out from under the cuffed hem.

"I guess so." He chuckled and pointed down. "Me and my chicken legs." Unsure of himself, he held out his arms for a hug. "It's so nice to see you again, Mike." While we embraced, he rubbed his hands over my back and moaned. "Boy, you've changed."

I felt his cock grow as he held me. The bitch in me wanted to push him away, but my cock begged to fuck him silly first. Let's face it: revenge sex is hot on several levels. Besides getting off, I'd get to string him along until he'd lower himself to beg in a way he'd previously thought beneath him. When we were still together, he'd teased me, made me feel like sex with me was a bore. Inside I chuckled because I was in control. Even though he nibbled on my neck, I acted as if I didn't notice. I wanted him to work for it. He would beg me to fuck him when I was through with him.

"What's the view like?" I pulled away from his embrace and sauntered to the glass doors, which opened onto a terrace. "Wow, breathtaking." I gasped at the blue sky and the view of the buildings around us. In the distance, I saw the hotel on the strip I'd heard about with the roller coaster on the roof, which I pointed to. "What's the name of that? The Cock Hotel?" I giggled. "That's a phallic symbol if I ever saw one."

Scott laughed. "That it is. It's called the Stratosphere Hotel. Would you like to go check it out?" He touched my arm. "I can get us a driver to take us."

"We have time." I smiled and patted his back, noticing he felt like he'd lost weight. "I'm kind of tired from my trip, so let's go to the pool, instead."

"Sounds good." Scott smiled and touched my hand resting on his shoulder. "I'm really glad you came, Mike." He pulled my hand to his lips and kissed it.

I gulped and felt guilty for a moment for wanting revenge. "Let's go put our suits on and hit the pool." I know, you're wondering if I faltered in my revenge plan. Well, let me tell you.

After I slipped into a skimpy suit and Scott slid on his usual down-to-the-knobby-knees swim trunks, we threw towels over our shoulders to head to the hotel pool on the third floor. I felt Scott's eyes devouring my body as he walked behind me. I glanced over my shoulder sporadically, but he was too intent on inspecting every inch of my backside to notice.

"Hey, we'll have to play tennis while I'm here." I pointed to the courts near the pool. "Where can we get racquets?"

"Oh, we can rent them." He nodded toward a stand nearby. "Actors and actresses used to sit in the pool and wave down at the people on the street," Scott said, glancing around at the pool area. "I think they've remodeled since then, though."

"Cool. I wonder what it was like back then." I lowered myself into the lukewarm water as I imagined socializing with the likes of Rock Hudson or Clark Gable. Shoot, I'd even settle for meeting Marilyn Monroe. OK, I'm a sucker for old movies. They don't make them like that anymore. "Can you imagine having a beer with the Rock? Oh, man."

"Be great. Wouldn't it?" Scott chuckled. "Or Clark Gable."

"Yeah, that's what I thought, too." I laughed. Scott's one of the few fags my age I know who's into the classic movies. "It's like you read my mind."

"Like old times." Scott caressed my thigh under the water. "I've missed you, Mike."

Not knowing what to say, I nodded for several long moments. "So, what have you been up to?" I asked to change the subject.

"Personally or professionally?" He leaned toward me as he waited for my answer.

"Personally first." Even though I felt extremely curious about his love life since me, I forced myself to act nonchalant.

He lowered his head and drew in a deep breath. "Michael, I need to be honest with you."

I felt my body stiffen at the use of my full first name. Pretending not to care what he had to say, I swished my legs through the water.

"I lied to you." He pulled himself onto the ledge and sighed. "I left you for another man." He bit his lips as he waited for me to forgive him or to explode.

I refused to do either. I didn't want to give him that kind of control over me again. "Oh, I see." I stopped kicking my legs and stared at the rippling water. "Who was he?"

"No one you knew. A coworker." He touched my shoulder and tried to turn me toward him. "It doesn't matter, now."

"What happened to him?" I stared past Scott with my jaw clenched. "Are you still with him?" Don't ask me why it upset me, but it did. I wanted to punch him, but I refused to give him the satisfaction.

Scott laughed. "No, we aren't together anymore. I was just a career move for him."

"Really." I knew I sounded smug at that knowledge, but I didn't care. "That's a shame."

"You don't mean that. I know you don't." He grinned at me as I focused on his face again. "I understand why, though."

"Do you now?" My anger seeped through my clenched teeth with each word I spoke. "Why am I here then?" I looked him in the eye and waited for his answer.

"You deserve the truth." He swallowed as he considered his next choice of words. "You're the only man who loved me for me, not my money."

"And you threw it away like nothing." I punched the water and watched it wave away from me.

"I know. It was a stupid thing to do. I took you for granted, and I shouldn't have." He stood up on the pool's edge and wrapped his towel around his shoulders. "I wanted to make it up to you." He pointed at me and said, "It looks like you're doing pretty good for yourself."

Pushing my insecurities aside, I rubbed my sculpted muscles and smiled. "Yes, I am."

He reached out and tweaked my nipple, which caused me to gasp. "You look delicious." He licked his lips and flicked his tongue at me. "Want to do it for old times sake?" He raised an eyebrow in my direction and smiled sheepishly.

My cock jumped in celebration at the opportunity to finally put our plan in action, but my heart begged me to throw a tantrum fit for a queen. I stared at him while I waited for them to battle it out. Scott returned my stare in anticipation. Before I responded, I jumped out of the pool and walked toward Scott. At first, he stepped away from me and gulped. I smiled as I stepped closer. "Only if I'm in charge." I stared into his eyes with our faces inches from each other. "Got it?"

"Uh?" His mouth hung open and he moaned. Swallowing his unspoken words, he nodded.

I could tell he feared giving me the control he'd so easily taken from me during our relationship. "Good." I glanced down at my towel on the ground and waited.

After several seconds, he realized why I was waiting. "I'm sorry. Here you go." He rubbed the towel over my hair and my chest. I knew he wanted to lick the pool water off my body because his tongue snaked out over his lips as he toweled me. "Is that good?"

"Yes, it is. We'll finish in the room." I turned and marched away from him, knowing that he'd follow like a homeless puppy. Power surged through me. This must have been how he felt when he took me home that first night.

We'd met at a bar close to Marian College, a small Catholic school on the west side of Indianapolis. I felt at home in the small-town feel of the city school, since I grew up in Sheridan. A group of us decided to check out the 3535, which used to be located near the Indianapolis Speedway. We were playing pool when he walked in wearing a leather jacket over his midnight-blue silk shirt. I flubbed my shot because my knees weakened at the sight of him. Seeing me staring at him with my mouth hanging open, he smirked and nudged his friends. I almost shrank when they laughed. He sauntered over and bought drinks for all my friends. Before I knew it, he walked away and expected me to follow him. At first, I wasn't sure whether he wanted me to, so I stared after him until my friends pushed me toward the door. When I came outside, he was waiting in his Porsche at the edge of the sidewalk. Without saying a word, he drove me to his house and fucked me. I never made it off my knees the whole weekend.

Remembering that weekend, I smiled at how the tables had been turned between us. He was mine now.

In the room, I pointed toward the ground as he'd done me several years earlier. "The towels need to be hung in the bathroom." I waved him in that direction as I plopped onto the sofa. "Oh, this is gonna be great." I bit my lower lip, while I waited for him to return. When I saw him crawling toward me, I raised my legs. "Remove these."

He obliged with a huge smile on his face. "Yes, sir."

"Rim me." I knew he struggled with his disgust for tonguing an asshole.

He gulped and moved toward me slowly as if he hoped I'd change my mind. I gripped his head and forced his face between my cheeks. After a few moments, he accepted his task and savored my ass. I tossed my head back and moaned at the sensations his tongue created. My cock stiffened with each lick until it throbbed like it never had before.

"That's enough. Turn around." Dazed, he pulled away and rested on his knees. I noticed his cock bobbing before him. "Do you have any condoms?"

"In the bedroom?" He moved as if he were going to stand. "I'll get them."

"On your knees." I stared at his stoop position.

"Sorry, sir." He lowered himself back onto his knees and crawled toward the bedroom. After he handed me the box of condoms, I motioned for him to position his ass toward me. "Is it going to hurt?"

"It will if I want it to." I laughed at my use of the line he'd used my first time.

He gulped and turned his ass toward me slowly. I could tell he hoped again I'd change my mind, but I wasn't going to. I wanted to see what it'd be like to fuck him because when we were together, he never let me. It was time for that to change. I slipped on a condom and drizzled lube on his asshole. I was so bad. I didn't warm it first and giggled when he jerked at the cold liquid on his sensitive hole. I know I'm such a bitch.

"Any last words?" I leaned over him and spoke into his ear.

He quivered and opened his mouth to speak but closed it without saying a word.

I nudged my cock against his tight opening and pushed a little. When I felt him jerk away from me, I withdrew for a moment. I inched in and spread him open. When I pushed in too fast, he pulled away from me. Once I buried my whole shaft inside him, I paused and gripped his hips. I gave him a moment to get used to me before I pummeled his ass. Even though I heard him gasping, I gave him no mercy.

When I thought he was close to coming, I leaned near his ear and said, "Don't come until I say so."

I pumped his ass so hard that his face rubbed against the floor, giving him a carpet burn across his cheek. Breathing heavily, I exploded and collapsed on top of him.

"Sir, can I come?" His voice was strained from holding it back.

"No, not yet. Maybe I'll let you come later."

The bitch in me teased him every moment during that visit, not allowing him to have relief. During a boat tour of Lake Mead, I rubbed against him as we moved about the boat. I pressed my cock against his ass while we rode the elevator down into the Hoover Dam. My excuse was all the people squeezed into the small elevator. I loved to hear him beg, but I stood firm against giving him relief. I teased him over dinner at expensive restaurants, while watching the light show, while seeing Elvis impersonators, and at the gambling tables. Ooh, I loved hearing him beg with every ounce of his dwindling pride.

On the last day, I jerked his cock until pre-come dripped from his slit. He clamped his mouth shut, hoping I was going to finally have mercy on him, but I didn't.

"It's time for me to go. My limo's waiting." I rubbed against him as I slung my bag over my shoulder. "Walk me down."

His mouth hung open. "You're leaving without . . ." He glanced down at his aching cock.

I walked away from him without answering, and he followed in silence. Downstairs, he hugged me but said nothing. When I approached the limo, I noticed I had the same driver and smiled. He opened the door for me and took my bag.

"Bye, Scott." I waved at him while he stood stunned on the sidewalk of the circular drive. "I had a great time."

He waved back, but I could tell by the look on his face that I had gotten my revenge. Hopefully, he had learned not to take a lover for granted, but I'll never know.

I could tell you about my trip to the airport with the luscious limo driver, but I don't have time. Maybe over coffee, next time.

REAR ENDED

LOGAN ZACHARY

SPASMS OF PAIN SHOT DOWN MY LOWER BACK. I squirmed in my seat in the waiting room. When would they call my name? Maybe I should've gone to the emergency room? If I passed out from the pain . . .

"Nick Stevens. Nick Stevens." A male voice called my name.

I pushed up on the armrests with all my might, trying to keep my spine straight and tight. The pain intensified with each bend or twist of my spine.

The man saw my pained approach and rushed to assist me. He took one of my hands and wrapped it around his neck, pulling my body next to his. "I'm Paul, Dr. Murphy's nurse. Lean on me. I'll help you to the examination room."

I put my body weight onto him. I could feel his tight muscled arms and shoulders. I knew he would be able to support me, even if I passed out. Despite the pain, I could feel the warmth of his body radiate into me, and as I took in a deep breath, his masculine scent caused a stirring in my loins.

"How long have you been having pain?" he asked.

"I was rear-ended yesterday after work. My car's bumper is gone, and my trunk looks like a compact car. I was a little sore a few hours after the accident and took a hot shower. This morning, I was stiff. I took a few aspirin and that seemed to help, but after lunch, my back began to spasm." At the mention of the word, another one hit the small of my back and radiated down my left leg.

"What would you rate your pain on a scale of one to ten? One being 'ouch' and ten being 'get me to the ER now.'"

I felt my knees buckle as I stepped, but Paul caught me and held me until my spasm stopped. I took a deep breath. "That was a ten."

"I could tell."

We walked past a scale. "I should get your weight, but with your pain, I'll say that you are 165 pounds."

I looked at him amazed. "How did you know?"

"I've done this job for quite a while." He ushered me into an exam room and helped me onto the table. He quickly took my temperature and blood pressure. "Did you have your seatbelt on?"

"Yes."

"That's good, but I'm sure that jarred your back even more." Paul typed the information into the computer for the doctor. "Are you on any medications?"

"Nothing, except for the aspirin I took for the pain in my back."

"OK," he said and walked to a cabinet above the sink and removed a hospital gown. He handed it to me. "Put this on. The doctor will be in shortly."

I reached for the gown when another spasm hit.

Paul stepped forward and held my body, stabilizing me until the pain subsided. After it passed he asked, "Are you going to need help undressing?"

My face flushed with embarrassment. How was I going to undress myself? And I didn't want this guy to help me. Despite the spasms, I had noticed his blond hair and easy smile, his white teeth and hazel eyes. I didn't want my erection springing free when he undressed me or when the doctor examined me, but no matter how bad the pain was, my body was already responding.

"I'll take that as a yes." Paul reached over and touched my shirt.

I pulled back and my back tensed from the sudden movement.

"Relax, let me help you. That's my job, you know."

"But . . ." I started.

"I've done this many times. You need my help, so let me." His hands started to unbutton my shirt and quickly opened the buttons. He pulled the shirttails out of my pants and slipped the shirt off. He pulled my T-shirt over my head.

I could hear the static electricity of the fabric across the hair on my chest, crackling from no fabric softener. I wanted to cross my arms over my chest to cover myself, but held them down at my sides.

"Lift up your foot," he said.

I swallowed hard as my shoes and socks were quickly removed. I'm a modest person and this was making me nervous. I took a deep breath as he unbuttoned my pants.

"Stand up, and I can help you out of those."

I was about to protest when he unfolded the gown and opened it.

He draped it over my chest and had me slip my arms through the sleeves. He tied the string behind my neck. At least, I had one layer of protection.

Paul smiled at me. "Almost done." He reached underneath the gown and unzipped my fly. He slid the pants down my legs and reached up for my underwear.

Which pair did I have on today? Panic flooded my mind when I couldn't remember. I hoped they weren't the bikini briefs. I tried to feel what I was wearing as his hand brushed up against my balls. "Sorry," he whispered, but I wasn't as his warm fingers slipped beneath the elastic waistband and stretched them open.

I could feel my arousal starting to stir as blood flowed to fill up my semi-hard penis. The glancing touch and new freedom made my blood surge and my organ swell. The underwear slipped down my hairy legs to join my pants, and I was loose and hanging free, or at least two things were—one wasn't cooperating.

"Sit down and I can finish."

I looked into Paul's eyes, hoping he didn't see the discomfort from my embarrassment.

"Here, let me help you. You must be in a lot of pain."

I just nodded my head as he helped me sit. I felt his hand slide across my bottom, tucking the gown behind me to stay closed as I sat. I lifted my legs as he bent to take my pants and underwear off. He gently folded them and placed them in a pile on a chair in the room. He placed my white Calvin Klein briefs on top of the pile. At least it was a new, clean pair.

"Did you want to lie back or stay sitting? Which is more comfortable for you?"

Neither.

"I think my back feels better if I'm lying down," I heard my voice say.

"Let me help you." He pulled out a drawer in the table to provide a place for my legs. One hand reached behind my back, and the other one scooped my legs onto the extender.

I could feel the gown tenting at my groin as I lay back. My erection had flipped up and rested on my lower stomach, but the material stood straight up.

Paul ran his hand down the gown in the center of my chest and paused just above my waistline. He grabbed the bottom hem of the gown and pulled it down.

I looked at my groin, afraid my bulge would be exposed, but he had pulled it just tight enough to cover me and lie flat over my body. I let out the breath I had been holding.

"That pain must be intense. I'll see if I can hurry the doctor. It's been a busy day. We're running a little behind, but I'll see what I can do." Paul smiled and left the room.

I closed my eyes and brought my arm up to my head and covered my brow. Think of something to get rid of my erection. Eighteen plus eighteen is . . . My mind tried to do the math as the pain returned. A spasm twisted in my back and I rolled from side to side, trying to find a comfortable position. I pulled up a knee to help release some of the pressure on my back. I felt a cold draft of air run up the gown and swirl around my aroused flesh. Great! That's the first thing I wanted my doctor to see, my raging hard-on as he opened the door. I pushed the gown down between my legs, covering myself as best I could. Just then a blood-curdling scream echoed down the hall.

At least, I hoped that the scream came from the hallway and not from me. There was running of feet and doors opening and closing as people rushed around outside my exam room.

There was a quick knock on the door and it opened. Paul returned. "The doctor has a small emergency in another room. It's going to be a while before he can get in here. Did you need me to drive you to the emergency room or can you wait?"

This wasn't happening. I could feel a tear run down the side of my face. "I . . . I think I can wait."

Paul held up a hand. "Wait a minute. I have an idea. I'll be right back."

My head fell back into the small pillow on the table and I closed my eyes. My hand strayed down to my groin; a wet spot stained the light blue material. Great! Deep breathing will help: one, two, three . . .

I must have dozed off for a few minutes, because I never saw the door open or the room's lights dim. I felt two warm hands slide up my hairy legs. They started at my ankles and glided up to my knees. The gown slowly rose with them. I could feel a cool breeze across my legs. The hair bristled and stood on end. Was I dreaming? Wouldn't the doctor have knocked? Announced his arrival? Started asking questions?

The hands rounded my kneecaps and massaged their way higher. The fingers were skilled and trained.

I opened my eyes slightly and saw Paul standing next to me. "What?" I began.

"Shhh. Just lie back and relax. Let me help you get rid of your pain."

I could feel the blood rushing back to my cock.

His hands worked higher on my thighs, his long fingers combing through the thick hair. I could feel him getting closer, closer to my . . . and his fingertips gently touched my balls.

Electricity ran through my body. I could feel the muscles in my back tense, threatening to spasm again.

"Relax," his voice cooed. "Relax."

Was I dreaming? Paul was a great-looking guy. If I hadn't been in so much pain, I would have paid closer attention to that. I was now. His hands worked magic on me. His thumbs ran up and along the length of my erection. They burrowed into the curly hair that ran up my chest.

A low moan escaped from between my lips.

His hands stopped in mid-stroke. "Am I hurting you?"

"Anything but."

His fingers combed through the hair on my chest, drawing the gown up around my neck. So much for modesty, I was fully exposed. His hands circled my nipples, instantly erect under his touch. He took each nipple between his fingers and rolled it slightly.

I closed my eyes and felt his hands work lower. They stopped above my cock and gently swirled around the tip. Pre-come wet his fingers and the mushroom head of my dick. He drew the sweet juice down the length of my cock and pulled it back up.

Once I was completely lubed, he stopped. "Hang on a second." He walked to the door and locked it. He returned and stood at the end of the table. He pulled his scrub top off, over his head, and tossed it on my pile of clothes. His hands untied his drawstring, and his pants slipped to the floor. He kicked off his shoes and looked down at me. His smooth chiseled chest glowed in the faint light, his nipples like perfect dots above a tight six-pack.

I looked down and saw a thick blond triangle at the bottom of his torso. He leaned forward and climbed on the table. His erection stood straight out in front. His hips paused just below my groin, and he leaned forward, his low-hanging balls bushing up against mine. A faint scraping of razor stubble pulled on my hairy balls, letting me know he shaved. His hands massaged my chest as he bent forward, laying down his cock on top of mine, matching me inch for inch. His sweet cream oozing down added to mine.

He ground his hips into mine, and despite my fear of spasms, my body pressed up against him. His balls rubbed against mine and slowly slipped between my legs.

I pulled my legs together and squeezed them. This time it was Paul's turn to moan. He reached over the side of the exam table, pulled a drawer open, withdrew a tube of lubrication jelly, and rolled it between his hands. He squeezed a palmful of lube out and then grasped my cock.

He ran his fist up and down my length, and then he went to his. With the added lubrication, our dicks dueled for position. I could feel the viscous gel run down my groin and between my butt cheeks.

Paul slid higher on my lap, letting my cock slip between his ass cheeks. He rode my length, and I felt my cock seek entrance. He smiled as the tip circled his hole and pressed down on it. I felt his ass open and welcome me. I slowly slid in. He rocked his hips back and forth, sending waves of pleasure through my body.

His hands continued to massage my chest. His fingers slid across my chest more easily now with the lubrication. The hair matted down to my skin.

I could feel a release building inside me and as I moaned, Paul stopped and slid off my dick. "Not so fast," he said, "and not without protection." With that he jumped off the table and opened another drawer. This time he pulled out a small, square foil packet. He tore it open with his teeth and quickly removed the sheer ring. He smiled and placed it on his cock. He unrolled the sheath down his erection. He stood at the table and rubbed more lube onto his protected dick.

He gently bent my knees up and slipped between them. His cock rubbed along mine. The near-climax sensitized my skin and I jumped at the contact. I bore down, stopping the eruption that was so close. One of his hands slipped down between my butt cheeks and dipped into the pool of lube. He slipped a finger into my crease and rubbed it up and down, his tip circling my tight hole. He twirled it around and around, pressing down in the center with each pass.

I could feel the tight sphincter muscle start to relax. My legs slowly rose up, exposing more of my ass.

Paul moved closer to me, his erection seeking a home.

I took a deep breath as his dick touched my hole. My pelvis rocked back and forth as he pressed into me. My legs rose higher as he entered.

He leancd forward and drilled down deeper. His girth filled me. His balls slapped against my ass. With each thrust of his dick, his shaved balls bounced off my tight cheeks. As he plowed into me, his cock hit my prostate, sending shivers up my spine and down the shaft of my cock. As the sensory overload intensified, he thrust into me harder and extended his head back, letting a low, guttural groan escape from his lips. His hand grabbed my cock and started to stroke the length of me with each pelvic thrust.

My legs extended and wrapped along the side of his neck, opening my ass even wider for his cock. His pace quickened and his hand squeezed tighter on my cock. His dick seemed to swell in my hole. His balls slammed my ass. My balls pulled up alongside of my shaft; pressure was building, building. My breathing was coming short and shallow, just the opposite of Paul's thrusts.

Paul threw his head back and thrust one last time. He pulled down my dick and covered the tip of my dick as the spasm hit. I sent a load of white, hot cum across my chest, and pleasure flooded over my body.

Paul drilled into me, expelling all of himself into me. Beads of sweat rolled across both of our bodies.

My legs relaxed as Paul slumped down on top of me. We lay there, enjoying the waves of pleasure that pulsated over our bodies.

Paul slid off the table and grabbed a few hand towels. After wiping me off, he gave me a fresh gown. He cleaned himself and slipped back into his scrubs. As he threw the towels in the laundry, there was a knock on the door. Paul rushed forward, unlocking and opening the door at the same time.

Dr. Murphy looked at Paul. "You look a little flushed. Must be working hard again."

He smiled. "Yeah, that's it. I'm working hard." He flashed me a killer smile, which I easily returned.

"So what brings you to us today?"

I sat up and glanced over at Paul. "Well, I've been rear-ended twice. Two times in two days. The first time must have knocked something loose, and the second time must have put everything back in place. Because I feel much better now." I reached above my head and twisted one way and the other.

Dr. Murphy scratched his head. "I'm glad I could help."

Paul stepped forward and smiled. "Me too."

"So am I," I said as I started to dress, "so am I."

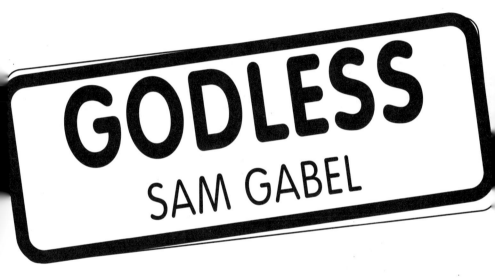

GODLESS
SAM GABEL

IT WAS ONE OF THOSE CRIES that begins as an uncontrollable plea, to demonstrate such an excruciating pain that it can move the hearts of even the cruelest of tyrants, but when it fails to halt your captor, it tears open an endless abyss within you, provoking you to draw on every tragic pain never told, never forgiven—numbing your heart to such a darkness that you can't even tell whether you're basking in a tub full of water or one full of tears because you've accepted the end of everything.

What moment the door broke down was irrelevant. Her screams

remained white noise, the slaps of her hands only flickers of an empty shell, but it was the endless repetition that served to shatter my spirit. At some point, she stopped. Perhaps there was a newfound submission in my pupils that frightened her into ceasing, the blankness in my eyes like waves returning to the sea. She feared taking responsibility, her demon, and retreated like an engine past exhaustion.

I sat there in my little pool. And slowly, feeling restarted: the red marks across my body deliciously igniting my revival. As I peeled myself up from the tub with wrinkles in my soaked fingers matching my tear-eroded eyes, heartbreak hit me: no child should ever pray to his god for his mother's disappearance—I was never meant to be born.

I wrapped the towel around me and felt someone's arms—protect me. As I crept down the hallway, there was reassurance in this rare solitude in the dead of night when even the haunts of the house slept, and the only noise you could hear were crickets' chirps and a slow hum of moonlight. Lying on my bed, my body demanded a corpse's rest, but my mind raced. I watched my ceiling fan turn, turn, turn.

In the stillness of fabric and the tangible coolness of the air conditioning, I imagined, similar to a song lingering in me, that there's a perfect man, in the same way I know the world is fundamentally good. I wish he could save me, fuck me, wish he could accomplish the sacred in sex: with every caress, he's saying, "I appreciate you," with every lick, "I believe in you," with every thrust, "the world needs you," and most important, when he comes, "I—need you." But in the concrete, I find the song less in the lyrics, just waiting.

Soon enough, my restlessness moved me to my chair, my eyes fixated on the screen, a world where you can become anyone and find anything. I typed in "a man who can save me," and it regurgitated a link urging me to find my Adonis. Getting lured in and setting up a profile was simple, and my pictures uploaded. I thought carefully what to set as my profile, hoping for something insightful, an inspiration for someone to love me.

"From every turn of the face, every gesture, we're all looking for the same thing—a connection. It is said we are created in God's image, perhaps not in the physical sense, but in the spiritual sense: we are all creators. We have the power, the potential, to enter our possibilities, our limitless conscience. I'm here hoping to create a connection. Perhaps someone will help me find the clay to do so."

Waiting for my profile and pictures to be approved by the site's staff, I browsed through profiles. Half of them were random penises. It was this ironic setting that slowly brought back my normal mental state, thoughts rather than uncontainable emotions. A welcome e-mail prompted me that my profile was now viewable by the public. Most of the e-mails I got were from older men, the kind of trolls who abused the infinite possibilities that the Internet promises.

There was one e-mail that stuck out from the rest: TOPGUN08. He didn't give me a long-drawn-out explanation of how he could provide the hottest night possible; his e-mail simply stated, "Hey." When I looked at his picture, there was a certain darkness that drew me to him, a certain pain I understood. He posed bare, open in a way that wasn't confident, but statue-like. It was almost as if he were proclaiming, "I'm here; this is my body," not "beneath this glamorous body is an equal hardness of insecurities." Unlike the other profiles, he had his entire gallery of pictures viewable to the public instead of leaving some locked. And in every picture, he didn't smile. It was the same look of rare disappointment, the one achieved by never having any expectations. I was hooked.

"Hey, what's up?" I responded.

Then I sat there in silence waiting.

"Looking for a boy to fuck tonight."

"I'm a boy."

He gave me his address and expected me there in an hour. I scoffed. Cocky.

I didn't have much time. Driving from the suburbs to the city in an hour was going to take some time management. I put on some jeans and a T-shirt and peered out into the doorway to find familiar darkness. I shut the door quietly and escaped to the garage. I took their keys and got into their car, not closing the garage door, hoping they wouldn't wake up. Then I left.

I drove, feeling that at any moment I was going to get caught. Or perhaps the phone would ring, and my parents would demand the whereabouts of the car. But none of my paranoia made it to reality. The drive was actually kind of beautiful. I think driving on the interstate at this time of night is the kind of moment that convinces you that life is important. The long stretches of road seem like predestined lines you're supposed to follow, choreographed by the stars above, and the red lights of the backs of vehicles remind you that they're like other fishes in this stream, each with a destination, a purpose—just like you.

Eventually, I arrived at the gates of his apartment complex and glanced at the clock: five minutes to spare. Great. I was getting kind of nervous. It would be my first sexual experience, and here I was doing it with a complete stranger. It kind of saddened me, but somehow, it felt essential. I believed in what I was doing right now, which was passing through the gates.

There was a surreal presence in the vibrant darkness of the apartment complex. The buildings themselves seemed drained, leaving gray remains. I saw kids behaving like adults, and adults as walking corpses. And in the midst of it all was Rick, with a look of obliviousness. There was something queer and erotic about his expression, his posture against the railing of his porch. He seemed to overlook my arrival, simply didn't give a damn. He had this numb visage glued on, and with his perfect physique, Rick knew he was the sexiest man alive. His lack of insecurities leeched the humanity from his face: a glance into his eyes would turn you to sex pulp.

As the car came to a complete stop, I froze, unable to quit staring at his eyes, which glanced at me sideways. He turned and disappeared into his apartment, the song emanating from the threshold serving as his seductive footprints. I somehow managed to get out of the car. Knocking on the door, I felt this rush of anxiety: it felt like fiction. The door opened, revealing—an older man, much older. Before I could stammer, "Hi—"

"Looking for Rick?" he grinned.

I tried to hide the relief in my voice. "Yes."

The door opened, leading me further inside the confines of Pandora's bed. I mustered a half-hearted smile as I stepped in, hoping it'd make him disappear. It did. Before he returned to his crypt, he managed to point me toward my destination. I mentally chuckled. If Charon had a human form, this guy would be it. Peering inside the room, I cautiously entered, observing Rick's reaction: indifference.

He lay naked on his bed, dark hair shambled in front of his face, with a cigarette puffing fumes that danced slowly to the ceiling. I eyed his dick; it looked glorious even when flaccid. Starting to undress, I was unsure how to reply to his continued jadedness. He still hadn't given me a glance. Naked, I crept toward him, on his bed, near him, but not touching. I lay content, staring into his face, that masculine, numb, and yet gentle face.

I caressed his smooth chest with my hand, surprised it didn't waver. He turned his head, his nihilism palpable. I wanted to melt as I looked into his eyes; there was this dark gloom to it, this impenetrable fortress that made you certain if you could conquer a fragment of his spirit for just a second, then you meant something. It felt ridiculous, actually.

I leaned over and tried to kiss him. My mouth opened and my tongue slid in, tasting this mixture of tangy watermelon and smoke. I stopped and looked at him, wondering why his mouth wasn't responding. Holding his cigarette in one hand, he used the other hand to push my head lower to his cock.

"Suck my dick." It was a statement, not a request.

I pleaded with his eyes. This wasn't how I imagined it to be, but I knew I deserved it. I looked down at his cock, still limp. And going down, standing it up with my fingers, I felt a form of liberation and craving as I bobbed my head down and up and back down again. I didn't even care about the slight taste of bitter used lube and the subtle odor of sweat. All I wanted was his cock down my throat, and I imagined that gush of come dripping down my throat. Was it wrong that I sought fulfillment by being his come dump?

His dick started to rise, to get firmer, and he put out his cigarette. He needed both hands: one to rustle through my hair, the other to guide it down at his desired rhythm. I thought it'd be normal to moan, but he had his own method of demonstrating his bouts of pleasure, through this shallow breathing that I found strangely cute. His head leaned back, and his eyes remained closed, as if he were in this faraway fantasyland, and the only way he could sustain that world was through the motion of my mouth sucking in and making that wet noise as it returned to the top of his shaft.

"Harder, deeper. Yeah, go all the way down."

His hand started to force my head down, making me gag periodically. Instead of disgust, he found a certain pleasure, a certain erotic high as my gags demonstrated pain, submission.

"I told you to go deeper. Don't you know how to give head?"

I didn't mumble. I just tried to go completely down, to have that whole shaft down my throat, and his balls at my lips: to be a good boy.

"Yeah, that's it."

My head continued to bob up and down. His stomach breathing seemed to match my own, going up when my mouth went down, going down when my head went up. Watery bitterness dripped down my throat, and I wished for more, imagining how delicious it would be going down my throat. He licked his lips, moving his whole body forward, and pressing me down on the bed. With his cock now out of my mouth, he needed another hole to slide it in.

He forced my legs up and grabbed the bottle of lube. As he dropped a bit in his hands, I wondered if it'd be enough. He slathered a thin layer on his dick and started to press his cock against my hole, its throbbing demonstrating a beg for intrusion.

"Do you have a condom?"

"I don't use them."

I felt something inside sicken, but my rationality couldn't resist; I raised my legs higher. I tried to relax, but his cock's intrusion met with a layer of muscle, not an open eager hole. He tried to force it in, but I couldn't budge. And when he tried to shove it in, I yelled as my hole started to pulsate in agony. He tried to slide it in more slowly.

"No, it hurts too much."

He frowned without moving his facial muscles. Grabbing a tiny bottle, he opened it and handed it to me.

"What is it?" It had a funny smell.

He thought of something before he answered, looking amused and pained at the same time.

"It's a bottle that helps you feel nothing. Whenever you want to feel me inside you again, just inhale it like it's your last breath of air . . . and think of me."

As I let myself go into the bottle, I also lost myself in Rick's eyes: they're both the same drug. This odd taste filled my mouth like bubble gum acid. My head started to drift as if there were a black hole inside it, a beautiful oblivion that drew my conscience to its heated center. As I closed my eyes and leaned my head back, Rick took his cue to slide his cock in my blooming hole. The first thrust was like finding God. I moaned in pleasure. There was no other feeling that could compare. But soon as the nova in my head started to explode just a little brighter, it was as if his cock disappeared. I could feel the head pounding at the back of my hole, but it was like the shaft was a shadow. It was like a spiritual javelin; I felt connected to his soul, could catch glimpses of it every time he thrust through me.

"Fuck, fuck, fuck," I moaned. I'd never felt anything like it. As the high started to wear off, I looked for the bottle again, craving for more, to ignore the pain, to accept the numbness—to be one with Rick. I opened the cap, and before I could inhale, he leaned and grabbed me toward him, spilling drops on his sheets. He laid himself down on his back with a big hard-on pressing up against my hole. I breathed deep into the bottle, and with each breath, his dick reached farther up my ass. That initial pressure turning into ecstasy. Straddling his cock, I felt I was at the top of the world. This was my favorite position, to look into his eyes, to see the pleasure I was responsible for. He'd do this thing where he would steady his thrusts, and then shove it hard up inside me, forcing a roar out of me.

In the midst of it all, I tried to grab his hair, but he smacked my hand away. Instead, I just pinched his nipples as I rode him. Jerking off my cock, I started to feel close, feeling my ass intensify as it wrapped around his throbbing cock. Fuck. I was going to come, and I think he started to sense it too because he pulled out immediately and turned me over, breaking my momentum.

Bent over, I gasped as his cock slammed into me. His thrusts were more relentless, frantic. I grabbed my cock and imagined what he saw, what he felt, imagined seeing his cock disappear into my hole, to see his pubes slam into my ass, to grab my cheeks, to see the red imprints, to own me. Shit, I was about to come. I felt it. My body dropped, pressed against the mattress, his cock sliding deeper inside me, his chest on my back, and his breath against my neck. He licked me, feeling his saliva on my neck. I felt that volcanic pressure in my dick, that build-up of come, and Rick was thinking the same thing as my ass rhythms changed, and his thrusts turned insane. His breathing got harder, and he started to moan. His grip pinched me, and I felt something.

Perhaps it was only a fragment of a second, but it was like a glimpse into god. My mind disappeared, and in that subtle space of infinity, I felt for once in my life, someone knew me: Rick understood my pains, my joys, and somehow it was a mutual understanding, I felt his struggles, his triumphs, and we shared a temporary wholeness. I shot into the sheets, the drama lost in fabric. Rick's cock jerked inside me like a thunderbolt before coming to a complete stop, his body collapsing on top of me, his sweat mixed with mine.

I felt fatigue; he had left my body beaten and battered like a whore, and I couldn't think of anything else in the world that I wanted more of. I remembered how just gazing into his face as he decimated my temple was like looking upon a god, that hope of seeking the unattainable; it was an excruciating ecstasy. And it was in these moments, amid all the repetitive drone of daily life, the gray and white, that I had found my blackest humanity. He was done; I had fulfilled my purpose, given him my worship.

I basked in the darkness, imagining how I would look right now if we were in a movie. I pictured a look of agony and vulnerability on my face: "What have I done?" But I looked beautiful as I pondered such a futile question. I glanced back at Rick and realized that he wouldn't open his eyes till I left. I started to pick up the clothes off his floor and felt some sort of half-paralysis as I put them on. I don't think I'll ever see him again. I somehow managed to leave, but I'd be lying if I said it didn't feel as if all the air had been sucked out of the room.

Driving home, I knew something inside me had died. My rationality, double-edged, returned, forcing me to confront my loneliness, my survival instinct, to once again—search for the divine.

THE SECOND IMPULSE

DAVID HOLLY

THE HOT WATER AND FUMES were making me light-headed. Sulfurous bubbles were bursting the pond's surface like farts from the underworld. Shifting away from a bubble, my hand touched Jeff's bare ass. A thrill shot through my dick head, which I masked by saying, "I'll bet this pool is radioactive."

"No," Larry said. "Well, slightly. Not enough to hurt us."

My face must have given me away. Chip's hand brushed the head of my cock. "Ben's got a hard-on," he sang out.

I felt my face flushing. My first impulse was to blame my condition on the hot water. I scarcely knew these guys, and I didn't know what they'd think about my dick getting hard while we four crouched buck naked in the small, geothermally heated mineral-water pond.

Larry and Jeff snickered at my discomfiture, and laughed harder when Chip added, "You think he's got a hard-on for our asses or our cocks, guys?"

My embarrassment was acute, but Jeff took mercy on me. "You're not alone, Ben," he said, rising abruptly from the milky mud suspended in the greenish water. I found his swollen cock head protruding within an inch of my lips.

My first impulse was to pull away, but not because there was anything wrong with Jeff's dick. It had a thick, juicy look, though the heat of the water had made it look a bit boiled and shiny. Jeff's circumcised head flared away from the shaft, and it seemed to be puffed up as if it wanted to spit at me. His pee hole was an actual slit, hooded with a tiny flap. The thought of the rich come that would spurt from that hole emboldened me to an act I would never have dared had I not been half-dazed by the fumes.

It was my second impulse that I followed. I touched the head of Jeff's cock with my lips. As I kissed his cock head, I closed my eyes so that I could not see the guys' reaction. However, I could not close my ears, so I expected to hear them say *something*. Their only response was utter silence. Amazed silence? Stunned silence? I could hear the bubbles of gas breaking the surface and the wind blowing down the blighted slopes. I could hear the hissing of the steam plume that vented not too far from our pond, a grim reminder of the volatile nature of the land we were occupying.

Better judgment told me that I should not suck Jeff's cock, especially with Chip and Larry watching, but my judgment was faulty due to the poisonous air, and naked impulse made me touch my tongue to that delicious cock. My lips formed a circle, a tight opening, through which the head of Jeff's cock passed. The weight of his cock head inside my mouth almost made me come. My entire pelvis throbbed. My asshole contracted and dilated in the hot water as my hands arose from the pool, almost as if they had a will of their own, and slid sensuously up Jeff's thighs. His hamstrings were tight from hours in the gym, and his buttocks were nicely rounded.

Gripping his ass with both hands, I took Jeff's cock deeper into my mouth. His buttocks were so firm that I could massage them as if they were melons while I licked the underside of his dick head and down his cock shaft. I fucked his dick with my tongue, controlling position with my head and by pulling his butt toward my mouth. As I traveled his cock, I found that I was taking him deeper, deeper, and closer to my throat than I had ever taken any other man.

Not that I had vast experience. Jeff's was only the third cock I had sucked. When I was younger, I sucked Brother Slim's dick a couple of times, which is when I found out how much I love men's jizz. Brother Slim was the youth pastor at my parents' church, and when I started rebelling, my oblivious parents encouraged me to go on Christian outings with Brother Slim. The "outings" consisted of visits to Brother Slim's sleazy little apartment in downtown Sioux City, where he showed me a lot of magazine pictures of men sucking cock or taking a big one up the ass. Then he taught me how to suck his dick, though Brother Slim never returned the compliment. (Brother Slim wasn't all that slim, either, being somewhat "corn-fed," as we used to say back in Iowa.) However, his cock was thick and his semen tasted better than custard.

I pulled back on Jeff's cock and popped my lips over his dick head, worrying the circumcised rim especially, while flicking his pee hole with the tip of my tongue. Jeff gasped when I did that. I nibbled a little, using my teeth just enough to excite him, to stimulate him to pump every drop of his semen into my mouth when he finally did come. I was careful not to bite or frighten him. I bit Captain Allen once, and he didn't care for it at all.

Allen Waverly was the guy my parents hired to paint our house one summer. My pop was a big-time Republican, and "Captain Allen" was our precinct captain in addition to being a professional house painter. Captain Allen usually worked with a helper, a high school boy named Springer. I always wondered about their relationship, because the first time I saw Captain Allen on his ladder, my gaydar pinged as though it were scanning incoming nuclear missiles.

Springer was the most gorgeous African American male I have ever seen, captain of our high school swim team—I attended every practice just to watch Springer saunter toward the pool in his brilliant green Speedo. Captain Allen was about ten years older, but no less gorgeous. Still, he was about a hundred times more masculine that Springer, who had an ass like a girl's and a mouth like black cherries. Captain Allen favored faded cut-off jeans and white T-shirts. His tight shorts and shirts showed off his powerfully developed figure, not to mention his most remarkable asset, the big cock that formed an impressive bulge in the front of his shorts.

I hadn't sucked a cock for a couple of years at that time, not since Brother Slim had gotten into the teensiest bit of trouble when he propositioned an undercover vice cop and ended up moving to another town (and probably another church where he could find more young males and introduce them to the joys of fellatio).

The day my parents left town for a three-day state Republican convention turned out to be the same day that Springer couldn't make it to work due to a sick grandmother. I hurried down to the yard to greet Captain Allen, and he was overly friendly as usual. However, he disappointed me when he climbed up his ladder and went to work painting our house (a lackluster white, of course, to match our picket fence).

I went up to my room. My window was open to let in the breeze, for the day was hot. I stretched out on my bed and thought about Springer for a while. Then I thought about Captain Allen. My cotton shorts were bulging by that time, so I slipped my hand into my waistband and started playing with my dick. I fiddled with it dry for a few minutes before I knew that I was going to have to jerk off. I pulled off my shorts and my T-shirt too, because I like to masturbate completely naked, spit into my hand, and started my long-practiced stroking.

I was picturing Captain Allen, and though I must have heard the ladder moving against the side of the house, I paid no attention to the sound or to the sudden appearance of a set of rungs directly in front of my window. I kept jacking my cock, faster and harder, and I was getting close to the point of no return when I saw Captain Allen's head appear at my window. The next instant his eyes met mine, he saw what I was doing, he paused briefly, and then he climbed up another two rungs so that his crotch was centered upon my window.

Then Captain Allen did something amazing. His hand lowered into my range of vision, pulled down his zipper, and let his cock bob free. He was hard as a rock. I had stopped beating my meat when Captain Allen heaved into view, and the hiatus had placed my impending orgasm on hold. I jumped from my bed, rushed to the window, and dropped to my knees. Captain Allen's magnificent erection, a thick, darkly complexioned, hooded cock, stood waiting for me. I closed my mouth around it and let it slide over my tongue.

I gripped Captain Allen's shaft, as Brother Slim had taught me, so I wouldn't gag. I worked the head of his dick, and as I used my tongue and lips, jacking him between strokes with my mouth, I jerked my own cock. I spit into my hand again to lubricate my swollen dick, and then I sucked hard on Captain Allen's dick. I heard him moan, and I wondered whether he was still sliding his paintbrush over the old boards of our house.

My dick grew heavier. At the same time, I felt Captain Allen soften slightly and then grow very hard. I knew that he was approaching orgasm at the same time I was. I vowed to make us come together. I sucked his cock with all my might, torturing the foreskin of his dick while I squeezed the tip of my own. Orgasmic tingles rushed through the head of my cock. I was committed to come, and I heard Captain Allen moan, "Oh, you cocksucker."

Somehow, I liked the sound of it: Ben Marshal, cocksucker. It had an official ring. Maybe I should have business cards printed. That thought was erased as I tasted semen, spicier than Brother Slim's custard but flavorful still.

Captain Allen's come hit the back of my throat, and I let it go down. I wanted his sperm in my stomach. I wanted to eat his load, swallow him whole. He came, moaning, hanging on a ladder fifteen feet in the air, and quivering from my cocksucking power. I sucked his cock until he had finished, and while I sucked, my pelvic muscles contracted and a burst of my jism splattered against the wall under the window.

While my memories swam before my exploding consciousness, I continued sucking Jeff's cock. I was hard, but I did not masturbate. Why not, I cannot really say, except that Larry and Chip were watching.

By then, Jeff was grabbing the back of my head as tightly as I was gripping his butt. He was fucking my mouth, and I was fucking his dick with my lips, tongue, and throat. As Jeff's dick reached the back of my throat, I swallowed hard, time after time. I tried to swallow his dick. At the same time, I slid my finger into his asshole, which was hot and tight but lubricated with the weird water of the volcanic pond. I was using the hot, slightly radioactive volcanic mud to lubricate his asshole so that I could slide my finger inside. More and more, I opened him up until my entire forefinger was rubbing against his prostate.

"Oh, the way you suck me, Ben," Jeff moaned loudly. "Oh, man, I'm gonna come."

I could hardly answer, since his dick was fucking my throat, but I pressed harder against his prostate, massaging the little gland enough to drive him to distraction.

"Oh, god, here I come," Jeff howled. I kept swallowing, his cock head penetrating into my throat. I knew that he was shooting his semen down into my esophagus, but there was no more hope of my tasting it. He was coming beyond compassion, beyond compare, and beyond any rationality whatsoever. I was the master of his cock, the ruler of his orgasmic universe. I had only to suck him, and he must obey.

"Oh, Ben," Jeff moaned. "I can hardly stand it. It's so good. Ah, Ben."

◆

I MET CHIP WHEN I SIGNED UP FOR A SUMMER ENGLISH COURSE at Clark College in Vancouver, Washington. That summer I was staying with my Aunt Donna, who insisted that I "better myself" rather than lounging around the house. Chip was taking the same course, and when I found out that he was the president of the Gay Penguins, I asked him about the club. Naturally, the club didn't have regular summer meetings, but he suggested we have lunch at Burgerville.

After we collected our food, Chip led me to a table occupied by his two friends, Jeff and Larry. We talked for a few minutes about the local scene. (All three said that it was better to go across the river to Portland, Oregon.) Before the meal ended, the guys told me that they were going on a weekend camping trip to hike around Mount St. Helens.

"Want to come along, Ben?" Chip asked.

"Sure," I agreed readily, never having taken a camping trip nor hiked more than a mile and a half in my life.

Right after class on Thursday, we piled into Larry's jeep and set out for the mountain. We parked in a remote location, loaded our gear, food, and water onto our backs, and set out over rough terrain. By the time we reached our camp, I was half-dead. I hurt all over, but we still had to pitch our camp, build a fire, and fix our food before we could eat and sleep.

Every rock that had spewed out of the 1980 volcanic eruption must have found its way under my sleeping bag. If the rocks weren't enough to keep me wakeful, my dread of a rattlesnake or mountain lion attacking me while I slept would have. I spent a night in near agony and decided that morning could not come soon enough.

Morning came far too early. I have to admit that breakfast was good: eggs, ham, and flapjacks cooked over an open fire. The food restored me, so that I set out with high spirits that lasted an hour. By the time we stopped for lunch, I didn't think I could walk another step. Nevertheless, I would have died rather than admit my weakness. Almost immediately after lunch, we ventured upon a landscape where the vegetation had not yet returned. The air reeked of rotten eggs, and great chalky deposits streaked the rocks. We passed a vent where steam and gas spewed out of the ground, testament to the molten lava beneath the thin crust.

Larry said that the white streaks were mineral deposits and the smell was a combination of hydrogen sulfide and sulfur dioxide, which escaped in the venting steam and bubbled up in the pools. Shortly thereafter, we came upon the small pond, about five feet across. The water looked like greenish milk, and as I stared at it, a smelly bubble broke the surface. Larry tested the bottom with a stout stick, finding it to be only about four feet at its deepest point. After he had tied a thermometer to the stick and measured the temperature at all depths, he pronounced it safe.

"Safe from what?" I asked, staggered that these guys seriously planned to get into that hell bath.

"We don't want to get scalded," Jeff said. "People have lost legs from wading into geothermal pools, those who weren't killed outright."

"The water is heated by the molten magma just beneath the surface. If we waded in and the crust was so thin that we broke through, well, it would just be too bad."

None of this information motivated me to soak in that pond, but the guys were already getting naked. I glanced at Jeff's thick cock and Chip's sculpted ass and the chest and arm muscles that Larry had worked for in the gym. For a moment, the reeking air nearly overcame me. I felt a minute of dizziness, and I was having trouble breathing. The air seemed to be burning my lungs. Then I glanced down and saw that I had completely undressed myself. The guys were already squatting down in the hot pond, so I waded in behind them.

◆

WHEN I PULLED MY MOUTH OFF JEFF'S DICK, he dropped back into the pond as if someone had biffed him. His hands slipped underwater, and I knew that he was groping his dick and balls to make sure they were still attached. Jeff wasn't the only one feeling his dick. My own cock was swollen with desire. Chip was standing up, so that his erection jutted up to his stomach. He was fingering the head of his cock, not really jacking but simply fondling and petting his toy. Larry was beating his meat furiously.

Jeff was still staring about with wonder. "That was the best," he moaned, "the blow job of a lifetime. Man, nobody has ever sucked me like that."

"Better than me?" Larry said, looking wounded to the core. He stopped jerking off in order to study my mouth.

"Ben, please, man," Jeff pleaded. "You just gotta do these guys. It's the only way they're gonna believe me."

I could feel my mouth widening into an ingratiating grin. "Sure," I agreed, mildly abashed that my new chums regarded me as an oral whore. "I could suck dicks all day," I added, trying to play the sophisticated gay man but sounding more like a cock-crazed newbie.

"Larry is closer to getting his rocks off, Ben," Chip offered. "You better suck him first."

Larry rose from the water. His cock was smaller than Jeff's, but it had a ferocious look. Vowing to tame the wild critter, I touched my lips to it. Chip dropped to his knees beside me, moving close enough to see. I bobbed my head on Larry's cock and worked his dick head with my lips. Larry moaned loudly. By that time, Jeff had recovered from his shattering orgasm, so he too pressed close.

I wrapped my tongue around the underside of Larry's dick and fucked him with my mouth. Meanwhile, I grabbed his butt with one hand and started jerking off my own cock with the other. Chip pulled my hand away from my dick. "Save it, Ben," he urged. "We have a surprise for you later."

Making Larry come took no time at all. Within a minute, he was shooting his semen onto my tongue. It was warm and sweet, and I let it slide down my throat.

Chip took a little longer, but not much. His cock was longer than Larry's but not as thick as Jeff's. I'm partial to the thick ones, personally, but I enjoy sampling every size and shape. I took the head of Chip's cock into my throat and let him shoot his spunk straight down. When he pulled out, I felt a distinct wooziness. I staggered, and the fellows caught me.

"Come on, guys," Larry urged. "We better get away from these volcanic fumes. We've breathed enough of this sulfur. Especially you, Ben."

"But what about my surprise?" I protested, as the guys loaded our packs and hiked naked over the hot landscape.

"Your surprise will come later," Chip assured me, taking me by the arm and forcing me to walk a little faster.

We did not have to hike far before we left the thin crust and the volcanic vents behind. We found a meadow where the wildflowers had returned amid a grove of young aspens. We pitched camp there, and after breathing in the pure air and enjoying a hearty supper, the guys proved that they were not like my first two lovers. Brother Slim and Captain Allen had been takers; my new friends took and gave joyously.

"You passed the test, Ben," Chip said. "You're one of us now."

"Ben, you've noticed," Jeff began, "that everybody got his rocks off today—except for you."

Here comes the surprise, I thought. The guys giggled with anticipation. "Who gets to suck Ben's dick, or do we take turns?" Chip asked.

Jeff shook his head. "I had something else in mind," he said. "Something I'll bet Ben has never done."

A funny feeling came over me. What was he going to propose?

"You just want his cock up your ass, Jeff," Larry taunted. "We're onto your wicked ways." He giggled again when he said it, so I guessed that it was a running gag.

"Like you guys don't?" Jeff taunted. "However, Ben sucked my dick first, so he gets to fuck me first. He can do your asses after mine, if he feels up to coming three times. How about it, Ben?"

My first impulse was to claim that I was an exclusive cocksucker. After all, I'd never done anything else. But my hands remembered the feel of Jeff's firm ass mounds, and my cock stiffened. I was hard to fuck his ass. I followed my second impulse. "Yeah," I said. "I want to fuck you, Jeff."

Jeff positioned himself face downward, and raised one leg toward his chest. The invitation was obvious, but I was not sure how to proceed. Eager to teach, Chip and Larry grabbed my dick, which was rock hard. They slipped on an extra-strength condom and lubricated the outside of the condom, nearly driving me to raptures as they rubbed the lube onto my wrapped dick. I wasn't sure that I could hold out, but the unfamiliar territory unnerved me. While I pushed my cock between Jeff's butt cheeks, my mind reeled at the novelty.

"Slide it in, Ben," Jeff urged. Chip and Larry watched with hot, eager eyes. When I pushed downward, I heard Jeff draw a deep breath. He opened readily so my cock slipped into his hot, tight chute. I pushed it in to the hilt, pulled back, and plunged home again. His ass felt like a thousand hands and mouths massaging my cock.

"Oh, that's good," I moaned, fucking like a real man for the first time. I thrust and rose, lifting my bare ass and plunging down, riding the push and pull of the flesh, and savoring the tingles in my cock as I fucked Jeff's wonderful ass.

"Jeff's ass is a great ride, Ben." Larry laughed as the throes of orgasm struck me hard.

Chip added, "My ass is better."

As I wrung the last drops from my swollen cock, I looked forward to many happy outings with this group.

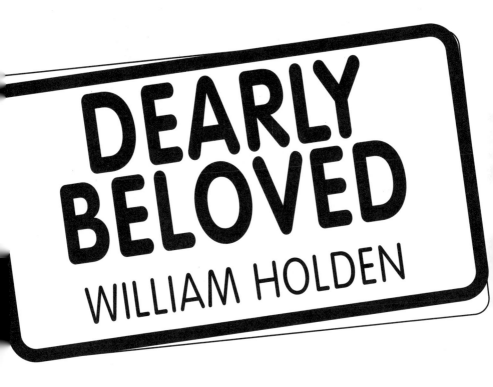

DEARLY BELOVED

WILLIAM HOLDEN

THE SCENT OF LEATHER WARMED BY THE HEAT and sweat of the men surrounded me as I walked into my small office. I sniffed my clothes and then my skin, trying to decipher whether the lingering smell was still coming off my body or just a vivid memory from the night before. I decided it was in my mind. I sat down at my desk. My head spun from the movement. Work was the last place I wanted to be. If I had known I was going to have to replace Brad this morning, I wouldn't have done what I did. Or maybe I would have, but at least I would have been more prepared for this. I don't go out very often cruising for men, and I certainly don't make a habit of going to all-night parties, but once in while I feel the need to express myself in ways I don't normally get to. Last night was one of those nights.

I looked at my watch. It was 9:30—too early for my sore, tired body. I had left the party only four hours ago. A message waited for me at home, telling me I had to be here for a 10:30 appointment. I closed my eyes in the hopes of getting a few more minutes of needed sleep. The visions of last night invaded my mind as I drifted off.

◆

I STOOD IN MY BEDROOM NAKED, looking at myself in the full-length mirror. My body was covered in black hair; the gray had just begun to make its appearance. My face was round and a bit chubby compared to the rest of me. My body while losing some of its firmness was still holding out at fifty. My cock, although never very thick, was impressive in length, with a slight curve midway up the shaft. My body seemed to glow in the dim light of the leather candles that burned around the room. Their scent enveloped me, licking and coating my skin. The CD player kicked into *Filthy Gorgeous* by the Scissor Sisters. I opened my walk-in closet; the scent of leather was stronger, more erotically charged in the smaller space. The glare from the sunlamps blinded me briefly as I made my way into the back. I would only wear my leather if it was warmed beforehand. I had always found that the energy and heat and the way it sticks to the skin, as if it were another layer of my body, brought out my deepest sexual fantasies. I turned off the lamps, gathered my clothes, and laid them out on my bed. In the background I heard the lyrics: "a dirty, puppy, daddy bastard." I turned back to the mirror. Yes, that was my song. I was a dirty, puppy, daddy bastard. At least I would be tonight.

I watched myself as I slipped my arms through the leather vest. My cock responded to the warmth of the vest as it caressed my back and shoulders. The front straps lay perfectly on either side of my nipples. I turned around to admire the crisscross of the straps on my back. The beat of the music coursed through me as I reached for the shorts. The leather pulled and tugged the hair on my legs as I slowly slid them up. The heat engulfed my cock and balls. I could feel my body temperature rising. Dampness began to build in my shorts. The small metal eyelets from the laced fly burned as they made contact with my skin. My cock expanded again, filling what little room remained in the shorts. The thin leather shaped and molded itself to every vein and curve of my crotch.

I moved over to the edge of the bed and slipped my feet into the boots. The bright white of my socks slid easily into the black shine of the leather. As I laced up the boots, I could feel the leather squeeze around my ankles and calves. I stood up and walked over to the mirror to inspect the transformation. The final lyrics, just in time: "'Cause you're filthy, ooh, and you're gorgeous." A smile crept over my face. I was ready, in every way possible. I shut off the CD player and blew out the candles. The scent of leather hung heavily in the air as I left my condo. I stepped out onto Folsom Street and began the walk of three short blocks to the party.

From the outside the warehouse looked deserted. The windows and doors were boarded up. The only light came from the moon and the few streetlights nearby that were still working. I walked around back. The hard leather soles of my boots made deep, hollow echoes in the empty alley. My heart raced with anticipation as I stood in front of the door. I hesitated for only a moment before opening the door and stepping inside. There were no hallways or other doors. The whole cavern of a room just opened up before me. The music pounded the rough walls and the worn floors. I could feel every beat. The air was already heavy with smoke. It smelled of leather and rubber and impending sex. The smells were intoxicating. I crossed the room to get a drink—and to get noticed. It worked.

Heads turned as I pushed through the crowd. I ordered a bourbon and Coke and turned back toward the center of the room. I could feel the leather shorts pulling on my mass of damp pubic hairs. They tugged and poked the tender skin of my balls. I leaned up against a pole that stretched from floor to ceiling. I ran my hand over my chest and down to fondle the laced leather straps of my fly. They noticed me. They kept their eyes fixed on me, waiting for more of a show. My cock lengthened under their stares, pushing itself against the hide. I could feel myself getting wet. The smells of sweaty leather and heated rubber drifted through the air from the crowd of men hanging around.

Men of all ages and types strolled by me, each finding something on me to touch or caress. A few were bold enough to kiss me or lick my neck. I closed my eyes briefly to feel the music, to smell the men. Someone stopped in front of me. His presence was undeniable— whiskey on his hot breath. I opened my eyes and looked up at him. He stood several inches taller than me. He had broad shoulders and a muscular build and was noticeably younger. His sharp jaw was covered with dark stubble, and his dark, black hair was cut short; premature gray at each temple glimmered in the dim lights. His dark green eyes stared back at me—into me.

He ran his hands down my chest, the rubber-palmed gloves he wore pulling my hair. Pleasure snaked through my entire body and converged in my groin. His chest and stomach were covered with a skintight rubber shirt. Each one of his muscles stretched and pulled the material as his hands moved over me. His nipples stood erect. I licked my lips at the thought of sucking them through their thin rubber coating.

"You like what you see?" His voice carried over the loud music and the other men with ease.

"Yeah, and I can't wait to see more of it." My voice wavered and seemed hollow compared to his. "I'm—" I paused briefly, not sure if we should exchange names. "Dan."

"Dan. I like it; it fits you. Like Daniel and the lions' den." He looked around at the crowded room. A brief smile crossed his face. "I'm Eric."

I was a little surprised by the biblical reference, but as he moved in closer to me the smell of his body, his sweat, the rubber scattered the comment. I could feel his body next to mine. His heat radiated off his leather. I closed my eyes and took a deep breath. Rubber mixed with leather. Sweat scented with desire. I couldn't resist the temptation. My tongue reached out for his chest. It slid slowly to the right, enjoying the rich, deep flavor of the rubber shirt. A hint of bear polish and wax covered my tongue and left me wanting more. I felt the lump of his nipple against my lips. I sucked on it, gently at first, then more forcefully, desperately wanting to draw the salty flavor of his sweat right through the fabric. The taste of the rubber invaded my mouth instead. I could feel the vibrations of his moans as my face pressed against his chest.

I glanced down for the first time and noticed the tight rubber shorts he was wearing. The codpiece, held on by metal snaps, expanded as his cock swelled inside. I moved farther down his chest, licking the smooth, soft rubber. I fell to my knees, licking the bottom edge of his shirt. He stretched his body over mine, his shirt coming up out of his shorts. His scent surrounded me. Beads of sweat began to form on the edge of his shirt. I moved my tongue underneath. The hair on his stomach pulled away from his shirt as my tongue moved along the edge. Each bead of sweat tasted like soap, salt, and rubber. With each taste, I could feel the pre-come oozing out of my cock. His moisture was running through me. I began to get drunk on his body. I knew I needed more of him.

Slowly I rolled up the edge of his shirt. Sweat caused the rubber to stick to his skin and body, but I forced them apart. His body trembled each time I pushed his shirt farther up. My tongue followed the shirt up, licking his sweat from the thin trail of hair that ran down the center of his torso. The smell of sweat and rubber grew stronger as I peeled his shirt up above his chest. His arms were still stretched over me, grasping the pole behind me. His scent pulled me in. I pushed my tongue up under his shirt and lingered there, savoring the taste and smell of his damp, musky armpit.

"You are a nasty thing, aren't you?" he groaned into my ear. "That's just the way I like it, hot and nasty."

I moved my left hand down his back, feeling his muscles ripple. My fingers slid easily over the rubber that covered his firm, tight ass. I pushed my tongue deeper, licking his salty sweat from the rubber as my hand reached around and fondled his crotch. My fingers toyed with the snaps that held the codpiece. I felt Eric tremble with anticipation.

As I released the first snap, his body shook against me. A soft grunt escaped his lips. I could feel his heart racing as I released another snap. Our bodies pulled closer together. My tongue slid farther into his armpit. One by one I released the snaps, his body trembling more violently with each pop. As the final snap released, his hefty cock fell forward. It was long and thick and hung heavily between us. I slid my hand down to feel his wetness.

He pushed me away and pressed me against the pole. The look on his face was pure, raw desire. His eyes gleamed as he stared at me. Out of the corner of my eyes, I could see the other men around the room, many losing their clothes just as Eric was. The sights and sounds around me made me hornier than I had ever been.

My thoughts snapped back to Eric. He was no longer concentrating on my face. His eyes were focused on the length of the cock hidden inside my shorts. I glanced down and saw every familiar vein pushing against the material. Eric's finger pushed my chin upward, forcing me to look at him. He leaned forward and slid his tongue inside my open vest. He moved slowly downward. His tongue chilled my sweating skin. He knelt in front of me. His tongue slipped over the polished leather of my shorts. He licked and caressed every inch of my cock. I could feel his moans vibrating against me.

He moved over to the center of my shorts and bit down on one end of the lacing. He pulled it free from the knot. His tongue wrapped around another section of the lacing and pulled it free from the small metal eyelet. Slowly the tightness of my shorts relaxed. The heat of his breath reached my skin. He continued down the lacing with his tongue, on one side and then the other, reversing the crisscross movement I had used to tie it. I watch him as he removed the last wrap of the lacing. It hung from his mouth like a thin snake. He spat it out.

My knees went weak as he moved his tongue into the opened fly, running it through the thick mass of my pubic hair. I grabbed his shoulders to steady myself as he yanked my shorts down to my ankles. My cock fell out against his face. Pre-come glistened on his cheek. My hot sweaty scent drifted around us. He opened his mouth and sucked me in—every inch, all at once. The muscles in the back of his throat tightened with the sudden penetration. Then they relaxed, and I slid farther in. His large hands, still in rubber, squeezed my ass. His tongue and throat pushed and suck every drop of pre-come out of me. He moved slowly yet gracefully up and down my shaft. Spit and pre-come formed at the edge of his mouth. It ran down his chin and neck, then splattered onto his rubber shirt. He rubbed it off his shirt and used our mixture to lube his own cock. He stroked himself until the head of his cock turned a bluish-purple.

He stood up. My hand instantly made contact with his prick. It was hot to the touch and more solid than any cock I'd ever had. I squeezed it down to the base as I let my fingers slip inside the cutout opening of his rubber shorts. His large, hairy balls lay in a pool of his own sweat. I pulled down on the edge of his shorts to release it. The sweat trickled onto the wooden floor between his legs.

Eric moved closer to me and grabbed my cock. My fingers wrapped themselves around his. We began to stroke each other. Our breathing became heavier. Then it became one. Eric laid his forehead on my shoulder. I laid mine on his. Our free hands wrapped around each other. We stroked each other, back and forth, enjoying the feel and the look of our two cocks connected. I could hear him breathing deeply. His body shook suddenly. He groaned. The thrill of knowing he was getting close brought me to my limit.

Our bodies convulsed together as if we were having one orgasm. I felt his cock release beneath my grip. Hot, white come splattered over my arm, my vest. I kept stroking him harder and faster as I shot my come over him. Both of us were out of breath, but we continued to pull at each other, back and forth, showering each other with more of our come. It slid off the hot leather and rubber. Panting, holding on, we watched its whiteness slide down the blackness, leaving a faint creamy trail. It hung on the edge of his shirt and my vest before slowly dripping onto our legs. Our bodies rocked slowly back and forth. We held on to each others' softening cocks. The rocking seemed to increase.

◆

A FAMILIAR VOICE IN MY EAR.

"Father? Father McCleary? It's time. We're ready for you."

The voice of my assistant, Melanie, shook me from my sleep. I looked up at her groggily, barely out of my dream.

"Father, are you OK? You're sweating."

"Yes, I'm fine. It just seems a little warm in here to me." I quickly glanced down. I was relieved to see that my robes covered the raging hard-on in my pants. I stood up and grabbed my service book and followed Melanie out into the sanctuary.

As I found my place at the altar, the bride began her walk down the aisle. The kitschy music echoed in the church, as it always does. I looked for the groom; his back was turned to me. He rocked nervously on his feet as his bride approached. The bride reached out for him to take her arm. They turned toward me.

It was Eric, holding the arm of his bride-to-be. Recognition set in on his face. He seemed equally startled, even a little scared. Then his tense face eased into a tight smile. Finally he winked at me.

I stood silently for a moment to try to compose myself. I cleared my throat and began. "Dearly beloved, we are gathered here today . . ."

FIRE AND ICE

SLY JOHNSON

DEAN COULDN'T BELIEVE WHAT HE HAD GOTTEN HIMSELF INTO.
Any sane gay man would have answered "Fuck off" or "No." He was
named after James Dean and for the most part was a good ode to the
icon. But if James had been asked to go with his ex-lover to a family
retreat for appearances' sake, Dean thought sure the answer would
have been no. When Todd made his frantic request, supposedly for
the sake of his mother who had survived breast cancer, Dean mumbled a "Yeah, OK . . ." followed by Todd's awkward "I'll pay for
everything, and send you the dates . . . Thank you so much." With

that, Todd's voice was gone, and Dean was left to ponder what he had gotten himself into.

It had been seven months since the breakup with a man Dean thought would be the love of his life, his equal, a healthy addition to his life. He had fallen hard, more than he knew he was capable of. Dean was hot in all respects, with a lanky, tight swimmer's build, blaring blue eyes, and sandy hair, but he acted as if he didn't know he was cute, which made him cuter. His lips were lush and delicious and added an exotic look to his otherwise very European look. Sex, hookups, flings, and dating were not hard for him to come by at all. But no one before Todd, with his Latin look, great sense of humor, and lush body, had ever made him feel that desire to settle down and be a one-man man. Ironically, after two mostly great years, Dean began to feel underappreciated. His attempts at furthering the relationship with the option of a commitment ceremony or shared mortgage were both declined by Todd. Sex got less and less frequent and actually less sexy when it did happen. Todd seemed content with coexisting. As the months rolled into years, Dean came across Todd's private e-mail account. Todd was not faithful, even though he had insisted they stay committed to one another.

The breakup was rather civil, undramatic, as Dean announced his discovery and moved out as soon as the lease was up. Now he was in a open floor-plan loft in the trendy gay and yuppie part of downtown. He never thought he'd end up there, but a mutual friend was leaving for Italy and he immediately sublet his apartment for a decent price. Dean felt at home; his neighbors were not as snobby as he'd imagined. Lots of single gay guys kept his mind off his newfound bachelor status. Dean sighed to himself after saying yes to Todd's crazy scheme; he needed a jog. He locked his apartment door and headed to the ground-level gym.

Dean impatiently pushed the elevator buttons. *Todd would like this place,* Dean thought. The elevator doors opened.

"Hey," said the man standing inside, in gym clothes as well. "I thought I was stuck there for a minute; we might want to take the stairs."

Dean smiled. He didn't remember the man's name, but he had helped him move a loveseat the day before that had gotten stuck between the elevator and the hallway wall.

"Let's risk it!" Dean said, stepping in. He was half joking, but the new neighbor hit the button for the ground floor and the doors began to close.

The hot new addition to the floor raised his eyebrows as if he were a child up to something. "A man of adventure—that's good. Name's Josh," he said, smiling a big smile and extending his hand.

Dean took it, surprised how not firm the handshake was for such toned arms. "Dean, nice to meet you. You used the gym yet?"

Josh shook his head and took back his hand. "No, got the brief tour. I'd rather see the rooftop garden, but if I don't work my abs now, I know I won't all day."

Josh was shorter than Dean, wider, not fat at all, but a little thick. He had adorable dimples, deep brown eyes, and fairly short brown hair. Dean stared at the little black wife beater Josh wore, quite sure his abs underneath would be fine. Dean realized he was getting aroused, not a good idea in his gym shorts, and looked away. "We can work out together and go up to the roof as a reward, if you'd like."

Josh bit his lower lip. "Mmm." He paused, seeming shy. "I'm kinda scared of heights," he confessed.

Dean smiled at how adorable this guy was. His choppy hair framed his face perfectly, and he was strong enough to be slightly vulnerable. "Well, it is high. Maybe one day if you feel comfortable; it's an intense view."

Josh smiled a big smile and said, "Cool. I'll take you up on the help in the gym, though."

With that the lights dimmed suddenly, and then the elevator thudded to a stop, pushing the men into each other and nearly to the floor. Josh grabbed on to Dean's waist for support. "You all right?" they both asked, answering, "Yeah, uh-huh" simultaneously. The emergency lights came on, giving the interior a candlelit glow.

"You're lucky; you don't need to work on your abs," Josh commented, pulling his hands away from Dean but still facing him. They stared into each other's eyes and Dean leaned in for a kiss. It was gentle, warm, and perfect. Their mouths parted and Dean gently slid his tongue to meet Josh's. Dean wondered if Josh's dick would be short and thick like his muscular body. Apparently Dean wasn't the only one thinking about Josh's dick, as without warning he pulled down his shorts. Exposing a shaved, thick, long dick that curved upward, he grabbed Dean's hand and placed it on him. Dean wrapped his hands around it, surprised at its thickness. They continued to kiss, both in awe of the other's technique, Dean still pulling at the twitching dick in his hand.

The lights came on and the elevator jarred back into motion. "Oh shit," Josh burst out, pulling at his shorts. The doors opened just as he pulled them up and put his throbbing dick under his waistband to conceal it. "Let's take the stairs up to your place, if that's OK?" Dean nodded and led the way. As soon as the door thudded shut to the otherwise empty stairwell, the two men looked at each other. "I didn't get to see yours," Josh said, staring at Dean. "It's semi now . . ." He pulled down his shorts; his erection was still impressive, and impulsively Josh fell to his knees. "Not here!" Dean said, and began to move up the stairs, but Josh remained, grabbing Dean, holding him firmly in place.

The heat of the near stranger's hands on his thighs felt searing, and the heat from Josh's breath teased his rapidly growing dick. Dean stared down as Josh's eager eyes and mouth. Now rubbing his chiseled jawline against the now rock-hard dick in front of him. Josh stared up, Dean's length looking huge next to his face. Josh was teasing him; he finally placed the head in his mouth. He moved his hands to explore Dean's toned ass. A sigh of pleasure, a guttural throaty moan, echoed through the stairwell as Dean threw back his head. The warmth and perfect movement of his new neighbor's mouth was almost unreal. Josh attempted a "Shh" sound and slapped Dean's ass in warning, reminding him to be quiet. Dean controlled himself, and Josh took more of his dick, almost all. Dean grabbed Josh's hair and pushed Josh's nose into his own trimmed groin.

After a few seconds, Josh slowly slid Dean's dick out of his mouth. It made him dizzy, but he almost hated to part with it. He sucked the large head one last time and released it. "My turn," Dean whispered as the coldness of the air hit his hot wet dick.

"Not yet," Josh whispered. With that, Josh's hand turned him around. Dean wasn't really into getting rimmed, but this guy was so hot and he rationalized that they were safe. The stairwell had no cameras and the doors opened with a loudness that would give them ample time to dress. All logical thought left his mind as soon as Josh gently bit his left ass cheek.

"You are perfect, " Josh said aloud and with sincerity, the last words he spoke before kissing his way to the center of an-hour-a-day Stairmaster-regimented ass. Dean was amazed by his warmth and gentleness, intoxicating and totally different from the aggressive blow job he had just received. Josh was gentle and almost loving, his hands cupping the barely tanned, toned ass and gently opening the main course within. Josh groaned as Dean's hardly visited exterior fought the good fight and then lost. He darted in deeper and deeper, until his nose was pressed to flesh, his tongue exploring and getting squeezed back in defiant exhilaration.

After what seemed like joyous hours, Josh stood up, kissing Dean's back up to his neck and gently probing his finger into the moist relaxed ass. Dean gasped in shock, and instantly clamped down, but the finger fucking continued, hitting his pleasure point with every single thrust. "Grab my dick!" Josh panted in a harsh whisper as he pushed himself face to face, his finger still working hard in Dean's ass. Dean did so; the thickness once again shocked him. It was lubed up naturally with the pre-come that had already saturated his shorts. "Wait!" Josh said, as Dean worked his hand fast on the moist head. Josh's eyes rolled back and he composed himself, pulling his dick away. "Your place!" he pleaded, pulling free of Dean's tight hole and pulling at his shorts. The two men booked it upstairs in seconds flat, jogged down the long hall while Dean fumbled for his keys.

Inside, Josh pulled for the first time at his wife beater. It slid up and over his abs and thick chest and onto the floor in mere seconds. His wet little shorts followed, exposing the scary thickness that was his dick. "You can afford the gym being closed for a day," Dean said with a smirk. He quickly undressed too, and they stared at each other, soaking in the raw sexiness, catching their breath. Dean stepped toward Josh finally, kissing him and roughly grabbing his balls at the same time. They were smallish in comparison to his dick and fit easily into his hands, filling his palm nicely. It was Josh's turn to groan with pleasure and he did so freely, without risk of public embarrassment. Even though they had been at it for a little while, Dean had so much to explore still, kissing Josh's neck, finding the spots that made him moan, and caressing his balls the whole time. He followed the defined collarbone down to hard little pinkish nipples, sucking hard without any foreplay. Josh groaned and the sound of his head thudding against the door made Dean smile for a split second.

The abs weren't magazine cover-ready, but they were damn close. Dean slid his tongue down from one erect nipple to the slightly salty belly button to a shaved groin. Worried a blow job would make him come in seconds, Josh grabbed Dean's face, pulling his chin up. "Um . . . do you have condoms? I mean . . . can you top me?" The inflection in his voice made Dean grin. He kissed the wide head of Josh's dick.

"Yeah," he said, getting up and heading toward the bedroom, emerging with a condom and lube. He quickly put it on; Josh looked scared and excited as he stared at the rock-hard latex-covered glory in front of him.

"You sure you want to do this?" Dean asked.

Josh nodded yes without hesitation. "Yeah, just bigger than I'm used too."

Dean caressed his face. "We can do it however feels best for you." Their eyes met and for a split second they had a mutual thought; perhaps under all the raw sexual attraction and the exhilarating heat of something a little naughty there might be a nice guy.

Josh leaned in, gripping Dean's dick as they kissed gently at first, tongues darting, lips interlocking, heat exchanging, and eroticism quickly taking over any logical thoughts that may have been rolling around. Josh loved the way he fit into Dean, who was taller and leaner, and the way his head bent down ever so slightly for their mouths to meet. Dean in turn loved the gentleness of Josh; even with his chiseled jawline and thick body frame, the softness of his personality came through somehow.

The kisses became increasingly passionate. Josh bit Dean's lower lip and tugged gently. Dean grabbed his waist and slammed their groins together. His hands traveled from Josh's waist to his big bubble butt. Josh moaned almost silently, putting his head on Dean's chest, soaking up the smells of this gorgeous man. "Come to the bed," Dean said, hands still exploring Josh's butt. They walked clumsily, torsos bumping, arms intertwined, until soon they landed on the comforter. Josh pushed Dean into the lushness of the infinite white bed and lay on top of him. Dean felt the heat of Josh's inner thighs pressing tightly against his back. The condom was still in place, and Josh gently stroked lube onto it. He took a big breath. "Let me get used to all this; it's been a while." Dean nodded a yes. He would not move until he was directed to do so.

Dean watched Josh's abs flex as he began to lean back. Dean was shocked yet again as his eyes fell from the sexy abs to the crotch he'd yet to taste. The base of the wide dick amazed him, extending all the way to a fat, stout head. Josh was hard, skin pulled to the max, glistening pre-come about to drop at any second. His cock didn't have any huge protruding veins; it was very sleek and the center tubing on the bottom was thick. The thick dick pointed upward, like a rocket ready to take off at any second. As Josh leaned back more and more, the gorgeous imagery directly above Dean and the pressure on the head of his dick became intense. Josh bobbed back and forth for a moment or two, then groaned.

Josh could not believe the fullness he felt, absolute fullness, as he stayed still, breathing deeply. The gentle throb of the huge head he was taking inside his ass pushed against his body's inner warmth. His own temperature rose and he shook slightly at the pressure he was feeling, as he was staring down at a classic Hollywood hunk with naughty lips. He pushed down gently, then a bit more; his gentle bobbing ceased. He needed a moment to relax. Dean appreciated the pause as well; he needed to collect himself against the tight gripping wonderfulness that engulfed the head and the next couple inches of his dick. He caressed Josh's thighs gently, scared that if he touched the giant rocket staring back at him, it would explode and the exchange between the two would be complete. Josh leaned down, for a kiss, his ass consuming the rest of Dean's dick in a gentle motion. The pain was over, in its place a warm twitching dick that he wanted more of. Dean groaned, but instead of taking control and thrusting like a madman, he reached up slightly and kissed the immediately looming mouth above his own.

Open mouths gave way to warm tongues. Lips caressed each other, and Josh began to buck up and down, no longer gentle. He sucked Dean's lower lip into his mouth, bucking the dick deeper into himself, filling up more than what he was used to. The wetness on Dean's stomach, the level of pre-come were almost too much; he put his hands on Josh's waist. They stopped kissing, and Josh nodded yes to Dean's questioning eyes. Dean grabbed the thick muscular legs that straddled him and the men rotated in a fluid movement. Josh groaned loudly as he landed on his back, his legs still gripping the torso of the man inside him. Dean thrust with steady pounding motions, pulling his large dick half out and then back in, each time all the way to the base. Josh groaned every single time, his eyes rolling back in his head, his mind thinking of nothing. All he could do was process the sensations his body was feeling. Both men began to glisten with sweat; Dean grabbed Josh's waist and pulled him to the edge of the luxurious bed. He got off the bed and stood up, his dick still inside his partner. Josh rested his legs on Dean's toned shoulders. He stared up at his ankles now lying on either side of the sexy face that stared down on him.

"Fuck me!" Josh nearly yelled as the men settled into the new position and the thrusting began. Dean fucked hard and fast in an uncontrolled fury as Josh twisted his body slightly, biting the comforter and digging his arms into the bed for support as Dean's force moved him back and forth. The sturdy bed began to squeak, and the men faintly heard a clank of something falling somewhere. A phone rang in the other room, but nothing else mattered. Their raw carnal attraction was now in full force. Josh in his contorted glory used his upper body strength to thrust back, gripping with his tight hole, contracting as best he could while Dean pounded in deeper. Dean grabbed the perfectly round ass cheeks and spread them. His movements were ultra-fast and stabbing, as far inside as he could go. Josh could take no more. His ass contracted uncontrollably, squeezing tightly, his back arched, and Dean stared in amazement as fountains of white washed over the muscles below him. The thick dick throbbed wildly, skin a dark swollen red, pushing fountains of white cream over Josh's abs, torso, and even his chin.

Dean could not take a second more and his final thrusts ended in the hottest orgasm he'd had in the last two years. Josh moved his legs down, and Dean collapsed on the man below.

Caressing Dean's hair, Josh finally spoke. "Wow . . . thank God the elevator broke." Dean nodded in agreement. He gently pulled himself out of the man below and slowly rose from the stickiness between them; "A shower too personal?" Dean asked, extending his hand to help the Adonis below him up. "No," Josh said, "I think not after all that. A shower would be great, a hot one!"

In the steamy, soapy shower there was no awkwardness as Dean talked about the city and Josh about his excitement at being there. "So, um, if you want to hang out again let me know . . . I'm recently single, which is what brought me here, so I'm not sure where I'm at, but I'm glad we . . ." Josh paused, not sure what to call what they had just shared. Dean looked at Josh; it was ironic they had ended up in the lofts for the same reason. "Trust me, I understand. No expectations, but I can show you the city sometime." Josh smiled broadly. "Can we take the elevator down?"

After the shower, now alone in the quietness of the apartment, Dean recalled the phone ringing earlier. He searched for the cell phone, which was in his long-forgotten gym shorts by the door. Two missed calls and one voicemail. He dialed the number and listened to the automated female voice tell him he had one new message.

"Dean, Todd here . . . Listen, um, I'm a dick. So much of a dick, in fact, that when Mom told me how glad she was we could make it and how happy she was we had each other in this crazy world, I broke down. I told her I'd treated you like shit and you left me with the house and everything we'd worked for. My emotions are crazy; I'm like fire and ice, and it was never because of you. She wants you to come, if you feel up to it. You can stay in another room by yourself. I asked her to cut you a check from my trust fund for half of everything I still have, it's only fair. I . . . I love you, and just wanted you to know I'm sorry. I've never said it, but I'm sorry. I hope you come. Let me know."

The apology felt great, really great, and for the first time Dean realized how wounded he still was. Now, with that apology and hearing the words from the source that Todd was what he was, Dean felt validated. He had tried to make the relationship work, and sometimes that's all you can do. He vowed to himself right then and there: no more fire and ice for him. He would never deal with someone whose emotions were hot and cold, open and then closed, for no apparent reason. Whoever would get his heart next would be 100 percent in need of it and vice versa. He headed to the bedroom joyous but exhausted; maybe he and Todd could be friends; at least he finally had closure. More interesting, though, was Josh; as Dean lay on the bed they had shared in his post-orgasmic bliss, he smelled their smells as he drifted into sleep.

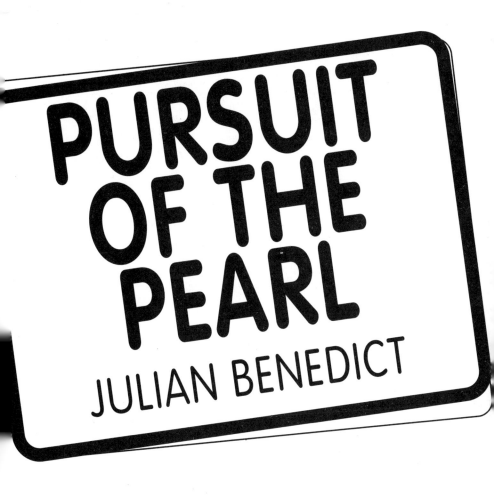

PURSUIT OF THE PEARL

JULIAN BENEDICT

I FIRST SAW HIM AT THE LEVANT PICNIC playing volleyball with people I presumed were company employees. Even though I'm the manager of human resources, I didn't know who he was.

My friends from my department didn't know who he was either, and I didn't ask anyone else for fear of looking too interested. He was beautiful; no one would argue with that. Even so, every conquest I ever had was exceptional. I'm particular. But this young man was . . . the only word I can think of is "extraordinary," and that doesn't begin to cover it. I glanced away from Cassie, my assistant, who was complaining about some company policy, and saw him but couldn't believe what I was seeing. This was a young man who could only exist in a sexual fantasy, although he was patently more than sexual.

I thought of a renowned verse from the Bible: *Who, when he had found one pearl of great price, went and sold all that he had and bought it.* Yes, I would do that. Everything I possessed was tawdry in comparison. I couldn't take my eyes off him until the game ended and he disappeared in the crowded park. Unable to find him again from where I was sitting, I used an excuse to go to my car and went searching for him like a common stalker, but he'd evidently left.

The rest of my day was ruined. I went back home, trying to resign myself to never seeing that agonizingly beautiful creature again, and resignation is almost impossible for me. I'm accustomed to getting what I want. I was wishing I had not seen him at all, but I knew if I lived to be a hundred, I would never forget him.

He could be anywhere by now; he might not even live in the city. What were the chances of ever seeing him again? Days later, I was still having tantalizing dreams of him, only to wake with an empty yearning. This was not only insane; it was humiliating.

After a while, the sharp edge wore off the tormenting obsession, leaving a painfully sweet memory almost too exquisite to be a reality, yet the experience had been so profound I would never be able to accept it as a meaningless incident.

On Friday, Colleen Burgess and I stopped off at the Lair for a few drinks after work. We often went there. Two years ago when she came to work at Levant, she made subtle advances that were nevertheless clear enough. She was hitting on me. Colleen is a lovely person and I'm sure that if I were inclined in that direction I would find her appealing, but needless to say, I am not.

I had become quite fond of her, and because she had value to me as a friend, I tactfully told her the truth about myself. She was surprised but accepting of it; we came to be more intimate friends than ever. I can't think of anything I cannot confide to her, and she has proven often enough that she feels the same way. These days there's only one thing I whine about when I've had a few drinks. It had been two months and I was still salivating over him to Colleen.

He was slender, his bones somewhat small for a male, sinewy in a mellow way, his skin a silky, honey tan. I remember how his white shorts, short and snug, looked almost snowy against the muscles of his thighs.

His thick amber locks glinted with dark gold highlights in the bright June sun; the tousled curls tumbled across his forehead and curled naturally around his ears. It brought to my mind the striking tresses of the marble sculptures of the young Greek gods, and with a warm rush I imagined him naked, assuming a casual stance, his countenance pensive, on a pedestal in the garden or great hall of a Greek palace.

He could have been Apollo or Dionysus, or better still, that beautiful Greek boy Antinous, lover of the Emperor Hadrian, who after the boy's untimely death had made him immortal, driven by his anomalous grief and bizarre obsession. But who in the hell was I to say that Hadrian's grief was anomalous or his obsession bizarre? Most of the world would never know what it was like to have a love like that, or how they would react if they lost it.

Yes, this could have been Antinous reborn: the melancholy eyes, the perfectly sculptured mouth, the full, succulent lower lip.

"You're doing it again, Troy," Colleen muttered over her scotch and water.

"Doing what?" I grumbled.

"You know what. Have you ever considered investing in a few sessions with a shrink? It might be worth your trouble."

"I'm not suffering from depression, Colleen. I just get lost in my thoughts sometimes."

"Not your larger-than-life sexual fantasy again? Damn, Troy, why the hell did you have to be gay? With your passion, you would have been the best lay I ever had," Colleen said, laughing.

"Fuckin-A, babe, I'd have screwed your ass off." She had nailed it. I was thinking about *him*. I wondered how long it would take for that vision to fade from my mind.

The CEO was throwing a pool party that weekend, the last week in August. I wasn't going, but that day in the bar Colleen changed my mind.

"There'll be a lot of good-looking hunks there," she said, "for both of us. And they'll be baring those glistening, tanned muscles. Doesn't that sound good?"

"What the hell, you've talked me into it," I conceded.

The big man's place was a palace on a few acres outside town, and it was worth attending his soirée just to see it. The pool was the biggest I'd ever seen, surrounded with gigantic tropical plants, fragrant flowers, and cascading waterfalls. It was spectacular. I'd heard the man was from old money. He couldn't have paid for this with even his yearly income.

There was food at hand everywhere and beautiful young Ganymedes in Speedos serving up drinks faster than you could slug them down.

"Now tell me you're not glad we came, Troy," she said with a giggle, already a little tipsy. We had climbed out of the pool and were stretched out in the sun on chaise lounges, drinking wine and nibbling canapés.

"Of course I'm glad, except that I can't seem to ditch that big daddy bear that keeps following me around," I grumbled, pulling my knit shirt down over my head. He was smirking at me from a raft in the pool as I spoke.

"What do you mean, Troy? That guy's gorgeous," Colleen said. "I wish he'd be interested in me."

"So do I, sweetie," I said. "He's not my type, and you know it."

"Yeah, you're still hung up on that pretty little thing you saw at the company picnic."

"I've given up on that, but yes, that has always been the look that attracted me, except that one was one of a kind. I wish you had seen him."

"Shit, me too," Colleen griped. "Then I wouldn't have to hear ad nauseum how divinely gorgeous he was."

"OK, asshole, I won't say another word about him."

"Don't call me asshole, shithead." She howled with laughter as she whacked me with a rubber flipper she'd picked up from the wet flagstones.

"Oh, God," I whispered with a gasp. I couldn't breathe.

Colleen was staring at me wide-eyed. "I didn't hit you that hard," she said, then, "Troy, what's wrong?"

"It's him." My voice sounded like a croak.

Colleen followed my line of vision to the celestial being who was talking quietly to one of the waiters as though giving him some menial instruction.

"Shit-fire, Troy. Is that who you've been brooding over all this time? I wish I'd known."

"What do you mean?" I said, never taking my eyes from him.

"I know him, Troy. That's our big boss's son, his only son, I might add. I met him one day when he was in the building. He was so eye-catching that I asked Julia—you know, the big man's secretary—who he was and she introduced me to him. He's a real sweetheart."

"You're telling me!" With the exception of my pounding heart I had regained a measure of my composure, or at least I had until a shapely brunette in a leopard-print bikini walked up and took his arm.

"There you are," she crooned. "I've been looking all over for you."

At my pathetic expression Colleen laughed and said, "Don't worry, Romeo, that little femme fatale doesn't have a chance with him; no woman does. Julia told me it's Chancellor's painful secret that his son has no interest in the ladies whatsoever. The big man keeps flaunting them in the kid's face with desperate hope, but David is kind to them only to pacify his father."

"Do you know? Does he have someone?" I was almost afraid to ask.

"I asked Julia that too, if there was someone in the company, but she said she was sure not. Any man interested in the old guy's son would no doubt find himself instantly unemployed."

Like I would give a damn about that job if I could have him, I thought. *Pearl of great price.* I had often considered the approach I would take on the off chance that I ever found him.

"Well, dammit, Colleen, are you going to introduce me or not?" He had a look of innocence about him that I knew how to approach.

"I'm not sure I want to be responsible for subjecting that child to you, Troy." It was intended to be a joke, but it wasn't funny.

"Child? How old is he?"

"Well, he's a sophomore at Lamar U, but his father has kept him on a pretty tight leash."

"Maybe it's time he broke free." I was intently watching the boy being pleasant to the girl who was hanging on his arm.

"Troy, I know you. I've seen you in action," Colleen grumbled. "I don't want you hurting this boy."

"It's never my intent to hurt anyone, Colleen, but believe me, in this case you don't know me at all. This is the one," I mumbled under my breath. "I'll have him or die for it."

"And then?"

"There's no 'and then,' Colleen. I make him mine and that's the end of it."

"I almost believe you."

"Have I ever lied to you? Believe me, Colleen. I'm in love."

"David," she yelled, and the boy turned.

"Colleen," he exclaimed, with a melting smile that made my stomach churn.

"My friend here wants to meet you," she said, with an abandon that implied it was totally in my hands, sink or swim.

I had no intention of sinking. While his attention was on Colleen, his expression was sweet, courteous.

"David, this is my friend Troy Hagen."

When those crystal green eyes met mine there was an instant arrest. I recovered first, and with a quiescent smile I winked at him. It was subtle yet shameless flirting. In his innocence he may have missed it, but his girlfriend didn't. She was glaring at me.

"My pleasure," David murmured, unable to disengage his eyes. He was blushing; not only had he not missed it, he liked it.

"You are incredible," I said softly, as though we were the only two people in the world. He blushed more deeply, unable to look away. My eyes narrowed, and I didn't even try to hide my wanton desire. If the chemistry had not been there, he could easily have looked away. I'm sure he'd had many occasions to do that. But the tension was volatile.

"I'd love to get to know you, David," I said, with genuine humility. "Away from here, someplace quiet?" He seemed to be tongue-tied as he stood there staring at me. "That is, if you would be interested?"

His lady friend was tugging on his arm and murmuring something unintelligible. He jerked his arm away—I think, unconsciously—and angry, she flounced off unnoticed.

"When?" he said, finally. It was a whisper.

Seize the moment, I thought. "How about now?" I was pushing my luck but might as well go for broke.

"I was about to leave the party anyway. I told Father I was going back to the dorm." His voice was timid yet sultry.

In his little Ferrari, he followed me to a piano bar I frequent. When he pulled in next to my car and opened his door I caught his hand and pulled him into my arms. I'd never wanted anything so badly in my life, and he was trembling. My lips instantly covered that delectable mouth and I was eating him. He was making enchanting little whimpering sounds that had me in flames. Then, struggling, he pushed himself away. "Too fast," he murmured, gasping, his voice hoarse with emotion.

"That's all right, baby. Let's go inside."

After we sat down in a plush booth in a dark corner, I reached across the table and took his hand. "David, you're calling the shots from now on, sweetheart. But please forgive me that one kiss!"

He smiled and it was angelic. "That's all right," he said. "I wanted it."

We talked for hours, and he was amazed that I wanted to know everything about him, that I hung on his every word. And the more he told me about himself, the more in love I was. He was a sensitive and naturally affectionate person, intelligent and spiritual. He was aware of who he was, had been since early high school, but told me timidly that he had never had a relationship. He had tried with girls several times to please his father, but it was painfully difficult. "My father can't know about this," he said, with a frown that I wanted to kiss away. "He would be very angry."

I wasn't the least afraid of his father. Nevertheless, I didn't want David to be subjected to a moment's stress because of me. We were together every evening after that day but took extreme care. Even so, I had the feeling we were being watched. The weather was usually beautiful and we spent time in the parks and took drives out into the country. I never thought I'd ever spend this much time wooing anyone, but this exquisite boy was the only one I'd ever found who was worth whatever effort and patience was required.

We had heavy petting sessions in my car on some remote country road, and we would be locked in long, lingering, deep kisses until our mouths were chafed. We were both so on fire it was merciless torment, but in his innocence he had the fear and modesty of a child and I wasn't going to push him. Yesterday he became so aroused as I was kissing him that he was on the crest of an orgasm. He tried to pull away, but I held on tight. "Let it go, baby," I whispered as I kissed and caressed, and he couldn't stop. He was climaxing, stiffening and crying out with little animal sounds as I held him to me, savoring him, crooning to him. I felt a little remorseful about it later because afterward he was so embarrassed.

Today I got an e-mail from Julia that Chancellor wanted to see me in his office this afternoon. As if I didn't know what the hell that was all about. I had been expecting it.

From his gigantic teakwood desk he sat staring at me as if I were some new breed of vermin. He didn't offer me a chair. Not that I would have taken one anyway. "Troy Hagen, manager of human resources, it says here." He had a manila folder open in front of him. "I'll get right to the point. You're spending time with my son every day, away from the public eye. What's going on?" He was trying to glare me down.

"Why are you asking me a question you already know the answer to?" I said, glaring back at him.

"So you don't even deny it. But I know my son, Hagen. You haven't scored yet. Now this is how it's going to be. You will not see him again; you will not even tell him why. You will not communicate with him in any way. If you do, I will know and you will find yourself unemployed within the week. The only reason I'm not firing you today is because it's going to take a little time to replace you. Do we understand each other?"

"I understand you perfectly," I said. I was quite sure he didn't understand me at all.

I went back to my office, typed up my resignation, put it in a company envelope, and dropped it in the outbox. On second thought, I took it back. I shouldn't show my hand until I knew exactly what I was going to do.

I was damn sure not going to give David up, not even if the bastard put a hit out on me . . . which he very well might do. I have money. I'm not extremely wealthy, but I am secure; I don't have to work.

For a while I communicated with David only via e-mail. I asked if he had a female friend he could trust, and his response was to mail me the address of Johanna Koontz, who lived in a large apartment house where I had to punch in the number and wait to be buzzed in. It was perfect.

He rushed into my arms the instant I entered. "I can't bear to be away from you," he murmured, covering me with kisses.

"Nor I you, my precious, but we have to talk."

"I can't let my father fire you, Troy. I'll go to him, try to make him understand."

"I think you'd be wasting your time, sweetheart. I was surprised when I got a good look at him. He looks nothing like you."

"Oh, no, Troy, he couldn't. He married my mother when I was ten."

I thought for a moment my heart was going to stop. "David, are you telling me that Chancellor is your stepfather?"

"Well, yes, but he's always been very good to me. He really loves me, Troy," David said, with the guilelessness of an innocent.

"When did he and your mother divorce?"

"When I was thirteen. I thought everything was fine; it happened very suddenly. I never did know why."

"It seems odd to me that you would go with your stepfather rather than your mother."

"My father insisted on it. He said I'd be happier here, not uprooted from my home and my friends."

"And that was all right with your mother?"

David frowned. "At first it wasn't, but he offered her a large settlement."

So Chancellor had bought the bitch off. As hard as it was for David to find fault with anyone, I could see that he was hurt by that.

"Baby, how does your father treat you?"

"He would do anything for me, Troy. He's always giving me expensive gifts without my even asking. My Ferrari was one of them. I wish he wouldn't do that."

"Tell me, baby, how does he act around you?"

"He's nothing like people would think. He's warm and affectionate, always hugging me, I guess like a real father would."

"David, has he ever done anything inappropriate with you?"

"Oh, no! Well . . . uh, no."

There was something he questioned. I could see it in his eyes.

I dropped my resignation in the outbox the next morning. Two hours later I was called into Chancellor's office.

"Hagen, you just made the biggest fucking mistake of your life. You think I'm going to roll over and let you have my son? You're a fool; you'll die first."

"I anticipated as much," I said calmly. "Therefore I came prepared." Now came the big bluff.

"I'll make a lurid story short. You're not David's father. You went apeshit over him the first time you saw him when he was ten. You married his mother to get next to him. She found out three years later that you were gay when she busted you with a lover. But you couldn't lose David in the divorce, so you bought her off. You have no legal right to him."

I thought the bastard was going to have a stroke. He rose up behind the desk, his fists clenched, his face a deep wine color. He was trembling.

"I'll kill you," he muttered.

"I believe you. I anticipated that as well. I put a letter in my safety deposit box explaining everything and naming you in case anything happens to me. My lawyer has the key."

"Now . . . David loves you. He's going to come to you to plead his case, to try to make you understand. You are going to be kind and supportive to him if you don't want me to tell him the truth about you. After all, Chancellor, you don't want to burn your bridges. You never know, David may tire of me and go back home to his dad someday."

"You son of a bitch!"

◆

MY PRICELESS PEARL WAS SAFELY AT HOME WITH ME IN MY BED, in my arms. I did it, and I'd never known it possible to be this happy. "Are you all right, precious?" I crooned, kissing his forehead.

"I think I'm dreaming," he murmured. "Father was so good about it all. He cried and hugged me and said that all he ever wanted was for me to be happy."

"And are you?"

"That all depends. Are you going to keep me?"

"I would die before I'd ever let you go," I whispered, pulling him up to me. My mouth went down on his and I was promptly overcome with an excruciating desire that sparked and spread through David like wildfire.

"Those clothes are coming off," I muttered. "I can't wait any longer." I was ripping at them and he was helping me, making those delightful little mewling noises, shivering against me. In an instant I was stripped, holding his luscious body to mine. I could feel him hard and hot against my belly, and my cock's agony of waiting was almost over. I was afraid I would erupt prematurely like a horny teenager.

"Take me, Troy," he said in my ear, his voice raucous with need.

"Oh god, baby, I want that so much. Are you sure?"

"I've never been more certain of anything," he whispered, his body shuddering.

With all the skill and gentleness I possessed I lubricated him, my fingers stroking lingeringly that little gland inside him until he was groaning . . . pleading. When I finally went into my virgin baby there was little pain, but I'd never been so aroused and I had to go in slowly to keep from erupting before bringing him to an intense, protracted orgasm. I prolonged it for a deliciously long time, and when he finally crested he cried out, his body arching, and I buried deep in him, kneading his sweet cock in my hand, feeling his fiery nectar ejaculate into my palm as my orgasm consumed me in violent shudders and I released into him.

"I have experienced the ultimate ecstasy, my treasure," I whispered, holding him close. "Now I can die happy."

"Not yet you can't," he said, laughing softly. "You've created a satyr, my love, and I'm going to be insatiable."

BAGGED

JAKE RICH

WHEN A COUPLE OF THE TRAINERS AT THE BOXING GYM mentioned hanging out after closing time one Friday night, I thought I'd died and gone to heaven. I can't get enough of that place; either I'm at work or working out at the L St. Ring. Hell, I get high just walking in there.

The sounds hit me first. There's the timer, buzzing out the three-minute round, thirty-second warning, and one-minute rest. Then there's the loud quick grunts keeping time with punch combinations on the heavy bags, the rhythmic three-beat of the speed bags, and the sound of air sliced to bits with jump ropes. And that's nothing compared to what you see.

First thing I saw was a heavy bag swinging on a chain from the ceiling. Then Jackson grabbed it with a bear hug and held it so another obvious newbie could try out the one-two combination.

"Keep your chin in, your elbows in. One. Two. See? That's better. One, two, one, two. That's it. Keep moving around the bag."

He let go of the bag and gave it a small push, so it had just a little swing to it. Then he saw me trying to figure out what the hell I was even doing there. The whole place was jumping, and I just stood in the middle of it, looking lost. The walls, floor, and air were vibrating, hands punching and feet moving and arms flying. Sweat dripped from everyone, and blood from a connecting punch to the nose splattered to the floor of the ring.

"Who'd you be?" Jackson asked, walking over to me.

"Phil. I'm new to here."

"Yea, you're new to here alright. You got Mexican wraps and gloves? Get changed, then come get me. I'll wrap your hands for you."

"Cool," I managed to say. "Thanks."

My head was already speeding like a freight train as I changed from jeans and boots to sweats and sneakers. Fuck, this guy's biceps were bigger than my head, for Christ's sake. How the hell did he get arms like that? I'd have bet his cock was just as thick. Damn, shit damn. He hadn't even said his name.

"Fuck me hard, please, Sir. And by the way, what's your name, Sir?" ran through my brain and down to my dick.

My nerves were live wires as I looked around for the hunk with no name. He was in the ring, working mitts with a young kid, couldn't have been more than ten years old. The round had just started, so I stood near the ropes and watched. I didn't really know what was going on, and I didn't really care. I just wanted to watch this hot guy move around the ring.

He was easy on the kid but worked him hard enough to sweat

some. The buzzer warned thirty seconds to go, and the kid barely made it to the one-minute rest. They touched mitt to glove and stepped between the ropes and out of the ring.

"Hey, Phil, got your wraps?"

I nodded and followed him over to a corner that was quiet, compared to the rest of the place.

"OK. First thing is to unroll and find the thumb hook."

"Why is it so long?" I asked, surprised by how much of it I unwound.

"Because you're going to need all the knuckle protection you can get. Now grab it and wrap it around and over the back of your hand like this."

Already I was confused and frustrated. Wrap this here, and then around there, and through that and back around here again. And do the same thing, only opposite, for your other hand. Shit.

"Can you slow down there ah . . . what's your name again?"

"Jackson. Jackson's my name."

"Glad to meet you, Jackson. So how'd you get biceps like that?" I asked as I unwrapped and rewrapped my right hand three times.

"Fried chicken."

"What? No, seriously, how'd you get your arms so big? I've always wanted huge biceps, but I can't ever make it happen."

"Fried chicken," he said again, and laughed.

Yeah, that's Jackson for you, always joking. But only half joking, 'cause when he's not training for a fight, he's sitting on the edge of the ring knocking back Micky D's burgers and fries for lunch. Every day.

◆

I'M HAPPY FOR THE INVITE, especially since I don't know the guys the way I'd like to. It's only been six months since I joined. Damn, six months, and I still don't have a clue how to throw a half-ass jab, much less a respectable one.

My first time on the speed bag, I hit it so hard I popped the thing. That's how I got the name "Freak" tagged on me. They took a liking to me right then and there. They rank on you all the time, if they like you. Pretty quick I figured I'd be one of the boys, especially with Jackson yelling out "Freak" whenever I walk in the place, and the whole time I'm there too. He's yelling out "Freak" and then laughing, making sure everybody hears him above the noise and hip-hop music.

I haven't even mentioned TJ yet. He's the other trainer that gets me hard. Totally the opposite of Jackson. More on the quiet side; he doesn't like loads of attention. For some reason, just about everything anybody says to him makes him blush. I'm always real careful about not getting caught looking at his package. Not sure if he'd just blush or punch me out. Probably both. Hard as I try not to, I end up staring right at it, looking and drooling and hoping that someday soon he'll take me up the ass.

He's always asking me what I'm doing over the weekend. He's single and a little lonely, like me. His fiancée broke up with him after he had another run-in with the law. Both he and Jackson have that in common; spending more than a night or two in the jailhouse. Jackson did a couple of years for a drug deal. TJ doesn't ever say what he was in for, and I figure it makes sense not to be asking him about it.

"What are you up to, Phil?" TJ said, walking over to me during a minute rest. "Anything good going on?"

"Yeah, I'm going to a party tomorrow night," I said.

"A birthday party?"

"Nope, this is no birthday party; it's a different kind of party," I said. "You might be interested in going . . . ah well, maybe." I'm thinking, what the hell am I doing inviting him along to Men's Leather Night? Am I fucking crazy?

"Knowing you, it's got to be something freaky."

The buzzer goes off, and I laughed as the place exploded with noise again. I got into stance for my next punch, then cocked my head toward him.

"Takes one to know one," I smirked, then threw three right hooks in a row.

His face turned red and he walked off toward the ring. I knew he would be after me to do mitts with him now.

He finished three rounds with a middle-aged guy, who's probably just a couple of years younger than me, and in better shape. Then he came looking for me, but I did my best to hide behind one of the heavy bags.

"Phil!" TJ yelled in my direction. "Let's go; you're up next."

Damn it, why hadn't I left before now? I already did three rounds on the speed bag, five rounds on the heavy bag, plus abs, leg work, and some shadowboxing. I'm beat and ready to crash.

"Nah, thanks but no thanks, TJ. I'm done for the day."

I preferred doing mitts with him instead of Jackson. TJ will work with you. He knows just how far he can push you and takes you just past that. Jackson flat-out pushes you over a cliff and laughs the whole time he's doing it.

"Phil. Let's go!"

Fuck. Ring time for me is like being worked over with a cat-o'-nine-tails. I fucking hate it while it's happening. But damn, it sure feels good when it's over.

"Alright, alright. Give me a second here."

I walked over to the ring, hopped up, and then awkwardly slid through the ropes. I ran my gloved hand across my forehead, wiping away sweat that's just about to fall into my eyes.

"Ready? Remember; put your whole body into it. Don't just punch out from your waist, follow it through with your shoulder, back, and legs. OK?"

I nodded my head yes and placed my hands and feet. TJ always started out with a straight jab; that's the hardest throw for me. Then he called out punch combos: one-two-five, two-four-two, three-four-one. I get confused as to which hand is which and which positions to use. That's nothing new. I always get confused, which always pisses me off. He moved me around the ring at a decent pace. I was getting better at combos, now that I knew my right from my left. The warning buzzer went off. Fuck, I really hated this part. For the last thirty seconds, TJ always wanted really fast four-fives. Do you know how long thirty seconds is, throwing nothing but four-fives?

"Go another round?" TJ asked as the one-minute rest starts.

"Yeah, sure," I said, breathing heavily.

A little over two minutes into the next round, I was toast. Got rubber for arms and couldn't catch my breath. I stopped, then doubled over, trying to force air down my lungs.

"You're not breathing right," TJ said. "Throw your punch breathing out, then right away breathe *in,* not out again. You're holding your breath. Come on, let's go. You got thirty seconds left on the clock."

I wasn't moving, just sucking down air.

"Phil, don't make me do mouth-to-mouth on you."

Still bent over, I turned my head and looked up at him.

"Yeah, you wish," I said, raising my eyebrows and laughing between gulps of air.

There was just no way I could do another round, and TJ didn't even ask. He did throw some encouraging words my way, which I thanked him for, and we touched mitt to glove. I pushed on the rope and bent down. I swung my leg out over the rope, trying to climb out of the ring. TJ opened the ropes wider for me, and I was moving through and then I planted face first, right into TJ's crotch. It happened so fast and was over so fast, I wasn't sure if it really happened. It did though, 'cause he moved in, just far enough for me get a good eyeful and a good whiff too. I sucked in the scent of his sweaty balls; it was just one gulp of air, but it was enough to get to me.

He didn't say anything, and I didn't either. I headed off to change, wondering what was going on with TJ. Maybe I really would get pounded by him. I was getting hard, and taking off my sweats didn't help any. I couldn't stop from giving my cock a couple of good spanks and then hurry up getting dressed. I already knew I'd be jerking off as soon as I got home.

I usually said goodbye before I left, so I walked out of the changing room to find TJ and Jackson. They were hanging out right around the corner, and I just about crashed into them.

"We're thinking of closing early tonight. John's not here, so he won't know anything different anyway," TJ said. "Give us half an hour tops and we'll head over to the Happy Swallow for a couple of beers."

"Ah, well, I don't know . . . sure, why not, I can hang out for a couple of hours. I'll just wait for you guys up front."

Holy fuck. First a face full of TJ, then a beer invite. Today sure went from shitty to awesome real fast. I'd been here before when they closed early because the owner had gone home. But I'd never been asked to stick around afterward.

I was punching and ducking away from my window reflection at the front desk, trying to calm my nerves. TJ was laughing in the back while Jackson was yelling about something. TJ stopped laughing; he was yelling back at Jackson. I couldn't hear what all the hollering was about, but it sounded bad. I was thinking, *What the fuck; I was sitting here waiting for these two and they started a fight.* Should I just leave or go back there? And do what? Break up a fight between a pro and semi-pro boxer? Yeah, right.

The shouting was still going on, so I decide to head home. I shoved the crash bar and banged my head on the door. It didn't open. I shoved it harder, thinking it was just stuck, and still nothing. Are you kidding me? I was locked inside the gym. Great. I rattled the door some, expecting nothing and getting nothing. Now what? Only thing I could do was find TJ and Jackson.

I walked back to the ring room. Most of the lights were off, and everything was kind of spooky. The yelling wasn't as loud now; I was hoping they'd calmed down enough we could still go for that beer.

"Hey guys, what's up? Can we go get a beer now? Or at least unlock the door so I can get out of here?" I yelled out as I made my way through. I was a bit disoriented walking in the low light.

"You ain't going nowhere." I heard Jackson's voice in front of me and to the right.

"Hey, Jackson! What the fuck is going on, man? Why you two yelling?"

"We're not yelling; we're just having loud conversation . . . about you, Freak."

"What about me?"

"Well, see, Jackson wants to do you first," TJ said. "And I think I should do you first."

"Do? Do what?" I asked, as I damn near shit my pants and got a hard on at the same time.

"Oh, yeah, like you don't know what TJ means," Jackson said. "TJ, let's show Freak here what you yelling about."

The lights turned on, and a hand gripped the back of my neck and shoved me to the floor. "Show us how many pushups you can really do," TJ said.

I scrabbled into position and started pumping them out fast. Jackson had his foot hovering above my ass, and pushed me down whenever I broke form. I didn't count how many I was doing, but my arms were shaking real bad and I knew I would collapse soon.

"Working hard, are ya', Phil? It's about time you did," Jackson said, pushing me to the floor, and keeping me there with his foot. I was crumpled up in a heap, my arms still quivering. I told myself to just go with this, don't think about it, just go along for the ride.

"Don't you think so, Freak?" Jackson said, real loud this time.

"You think we don't see you hiding in the bag corner, but we do," Jackson said. "I see you all the time hiding back there."

"Now get up!" Jackson grabbed the back of my belt and pulled me up to my feet.

He still had a good hold on me when he reached around to the front and unbuckled my belt. TJ stepped in and pushed my jeans and boxers down to my knees. It was pretty obvious to all of us I was really enjoying TJ and Jackson's attention.

"Look at that! What you got going on there, Freak?" Jackson said, laughing.

I felt heat rising up my face, and I knew I was blushing. TJ laughed, and his face turned beet red too. Maybe it was my imagination, but his sweats seemed to be bulging out more than usual.

"It's time we see just how much you got, Freak." Jackson tugged at my T-shirt. I lifted my arms up and he pulled my shirt off. "TJ, help him out of his pants there."

I got pushed back down to the floor, and TJ pulled off my boots and jeans. Now I was totally naked, with a boner. All I could think was, *I hope they plow my ass but good.* I wanted it so bad it hurt.

TJ picked up a pair of wraps and roughly taped up my hands. Keeping his eyes locked on mine, he pulled me up into the ring, where Jackson was waiting.

"You're bragging about fighting at Golden Gloves next year. By then you might get lucky and not get killed in the first round," Jackson said. "You're lazy. You're out of shape. You have no discipline. You can work a lot harder than you do, and starting right now that's what you're going to do."

I was in the center of the ring, following orders: round after round of jumping jacks, crunches, running in place, sidestep running, medicine ball work. Over to the speed bag, back into the ring. Two rounds of foot work, then over to the double end bag for three rounds. I was worn out; I was crashing and my dick was going soft.

"Please, guys. Can we stop now? Please?"

"You stop when we say you stop," Jackson said. "Next three rounds you're doing inch worm."

I fucking hated doing the inchworm. But sticking my ass in the air in front of TJ and Jackson is hot as hell. When I bent over, Jackson took a swipe at my ass with a doubled-up jump rope. The sting brought up more heat, and beads of sweat dropped to the floor. My dick got hard again.

"Hey, TJ! Look what Freak's up to," Jackson said. "You really like getting your ass beat, don't you, Freak? Bend over and grab your ankles, boy."

Again, I did what I was told. I closed my eyes, held my breath, and waited. And waited some more. Fuck, what the shit was going on? Would somebody please pound my ass, already!

I heard some noise, so I opened my eyes. I watched TJ give Jackson a blow job upside down. I could hardly keep from grabbing my dick and jerking off. I was whimpering to myself. Or at least I thought I was.

"What's the matter, Freak Man, you got blue balls?" Jackson said, pulling out of TJ's mouth. "You want my junk, Freak Man?"

"He's been checking out my junk since his first day here," TJ said.

"Is that right?" Jackson said, laughing. "If you want it that bad, then worm your ass over here."

I dropped to the floor, embarrassed that TJ knew I'd been staring at his package all this time. I worked my way over, ending up on my stomach at Jackson's feet.

"Pick him up, TJ, and sling him over the ropes."

TJ picked me up and damn near threw me over his shoulder, then put me inside the ring. He brought me to a corner, bent me over, and told me to wrap my arms around the corner cushion. I did as he said. My arms and legs were shaking. I think it was mostly because I was excited, that and muscle fatigue too. I concentrated on stopping or at least slowing down my jitters. I leaned my head into the cushion, and that gave me some relief.

I heard TJ spit into his hands, just as the three-minute buzzer went off. Without a word, he found my hole and pushed his cock through. Something close to a scream came out of me, and it wouldn't stop.

"Fuck! Why you screaming like that? Shut the fuck up or I'll fucking shut you up!" Jackson yelled.

I bit down hard on my lip. TJ banged me so fucking hard my head crashed into the cushion every second or so. He kept pumping for the whole round. He pulled out for the one-minute rest, and I saw Jackson out of the corner of my eye.

Jackson jumped into the ring, doing his usual footwork waiting for the next round to start.

"Get ready, Freak, 'cause here I come."

He spat on my hole, then pulled me open and spat inside. He slid right in and laughed as he pounded me hard. I tasted blood as my teeth cut through my lip. I held on with one hand, grabbed my cock with the other, and yanked off, spraying the cushion and my arm.

"Figures you couldn't last two rounds, Freak," Jackson said. "I got at least two more rounds left in me. How many more you got, TJ?"

"You're not beating me out, Jackson. If you got two more rounds to go, then I got three."

I licked the blood from my lip and got ready to go the distance.

LODESTAR

MARK WILDYR

A PENETRATING CHILL PULLED ME FROM MY SLEEP as the distant rumble of thunder and ghostly flashes broke the half-light of dawn. I abandoned the bedroll to find my two companions scanning the Little Humps, a line of low hills to the west of us.

"Rain?" I asked, scratching my bum where a rock had rendered it sore.

"Ain't thunder," Hap Auslander replied. "Somebody gittin' the shit stomped outa 'em."

"Military guns. Big ones," Henry Nettles added. "They's a Injun town over yonder."

Hap tied his bedroll on Speckles, the Appaloosa he rode. "Best be gittin' a move on. Keep a sharp eye out. Any stragglers is apt ta be tetchy."

We took the trail in single file, with me bringing up the rear. We were half a day on the path before Henry Nettles, who had the lead, hauled up and pointed west.

"By, God, it's the troopers that done it!" Hap shouted as a row of horsemen appeared on the horizon. We waited silently while the blue line approached. As the riders began to pass, a man broke ranks and rode over to us. Two others fell in behind him. The fella in front, a runty man with gold all over his hat and on his shoulders, pulled up and gave us the once over.

"Major Elijah Raintree, commander of the Southfork Militia at your service. Who might you be?"

"Hap Auslander of St. Jo. This here's Henry Nettles outa Independence. The young'un's Jim Tobar, a eastern man. We be bound fer Fort Johnson. You fellers wallop 'em good?"

"Old White Hair's outfit won't give no more problems."

"White Hair?" Nettles asked in surprise. "White Hair wuz under paint?"

The major's eyes went flat. "They're all under paint, far's we're concerned. The whole countryside's on fire."

The major favored us with a personal account of his heroic attack on the red heathens while his column of two hundred or so blue-clad soldiers and four wheel-mounted guns passed, leaving a broad trail on the prairie flats. In grandiose words rasping out of a thin, bony breast, he proclaimed that particular brand of murders, rapists, and thieves finished. His parting words sent a chill through my heart and left me wondering what this popinjay did for a living when he was not murdering human beings.

"Should you encounter any survivors, you have my authority to dispatch them forthwith. I want no living heathens left between the Bent Fork and Elk Mountain Rivers."

Henry Nettles waited until the major and his aides were out of earshot. "Hell, ol' White Hair wuzn't no war chief. Thet's why them bluebellies had sech a easy time a it."

"A Injun's a Injun, Nettles. Wouldn't go 'round takin' the red man's side, I wuz you," Auslander cautioned. "Let's be on our way."

As we crossed the trampled earth marking the column's passing, Henry Nettles's head wobbled on his thin, wrinkled neck. Auslander, a thick, squat man with grizzled hair and beard, gave me the nasty eye, making me wonder once again why I was in the company of these men. I had never contemplated the frontier until events conspired to place me here.

◆

TOO YOUNG TO FIGHT IN THE WAR BETWEEN THE STATES, I watched helplessly as that bloody conflict destroyed my family. It killed my brother outright and maimed my father into a grave two long years coming. My Aunt Bella, a well-settled widow, took me in when the fever carried off Mom. Perversely, life grew easier, but Providence has a fine set of scales and knows how to balance them. I would likely have married Mistress Penelope Greenstem, to my eternal regret, had not her younger brother, John, pursued me into the hayloft where we learned that males can pleasure one another without benefit of the opposite gender. In time, we were discovered with John's rod firmly planted in my fundament. Yet I was proclaimed the pederast—one of Satan's foulest demons. Aunt Bella hastily sent me on my way with a small packet of coins, the law and the rector of the Puritan Church dusting my heels. That was near onto a twelve-month past.

The fabled Santa Fe Trail beckoned until a chance encounter with skinny-shanked, pot-bellied Henry Nettles inclined me toward accompanying him to Fort Johnson, where opportunities abounded for industrious young men. Twice my twenty years, Nettles was not totally disagreeable, although his manners and morals required a smidgen of understanding. But who was I to complain about morals? It is not clear why he craved my company since my obvious assets were limited to a few silver and copper discs in my pockets, an excellent repeating rifle, and Nellie, my good mare.

A week out of Independence, Hap Auslander, an old associate of Nettles, joined us on the trail. I neither liked nor trusted this grum, battle-hammed ruffian. To make matters worse, Nettles coarsened under his influence. The deeper we penetrated the plains, the more uneasy I became, especially when Auslander cast an ugly, speculating glance my way, leaving me to wonder if I trailed the foul stench of sodomy in my wake.

◆

TWO HOURS DOWN THE TRAIL, Nettles hauled his horse to a stop. The hair on my neck bristled. Even to my tenderfoot eyes, the pony grazing on the trail ahead was an Indian horse. Small, spotted, and haltered with buffalo hide, it had a bright blanket tied across its back and a vivid red hand painted on one rump. Rifle in hand, Nettles reined to the right as Auslander continued up the trail, leaving the left to me. My mouth went dry as we crept through belly-high grass. My heart tumbled into my bowels when Nellie broke the pinto's trail. Something lay on the ground. I dismounted and crept forward. An Indian lay face down, his head obscured by long black hair. I judged him to be tall and slender yet well-built. Suddenly, someone shoved me roughly aside. I struggled to bring my rifle around.

"Hold it!" Hap snarled, kneeling beside the body. "I ain't no red devil."

"Shit, Hap!" I gasped, indulging in a rare vulgarity. "Give a body some warning."

"A man give warnin' in this country, he's apt ta meet 'is maker." He turned the body over, drawing a gasp from both of us. "This heathen's still breathin'."

The Indian was young and comely. I would have thought him a beautiful woman, but for the heavy chest muscles and flat, ribbed belly. His manhood was scarcely concealed by a loincloth. The only other articles of clothing were short deerskin moccasins. A bloody bruise marred the right side of his broad forehead.

"Hellfire and damnation!" Nettles exclaimed as he joined us. "He alive?"

"Yep," Auslander replied, his piggish eyes sweeping the inert form. My examination was little better. I was seized by the same emotion as when John first exposed himself to me.

"Lordy! He's purty as a woman!" Nettles chortled.

Auslander's stubby fingers prodded the youth's breast. One finger rested on a dark brown aureole. "Help me git 'im on that pinto."

"Ain't ya gonna scalp 'im?" Nettles asked as they bound the unconscious Indian and slung him belly down on his pony. Auslander made no reply.

We traveled perhaps another hour before a grove of trees in the distance signaled water. Hap led the pinto to a shallow pool and shoved the Indian over the side. He hit the water on his back and sat up without uttering a sound.

"Playin' possum, ya fuckin' whoreson! I oughta take yer scalp right now!"

The bronzed youth sitting in a foot of water held his tongue.

"He don't talk 'merican, Hap," Nettles opined.

Auslander waded into the water and grabbed a handful of the Indian's hair, placing his knife to the scalp. "Ya unnerstand this?"

The young man sat absolutely motionless. Overcoming his blood-lust, Hap hauled his prisoner onto the bank. The bound Indian fell against a tree, opening the cut on his forehead. I rushed forward and pulled him upright, feeling the strength in the muscles beneath my hands. As I worked to staunch the flow of blood, my rod began to harden.

"How come we ain't killin' 'im?" The longer Henry Nettles was around Hap Auslander, the more offensive he became. Only a few hours back, he was concerned by the attack on White Hair's camp. Now he seemed anxious to kill one of the chief's people.

"I aim ta take 'is crown, Henry. And I'm gonna make a travelin' bag outa that purty hide, too. But I got plans fer 'im first. Like you said yerself, he looks womanly."

"Thet I did," Nettles crowed. "A purty woman wuz whut I sed. We gonna leap 'im, Hap?"

"I kinda fancy that mouth."

Revolted by the idea of these gross men touching a helpless man, I spoke up. "That mouth has teeth. You're apt to lose part of your anatomy."

"I do, he be dead."

I looked down at my patient. My hand still held a tattered rag against his forehead. My leg touched his shoulder. "He figures he's that anyway."

"Meybe I'll slit 'is throat first."

I shrugged with feigned calmness. "Thrumming cadavers in any orifice doesn't appeal to me."

"Cadavers? Orifice? Whut kinda Yankee doodle dandy is ya? Keep it up, I'm apt to figger on some white meat with the dark."

"You better kill me first."

Auslander smiled nastily. "Kinda goes without sayin', don't it?"

Nettles stepped in before things deteriorated further, declaring he wasn't having a cold cap tonight, Indians or no Indians. He wanted hot food, even if it was the death of him. The fire he laid cooked victuals but provided scant protection from the elements.

I spread my blankets on the far side of a little rise in the glen to put distance between me and a probable rape. Wrapped in my blankets, I peered over the hillock and recoiled. Auslander had laid the Indian directly on the other side; I stared into his black eyes from a distance of less than two feet. Unsettled, I lay back and closed my eyes. I do not know how long I slept before a persistent hiss woke me. Cautiously, I lifted my head. A stray shaft of moonlight reflected in the Indian's eyes.

"Help me, and I will lie with you," he whispered.

My mouth was open in shock when Auslander's voice called out, "Whut's goin' on?" The Indian immediately uttered something in his own tongue.

"He's a prayin'," Nettles ventured.

Auslander moved on his prisoner. There was the sound of a struggle, harsh blows on naked flesh. The Indian began to chant.

"Ya miserable bastid," Hap cursed. "Whut's he doin' that fer?"

Nettles cackled. "'At's 'is death song, Hap. He's tellin' ya ya'll have ta kill 'im 'fore ya kin fuck 'im."

The Indian's chant faltered as Auslander struck him repeatedly. Without thinking, I rose and rushed through the darkness, butting into the bully with a loud grunt. Nettles intervened before the enraged man assaulted me.

"Damnation, Hap. The kid wuz comin' ta help and tripped. Didn't mean no harm. Let's git some sleep. Ya kin cover the Injun later. Better in the daylight anyways."

The danger past for the moment, I lay back in my blankets and tried to stop shaking. The Indian had spoken in English! He understood what was in store for him. That made him dangerous. I should have told my companions but did not. This was different from John and me. This was evil! Nonetheless, the handsome heathen's words rattled around in my head.

In the morning, the Indian's calm eyes studied me carefully as I hand-fed him breakfast and a cup of water. Ignoring my companions' coarse laughter, I self-consciously held the big staff free of his girdle while he took his morning pizzle. My roger rose stiffly in my trousers.

◆

I KNEW WE WERE HEADED for some scalawag trader's camp along the trail but had not realized we were so close. In mid-afternoon we approached the post situated in a grove of cottonwoods on a small, fast stream. The paint-starved main building—which leaned drunkenly windward—was flanked by a smaller outhouse and a sagging necessary situated downwind. Our party caused a minor commotion. The trader, a one-eyed, greasy man named Tate, greeted my companions by name, as did the customer at the bar, a jadish character who went by the handle of Hoover.

"Damnation, Auslander," Trader Tate said, squinting at our captive. "Whut ya doin' with White Hair's son?"

"Who?" Hap asked in astonishment.

"That Injun ya got tussled up; he's White Hair's kid. Name's Lodai."

"Be damned," Nettles said. "We come acrost 'im on the trail. Figger he pulled it when the troopers hit."

"Heard 'bout that. Apt ta bring more trouble than profit. Old White Hair was all right." Tate turned to the captive. "Yer old man git away, Lodai?"

The Indian made a noise low in his throat. "No."

Hap turned on him abruptly. "Ya talk English?"

Tate laughed. "An old papist priest went ta live with 'em years back. Taught the young'uns ta talk it. Whut ya doin' with 'im, anyhow?"

"Commandin' officer a thet militia commissioned us ta kill any stragglers we come 'crost."

"So how come he ain't dead?" Hoover asked from the end of the bar.

Auslander didn't answer the question directly. "Ya got women close by?"

Hoover caught on immediately. "No closer'n White Hair's camp, and them won't do ya no good."

Hap turned to Tate. "Ya got objections?"

"Not 'less ya gonna be hoggish," the trader said, proving himself a false friend.

Auslander laughed, a sound not pleasant to the ear. "Plenty fer everbody. Right now, I wanta wet down the idee."

"Lock 'im in the outbuildin'."

Seeking escape, I headed for the necessary, alert for the rattlesnakes Tate had cautioned about. I encountered no cold-blooded reptiles, but if I had, they would have been preferable to the four drinking inside the trading post. I exited the foul one-hole shack as Auslander and Nettles returned from locking Lodai in the outhouse. When they were safely inside, I eased over to the building, lifted the wooden latch, and slipped inside.

"You all right?" I asked, pulling a hog-tied Lodai to his feet.

"You will help?" His deep voice sent gooseflesh down my back.

"If I can figure a way without getting myself in trouble."

"You can come with me," he said, a frown of worry creasing his brow. "My hands are dead, and I will need them to work when the time comes."

It took overlong to cut the cruel knot without slicing into his flesh. Lodai almost cried aloud as the blood rushed back into his hands.

"I will be back. I want to see what they're up to," I whispered, beginning to realize the consequences of my actions.

All conversation died abruptly when I entered the post. The room was unnaturally quiet; evil emanated like a green miasma from the table where the four men huddled. In that instant I determined my better chance lay with the Indian.

Hap boomed in an overly loud voice. "Thought ya fell in." The other three laughed. The spell was broken, and they resumed talking.

I interrupted, hoping my voice sounded normal. "I'm gonna water the horses. Can I use your stock tank, Mr. Tate?"

"That whut it's fer."

"Want me to water yours, too, Mr. Hoover?"

"Right kind a ya, son."

The hot animals eagerly dipped thirsty muzzles into the big tank. After transferring Lodai's rifle and bow to his pony, I hid our two mounts behind the outbuilding, leaving the others to over-fill their stomachs. It was cruel but better than hamstringing them.

Lodai stood ready to fight when I slipped through the door. "I've got horses and weapons and food to sustain us for awhile."

"Good," he grunted, starting for the door. I stayed him with a hand on his arm; his firm, silken flesh set my fingers to trembling.

"I need your promise, Lodai."

He looked me level in the eye. "You have my promise."

"N . . . no," I stuttered, thrilled by the reaffirmation. "I want your promise not to kill them."

He frowned. Clearly, that was not his wish. Then his expression eased. "This promise I give. We will run away like children." He started for the door. "Unless they catch us. Then I will kill."

I dropped the latch on the door, hoping it would be some time before the men in the post discovered we were gone. Lodai eyed the three horses around the water tank. "Don't worry, they're bloated," I said, tugging him around the corner of the outbuilding. We mounted and headed back down the same trail we had traveled earlier in the day, keeping the outbuilding between the trading post and ourselves. Once over the rise, Lodai slowed his pony to a walk.

"Don't wind them."

"Lodai," I spoke my unease openly, "I'm lost if you betray me."

"I will not betray you, Jim," he answered, surprising me with my name. "Give me some of that pack in case we have to run for it."

Night fell with no sign of pursuers, but Lodai traveled deep into the darkness. We sheltered for a short while in a small wash but were on the move again by dawn. We stayed on horseback all day. When the light began to fail, Lodai drew Red Hand, his pony, around and searched the distance behind us.

"They come," he said, resuming a leisurely pace. "They are far behind. They will keep coming tonight but not gain much ground. Tomorrow is the time to hurry."

We traveled the night through. Under a bright hunting moon, Lodai halted in the middle of a broad, shallow stream and instructed me to dismount. Taking only my rifle and blankets, I waded to the northwest, trying to reassure myself he was traveling south—with my Nellie's reins in his hand—to lay a false trail, not to abandon me on this broad, lonesome prairie. The icy water soon bent my fears into concern for my numbed feet, but I resisted the temptation to walk the bank. Draping the blankets around me helped until I fell headlong into the water. Slogging along against the current made the journey seem longer, but sometime in mid-morning, I found the pile of big boulders Lodai had described and designated as our meeting place. Climbing into the midst of the stones, I dozed on the sun-drenched rocks like a cold-blooded serpent, moving with the sun until

I was dry, then seeking the cool shade. I woke in the afternoon to find Lodai asleep beside me. An hour later, we set off single-file up the stream once again, but Nellie fought the rushing water this time, leaving me free to watch the play of muscles in Lodai's broad back. The way his flaring ribcage shrank to a narrow waist took my breath away.

"Soon we will come to a good camp," Lodai called back to me. "We will rest tonight and tomorrow. Tomorrow night, I will keep my promise." Those simple words sent a tingle through my scrotum.

The camp he chose was a wooded hollow with a small spring for water and a ring of low hills providing protection against the wind. After tending our needs, Lodai climbed a ridge for a careful look around before joining me in rest. I drowsed fitfully in my blankets until he returned and then slept the day and night away without waking once. I stirred in the morning as he came back from his toilet. Clutching my blanket around me, I cleaned up before rustling some breakfast from the stores we had brought. We ate in silence.

Later, when I joined him as he kept watch from a vantage point, I tried to express understanding for his grief by explaining the loss of my family. He looked at me for a moment.

"Did you see your mother and father ripped apart? Your sister with her guts falling out? I was glad to be dying. When I woke up, I hated myself because I was alive. The soldiers were coming among us then," he continued. "I crawled on my hands and knees like a dog until I found Red Hand and came down out of the hills. Why didn't I charge the blue coats? I am not a coward, but I failed to kill a single one of them."

"It was not cowardice, Lodai. It was shock. But even in shock you knew not to throw your life away uselessly."

"We were at peace," he said. "White Hair had talked with the headman at Fort Johnson. We knew the militia was approaching but had no fear of them. We sent our shaman and two warriors to greet them. And then the shells started to fall."

"Do you hate me for what they did?" I asked, touching his bare leg.

He met my gaze. "I do not hate you." He sighed. "Our time is passing. Our Way is going. Soon our children will have to pretend to be white. It is better my father did not live to see this."

We sat in silence until I could no longer remain silent. "Lodai, why did you make me the promise?"

"So you would help me. But I understand what you ask. When you first touched me, your staff grew hard. And I saw the look in your eyes."

I noted that my hand still rested on his thigh. I left it there as my yard reacted to him, stiffening and lengthening. "Have you ever lain with a man?"

"Never. Only with a woman."

"Then how do you know you can do it?"

He looked at me again. "You stood up to Auslander, got him off me that night. That took courage. I can respond to a brave man." At length, he asked his own question. "Have you?"

"One. A boy, really. We both were. One day his father caught us, and I had to leave."

"Do you have feelings for him?"

I considered the question. "He showed me my true self, Lodai, so he was important to me in that way." I scanned the Indian's handsome features. "But he was never important to me the way you are." Lodai's face closed up, and I realized he intended to honor a commitment, nothing more. Removing my hand from his thigh, I released him from his promise.

He shifted around to face me. "I gave my oath. This night I will lie with you unless you refuse me."

"I do not have the strength to refuse you, Lodai."

"Then we will lie together this night, Jim Tobar."

My heart hammered. Unable to speak, I nodded mutely.

He paused before speaking again. "They were going to rape and kill you, too. Before they knew I spoke English, they talked about it. They had already divided up your horse and rifle. I said nothing because I was afraid you would think I was lying to get your help. Do not worry," he added. "They would be here now if they found my trail."

"Then why do you keep watch?" At his look of his pain, I added quietly, "To see if any of your people show up."

"Most will go to our kinsmen. There is strength in numbers." After a long silence, he stood and looked down on me. "Now."

Our preparations were almost surreal. We ate. We bathed. Lodai braided his hair while I scraped the sparse bristle from my face. I watched him, not quite able to believe what was going to happen. One thing I knew; he would not fumble around like John and me. This man would be firm in his lovemaking.

At sundown, Lodai laid a modest fire and spread his horse blanket. "It is time," he said, loosening his breechclout. I experienced paralysis for a moment before recovering the use of my limbs. Then we stood naked and examined one another frankly in the twilight.

"You are a handsome man. I am proud that you want me," Lodai said quietly. The words sounded true.

Strong arms closed about me. His lips touched my face, but I felt them in my stones. My pipe pressed against his sac. Burning with excitement, I slid down his torso, tasting, licking, feeling. His skin was taut satin; his muscles hard and unyielding. On my knees, I buried my head in his bush, inhaling his maleness. I sucked his flaccid pipe into my mouth, running my tongue along the underside; my hands caressed his thighs, probed his testicles, moved across his smooth bum. His rod stirred.

I sucked at him again, and he grew, overfilling my mouth. The strength of his erection forced me backward. He pulled my head into him, thrusting tentatively at first, and then with growing confidence. I opened my throat to receive him, drawing a breath when I could. Steadying his pipe with one hand, I explored with the other. He pumped himself into me for an eternity before his breathing became labored; his thrusts urgent. Finally, he drew almost out of my mouth and speared me deeply, exploding and flooding my mouth and throat. His yard, his pipe, his staff, that hard penis in my mouth was different from John's. This was a strong man's cock; John's had been less.

The aggressiveness of my oral assault and the strength of his reaction took him by surprise. I held him in my mouth until he went soft. Then he lay back on the blanket and pulled me into the crook of his arm. My pipe pressed eagerly against his thigh. Unwilling to spoil the afterglow, I did nothing, said nothing. Gradually my erection abated. His hard, lithe body warm against mine was pleasure enough.

Suddenly, he rolled atop me. "I did not expect the thing to be so powerful. It was a thing to remember," he mused.

Lodai studied me in the darkness. Then he gave me a proper kiss. I went weak. He forced my legs apart. His yard pressed against my stomach. This was something new . . . John had always taken me while I lay on my belly. Lodai lifted my legs to his broad shoulders. My fundament rose to meet his pipe. His hand spread my buns. My flesh parted for his manhood; my bum flamed with his penetration.

Lodai entered me in one long thrust, pausing only when he was fully seated. His stones dangled against my buttocks and his silky groin hair teased my inner thighs. Eventually, the burning pain eased, allowing me to enjoy the hard penis sheathed within my tube. Handsome, sensual, confident, he was the most man I had ever known. I stammered a question as he began to pound me.

"Lo . . . Lodai? What . . . does that . . . mean?"

"Lodestar," he answered easily. He had not yet worked up a sweat.

"Lodestar! Polaris. The guiding star! That's what you are," I gasped as he drove into me harder. "My guiding star. I love you, Lodestar," I murmured, hardly conscious of what I said.

Delirious with joy, mad with strange, wonderful sensations, stretched to capacity by his staff, I was lost. He rose above me and grasped my aching pipe as he beat himself against my body. He held me while I shot my seed, and then filled my channel with his sperm. He held me to him, releasing my poor shrunken pipe only when he left the blanket for water to cleanse us. Almost comatose, I was barely aware of him as he settled back into the blankets.

◆

THAT WAS A LUNATION AGO. Since that wonderful night, we have moved to an abandoned settler's cabin high in the hills, where we will winter. Lodestar is a bold and imaginative lover. He has fed me his seed orally, rectally, on the belly, on the leg, in my hand, and in the middle of my chest. What he has not done is verbally express his feelings.

Today, he returned in a new pair of buckskin leggings. His breechcloth was freshly laundered, and he wore a short deerskin vest across his chest. A choker of small animal bones draped his strong neck. His hair, braided and bound by a hairbine, was adorned with two hawk feathers. He held out a vest and a leather hat, both fashioned from deer hide by his own fingers.

"These are my bridal gifts, Jim Tobar," he intoned solemnly. "I come to take you as my *winkte* wife. I want you as my mate. Will you have me? For as long as we live?"

Speechless, I nodded, a happy smile breaking across my lips. He stripped off his finery and gave me the thrumming of my life. Even *he* was not prepared for the powerful ejaculation that came. My Lodai, my beautiful Lodestar, had proclaimed his love the best way he knew how. And he did it magnificently!

ABOUT THE CONTRIBUTORS

GAVIN ATLAS has been published in *Island Boys* (Alyson) and *Hard Hats* (Cleis). He also has two erotic short stories available at www. Forbid denPublications.com. Gavin lives in Houston with his wonderful boyfriend, John, and he can be reached at www.GavinAtlas.com.

SHANE ALLISON is the editor of *Hot Cops: Gay Erotic Stories* and *Backdraft: Hot Gay Erotica.*

JULIAN BENEDICT is divorced and living alone with his two dogs and three cats in the foothills of the Rockies. He has three adult sons who have their own lives and is finally free to live as he chooses.

"Many people are happier living a structured life," he says, "but I am just the opposite. I am grateful that I can devote all my free time to writing, the one thing which fulfills me like nothing else."

He has written one nonfiction book and three novels and discovered in the process that some of the erotic scenes would quite naturally become so sexually intense that he knew they would never be accepted by any publisher outside the erotic genre. Yet unable to bring himself to compromise his writing he chose instead to explore a genre that would not stifle his self expression.

Stories that have been accepted in the year that he has been writing erotica include one for *The Longest Kiss* anthology with Chrissie Bentley.com, five pieces with Hotspot Books for the anthology *Mammoth Book of Erotic Confessions*, and one piece with Black Velvet Seductions for the anthology *Righteous Sin.*

Since he was inspired to write his first gay erotic piece he has been obsessed with writing gay erotica and has written over a dozen stories.

R. KRAMER BUSSEL is an author, editor, blogger, and reading series host, with books that include Lambda Literary Award finalists *Up All Night* and *Glamour Girls*, as well as *First-Timers, Secret Soles, Ultimate Undies, Sexiest Slaves, Spanked, Rubber Sex, Crossdressing*, and the nonfiction anthologies *Best Sex Writing 2008* and *2009*. Bussel's writing has been published in Afterellen, Afterelton, Cleansheets, *Diva*, Huffington Post, Mediabistro, *Newsday, New York Post, Time Out New York, Zink*, and other publications. Bussel hosts the In the Flesh Reading Series in New York City, is a former sex columnist for the *Village Voice*, has appeared on the Martha Stewart Show to talk about cupcakes, and coedits the blog Cupcakes Take the Cake (cupcakestakethecake.blogspot.com) when not writing dirty stories.

J.M. COLAIL lives in a suburb of Detroit with her dog and she is working towards her degree in anthropology. She is still looking for the girl of her dreams, but having fun along the way. She is the author of the erotic novel, *Toren & Wes*.

RYAN FIELD is a freelance writer who lives and works in New Hope, Pennsylvania, and Los Angeles. His work has appeared in many anthologies and collections by Alyson Books. One of his favorite short stories is "Showy Joey," in a book titled *Slow Grind*, released by Alyson in 2000.

SAM GABEL attended Georgia State University to pursue philosophy and continues to find inspiration in native Atlanta to fuel the crux of his writing.

WILLIAM HOLDEN is the author of more than twenty-four stories of gay short fiction. He has served as fiction editor for *RFD* magazine, completed five bibliographies for the American Library Association's GLBT Round Table, and written various encyclopedia articles on the history of gay fiction. He can be contacted by visiting his Web site, WilliamHoldenOnline.com.

DAVID HOLLY lives in the Pacific Northwest, where gay sex among college students and volcanic eruptions are facts of everyday life. David Holly's stories have appeared in *Dorm Porn 2; Tales of Travelrotica for Gay Men*, Vol. 2; *My First Time*, Vol. 5; *Ultimate Gay Erotica 2008;* and *Cruise Lines*. Readers will find a complete bibliography at www.gaywriter.org.

SLY JOHNSON currently lives in Orlando with his boyfriend and their pug, Peewee. In addition to running the night shift of an emergency call center, Sly is currently completing his first novel.

REX LANDRY is a resident of Atlanta, GA, and has written several other gay erotica short stories that have been published. Rex has finished two novels of another genre and is currently working on several more gay short stories for an upcoming compilation of gay erotica.

KEN O'NEILL is a writer, actor, and marriage equality activist. His first manuscript, "The Marrying Kind," a comic novel about a gay couple who start boycotting weddings, is currently being shopped by Katherine Fausset at Curtis Brown.

NEIL PLAKCY is the author of *Mahu, Mahu Surfer,* and *Mahu Fire,* mystery novels set in Hawaii. Editor of *Paws and Reflect: A Special Bond Between Man and Dog,* and *Hard Hats: Gay Erotic Stories.* www.mahubooks.com

JAKE RICH'S work appears in the 2006 Lambda Literary Award—nominated *Rode Hard, Put Away Wet,* Suspect Thoughts anthology of lesbian cowboy erotica, and *Hard Road, Easy Riding,* an anthology of lesbian motorcycle erotica by Haworth Press. His short story "Be Daring" will be included in *Drag King Anthology,* edited by Rakelle Valencia and Amie M. Evans (forthcoming 2009 from Suspect Thoughts).

MICHAEL ROBERTS is featured in the Alyson Books anthologies *Dorm Porn, Dorm Porn 2, Ultimate Gay Erotica 2007,* and *Frat Sex 2.* For STARbooks Press, he appears in *Ride Me Cowboy* and *Service with a Smile.* One of his stories is in the "It's Too Big" segment at www.cruisingforsex.com, and he has published in several leading adult gay magazines.

ROB ROSEN is the author of *Sparkle: The Queerest Book You'll Ever Love.* His short stories have appeared, to date, in more than fifty anthologies, most notably *Mensch: On Being Jewish and Queer; I Do/I*

Don't: Queers on Marriage; Best Gay Love Stories 2006; Truckers; Best Gay Love Stories: New York City; Best Gay Romance; My First Time, Vol. 5; *The Queer Collection: Prose and Poetry 2007; Best Gay Love Stories: Summer Flings; Ultimate Gay Erotica 2008; Hard Hats; Backdraft: Fireman Erotica; Ride Me Cowboy—Erotic Tales of the West; Cruise Lines; Service with a Smile: Fun with Couriers; Contractors and Plumbers; Boys Caught in the Act; Frat Sex 2; Best Gay Romance 2008* and *2009; Surfer Boys; and Bears: Gay Erotic Stories.* His erotic fiction can frequently be found in the pages of *MEN* and *Freshmen* magazines. Please visit him at his Web site, www.therob rosen.com, or e-mail him at robrosen@therobrosen.com.

FRED TOWERS lives in Indiana with his husband of 10 years, Mel. He's editing Nerdvana for Starbooks Press. He was published in *Bearotica* from Alyson Publications, *Muscle Worshipers* from Starbooks Press, *Ultimate Gay Erotica 2008* from Alyson, and *Flesh to Flesh* from Strebor Books. He writes book reviews for gay male fiction for the Rainbow Reviews Web site. Email him at fredtowers at yahoo.com.

MARK WILDYR was born and raised an Okie. Mark Wildyr presently resides in New Mexico, the setting of many of his stories, which explore developing sexual awareness and intercultural relationships. Approximately forty-seven of his short stories and novellas have been acquired by Alyson Publications, Arsenal Pulp, Companion Press, Green Candy Press, Positronic and Southern Tier Edition of Haworth Press, STARbooks Press, Cleis Press, and Freshmen and men's magazines.

LOGAN ZACHARY is an occupational therapist and mystery author living in Minneapolis, MN, where he is an avid reader and book collector. He enjoys movies, concerts, plays, and all the other cultural events that the Twin Cities have to offer. His stories can be found in *Rough Trade, Hard Hats, Taken By Force, Boys Caught in the Act, Ride 'em Cowboy, Service with a Smile, Surfer Boys,* and *Best Gay Erotica 2009.* He can be reached at LoganZachary2002@yahoo.com.